Praise for *He*

"If you are looking to read a rom
inside, then *Heiress for Hire* is a must-read." —*Romance Junkies*

"McCarthy transforms what could have been a run-of-the-mill romance with standout characterizations that turn an unlikable girl and a boring guy into two enjoyable, empathetic people who make this romance shine." —*Booklist*

"Amusing paranormal contemporary romance . . . Fans will appreciate Erin McCarthy's delightful pennies-from-heaven tale of opposites in love pushed together by a needy child and an even needier ghost." —*The Best Reviews*

"One of McCarthy's best books to date . . . *Heiress for Hire* offers characters you will care about, a story that will make you laugh and cry, and a book you won't soon forget. As Amanda would say: It's priceless." —*The Romance Reader* (5 hearts)

"A keeper. I'm giving it four of Cupid's five arrows."—*Bella Online*

"An alluring tale." —*A Romance Review* (5 roses)

"The perfect blend of sentiment and silly, heat and heart . . . priceless!" —*Romantic Times* "Top Pick" (4½ stars)

"An enjoyable story about finding love in unexpected places, don't miss *Heiress for Hire*." —*Romance Reviews Today*

continued

A Date With the Other Side

"Do yourself a favor and make A Date With the Other Side."
—Bestselling author Rachel Gibson

"One of the romance-writing industry's brightest stars . . . Ms. McCarthy spins a fascinating tale that deftly blends a paranormal story with a blistering romance . . . Funny, charming, and very entertaining, *A Date With the Other Side* is sure to leave you with a pleased smile on your face." —*Romance Reviews Today*

"If you're looking for a steamy read that will keep you laughing while you turn the pages as quickly as you can, *A Date With the Other Side* is for you. Very highly recommended!"
—*Romance Junkies*

"Fans will appreciate this otherworldly romance and want a sequel."
—*Midwest Book Review*

"Ghostly matchmakers add a fun flair to this warmhearted and delightful tale . . . an amusing and sexy charmer sure to bring a smile to your face." —*Romantic Times*

"Offers readers quite a few chuckles, some face-fanning moments, and one heck of a love story. Surprises await those who expect a 'sophisticated city boy meets country girl' romance. Ms. McCarthy delivers much more." —*A Romance Review*

Praise for the other novels of Erin McCarthy

"Will have your toes curling and your pulse racing." —*Arabella*

"Erin McCarthy writes this story with emotion and spirit, as well as humor." —*Fallen Angel Reviews*

"Both naughty and nice . . . sure to charm readers." —*Booklist*

Sucker Bet

Erin McCarthy

BERKLEY SENSATION, NEW YORK

THE BERKLEY PUBLISHING GROUP
Published by the Penguin Group
Penguin Group (USA) Inc.
375 Hudson Street, New York, New York 10014, USA
Penguin Group (Canada), 90 Eglinton Avenue East, Suite 700, Toronto, Ontario M4P 2Y3, Canada
(a division of Pearson Penguin Canada Inc.)
Penguin Books Ltd., 80 Strand, London WC2R 0RL, England
Penguin Group Ireland, 25 St. Stephen's Green, Dublin 2, Ireland (a division of Penguin Books Ltd.)
Penguin Group (Australia), 250 Camberwell Road, Camberwell, Victoria 3124, Australia
(a division of Pearson Australia Group Pty. Ltd.)
Penguin Books India Pvt. Ltd., 11 Community Centre, Panchsheel Park, New Delhi—110 017, India
Penguin Group (NZ), 67 Apollo Drive, Rosedale, North Shore 0632, New Zealand
(a division of Pearson New Zealand Ltd.)
Penguin Books (South Africa) (Pty.) Ltd., 24 Sturdee Avenue, Rosebank, Johannesburg 2196,
South Africa

Penguin Books Ltd., Registered Offices: 80 Strand, London WC2R 0RL, England

This book is an original publication of The Berkley Publishing Group.

Cover art by pinglet
Cover design by Rita Frangie
Text design by Tiffany Estreicher

First edition: January 2008

Library of Congress Cataloging-in-Publication Data

McCarthy, Erin.
Sucker bet / Erin McCarthy.— 1st ed.
p. cm — (Vegas vampires ; bk. 4)
ISBN 978-0-425-21718-4
1. Vampires—Fiction. 2. Las Vegas (Nev.)—Fiction. I. Title.

PS3613.C34575S83 2008
813'.6—dc22

2007032844

PRINTED IN THE UNITED STATES OF AMERICA

10 9 8 7 6 5 4 3 2 1

One

To: Slash87@gomail.com
From: QueenieG@aol.com
Subject: Private—off vamp slayers' list

Hey Slash,
About what Vixen said . . . if the slayers' loop has plans to meet up somewhere, I'm going to be there. I want to get stake training from those more experienced than me, and I absolutely *have* to meet you. Is everyone meeting in Vegas? I live in Vegas, so that would be brilliant.

Smooches,
Queenie

Gwenna Carrick hit the send button and tried not to laugh. Smooches? Egads. She was appallingly bad at being both forceful and flirty, especially in an electronic format. Slash probably had no idea she was attempting to hit on him, which she knew she should regret, but didn't. If she could gain his confidence without the bloody mincing, she was all for it, because her experience with men was limited to her brother and her ex-husband.

Which was even more dysfunctional than it sounded, given they were both egotistical millennium-old vampires and controlling to boot.

It might also explain why she absolutely loved her fake online persona of QueenieG, who said what she wanted straight out and had a tendency to get a bit bossy when she thought she was being ignored. There was something absolutely liberating about being anonymous on the vampire slayers' loop, without any of her very long life's baggage weighing her down. Gwenna liked the power, the giddy feeling she got when she just dashed off an e-mail to the loop.

And it was amusing to be, in fact, a vampire, right smack in the midst of zealous anti-undead slayers. It wasn't often she got to be the sly, clever one, and she was enjoying it. So much so that it was getting addictive.

Her brand-new mobile phone rang on the desk next to her. "Yes?" she said, seeing on caller ID—brilliant invention—that it was Ethan, current president of the Vampire Nation. And her overprotective yet endearing brother.

"Hey, Gwen. Brittany had her baby tonight. Healthy girl, everyone is doing fine."

Gwenna smiled, relieved and ecstatic to hear that Ethan's sister-in-law had delivered successfully. She and Brittany Atelier had got close in the last few months as they had found a common thread in being the only two Impure women ever to conceive a child with a vampire.

"Is she up for visitors? I'd love to pop by."

"I think she'd be disappointed if you didn't pay a visit."

"I'll be right over." Gwenna said good-bye to her brother and turned back to her screen to shut her computer off.

One hundred and seventeen new messages on the vampire slayers' loop in the last twenty-four hours, many of them written in what she was starting to suspect was a secret code. Hints at a meeting. Implications of a planned attack on vampires.

Something was definitely in the works, and she wanted to know what it was and when it was going to happen.

Before she headed to the hospital, she dashed off another e-mail to the moderator requesting a reminder to the loop to trim posts. That always sent a flurry of responses to the list, distracting from the current topics, and muddying the waters. Then she tried to e-mail FoxyKyle, who, despite her ridiculous name, was the undisputed class president of the slayers' loop, with Slash87 being something comparable to VP.

FoxyKyle's e-mail was set to private. But Slash had sent her an Instant Message.

Queenie,
I'm in Vegas right now, too . . . wanna get together?

S

Slash was in Vegas? What did that mean? The question she'd never been able to answer was if the majority of the slayers' loop were just playing out a fantasy, or if they were all true slayers. Her instinct told her only a handful were slayers in the truest sense, those who had actually killed a vampire, or were planning to, and she was sure Slash and FoxyKyle fell into that category.

She clicked Reply.

Absolutely. Time and place?

His response came immediately.

Tonight. How about ten o'clock, at the Harrah's monorail station. Meet by the ticket machines.

Gwenna hadn't been born yesterday—not by a long shot. There was something odd about a request to meet at a rail stop, but she had to take into consideration Slash was a slayer, or at least aspired to be one. He probably enjoyed the subterfuge and intrigue. Meeting in Starbucks just wouldn't have the same ring to it.

Sure. See you then.

She'd swing by and meet Slash, assess him face-to-face, instead of just on-screen, then zip over to the hospital to see Brittany and the baby. Gwenna shut her computer down and stood up, curious as to why Slash wanted to meet her. She knew her reasons, but what exactly were his? Wondering if Slash and FoxyKyle had known each other prior to the slayers' loop, she figured she would have to get creative and track down Foxy later. Gwenna thought it wouldn't be that difficult. She was a dab hand with the computer. There hadn't been much else for her to do in York, where she'd been in a self-imposed exile for the last three hundred years. The Internet had saved her sanity in the last decade as she'd rattled about that castle entirely alone.

No longer. She was back in the real world. The past was dead and gone.

Or knocking at her door. Gwenna groaned, knowing before she even heard the doorbell that her ex-husband, Roberto Donatelli, was standing outside her hotel suite. She had an acute sense of smell and she knew his scent, a mix of expensive cologne and alcohol. And while it probably wasn't entirely logical, she was just always aware of him. He was like a toothache one tried to ignore, but instead had you reaching for the aspirin at regular intervals.

"Damn." She stuck her tongue out, knowing he couldn't see her, but enjoying it nonetheless. Then she added a series of obnoxious facial expressions and a rude gesture or two to work it all out of her system as she walked across the room. Pasting a polite smile on her face, she opened the door.

"Hi, Roberto. What brings you by?" Gwenna kept the door mostly closed, wanting him to take the hint, knowing he wouldn't.

"Hello, my beautiful wife," he said with a charming smile, leaning in to kiss her cheek. "I just missed seeing your lovely face."

It took everything in her not to correct his use of the term *wife*, given that they had been granted a vampire divorce three centuries ago, but he had wanted to irritate her, and she refused to give him the satisfaction. She accepted the kiss, than said airily, "Well, you've seen it, so I guess you'll be on your way now."

His smile disappeared and deep lines of annoyance marred his smooth forehead. "Since when do you talk like that? This city has had a negative effect on you . . . since you've been living in Vegas you've gotten—"

"A backbone?" she asked dryly. God knew he must despise that. Their entire marriage had been based on him dominating her.

"No. Nasty. Impolite."

She rolled her eyes.

"See? That is what I'm talking about. This isn't like you, Gwenna."

Everyone thought they knew her. They expected her to sit down and shut up, and for most of her life she'd done just that. But while she would always strive to be a kind and compassionate person, she no longer wanted to be an undead doormat.

"Maybe this is the new me."

"Well, it's highly unattractive."

Any patience she'd been trying to hold on to disappeared. "Why the hell are you here? And how did you get into the casino anyway?"

"I'm vice president of the Vampire Nation. We had a series of cabinet meetings in your brother's offices."

"You're not supposed to come up to this floor." Immediately she regretted making such a petulant statement. She sounded like a six-year-old.

"Why not?" He leaned toward her, suave and sophisticated in his dark charcoal gray suit, his hair trim and tidy, little flecks of silver on either side of his temples. "Are you afraid of me, my dear? You know I only have your best interests in mind." He brushed her hair back off her cheek softly. "I love you."

She hated when he did this. Back when she was mortal, his words and charismatic touches had made her weak in the knees and willing to give up her virginity to him. Now it just grated on her nerves and made her wish she really did know Slash's staking skills. There were times she'd love to just skewer Roberto like an Italian shish kebab.

"Right, then. You love me. Is there anything else you'd like to tell me before you leave?"

He dropped his hand and the false charm. "Have you talked to my daughter? Has Brittany had the baby yet?"

Just when she thought she had the upper hand on him, he was utterly brilliant at ripping the rug out from under her. It hurt like hell that he had a daughter, conceived with no forethought in a random moment of selfish pleasure in the back of a seventies strip club, when Gwenna herself would never be a mother again.

"I'm not at liberty to discuss Brittany or her baby with you."

Roberto frowned at her. "Just tell me if she's alright."

"She's fine."

"And her due date is next Friday?"

"Yes." That was the truth after all. No need to mention that she'd already given birth.

"Aren't you going to invite me in?" he asked, gesturing toward her suite.

"No."

"Gwenna," he said, his voice exasperated.

"What?" She felt just as annoyed. What in hell did he want from her? He'd already had the best three hundred years of her life, and while she probably had a pound of flesh to give him, she wasn't feeling generous. Or masochistic.

"We were happy together."

Oh, God, he was going to take it there.

She sighed and leaned on her door frame. "Sometimes. Sometimes not. Now will you please just go? I'm not in the mood to play this game tonight."

"I'm not playing games. I love you."

Roberto touched her face again and she shivered, which he mistook for passion. He leaned closer, while Gwenna gathered her resolve. There had been a time when she would have just let him, simply because it was easier. Easiest still had been locking herself away in York and never having to deal with him. But she refused to allow him such total control over her anymore.

Roberto's fangs let down as he bent his head. Gwenna clapped her hand over his mouth to prevent his teeth from sinking into the flesh of her neck. "We're divorced, Roberto. And I don't need a fuck buddy."

She darted back into her suite and closed the door on his shocked and appalled face. Hands shaking a little, she listened to him shout her name in utter horror. She'd never used the *f* word before. Maybe she'd thought it to herself, but it had never crossed her lips. And she'd done it with such force and vehemence. It was seriously liberating, and she felt an adrenaline-like rush rip through her.

"I can't believe you just said that . . . Gwenna Donatelli! Open this door." He was screaming and pounding so hard, the door shook.

"It's Gwenna *Carrick*, damn it!" she yelled right back.

She never yelled. Ever. And the total silence from his side of the door confirmed that for the first time in almost a thousand years she had shocked Roberto into complete speechlessness.

Let the past stay where it belonged. She was ready for a new millennium.

Nate Thomas focused on the woman in front of him, trying not to think disparaging blond jokes as he ignored the crime-scene team scuttling around the body. Either he was running on too little sleep, or this woman was a dimwit, because they'd been talking for ten minutes and he'd yet to figure how the hell she'd managed to stumble across a murder victim behind a monorail ticket vending machine.

"So you came here from the casino, the Ava?" he asked carefully.

"Yes."

"Why? Where were you going?"

"Here." Her finger pointed down to the ground as she hugged her thin arms to herself.

"To Harrah's?"

Her head shook slowly. "No, to here. This spot."

"Right here. In the station. This was your destination?" He didn't think many women would consider hanging out at the train station on the Strip a good time for a Thursday night, but hell, what did he know about the opposite sex? Diddly-squat for the most part.

A quick sweep from head to toe showed this particular woman to be five foot one or two, a hundred and ten pounds, fair skinned, blue eyes, delicate facial features, and short fingernails, painted a vivid red. She was dressed in loose jeans, way looser than current fashion dictated, a form-fitting red T-shirt, and brown leather sandals. No earrings, no makeup except for that shiny lip stuff, and no watch. Large ornate gilded ring on her right hand, which was almost overpowering for her small fingers. Not a hooker, that he could say with certainty, but otherwise not easy to read.

Nervous eyes darted left and right and had trouble meeting his. "Yes. I was planning to meet someone here."

That was progress. "Who?"

"Um. A guy."

Or not. Nate really was tired. He'd been up for seventy-two hours, easily, and he had a pounding headache. He shouldn't have even answered this call, but he had the most experience, and several other detectives were on vacation for spring break. But his brain was foggy, his patience thin, and his witness was either intentionally uncooperative or not the brightest bulb in the pack.

"What guy? A friend? A boyfriend?"

"Well, not exactly a friend. Definitely not a boyfriend. More like an acquaintance."

"What's his name?"

"I don't know his real name."

Nate stared hard at her. Was she a user? Meeting a dealer? That would explain the fact that she looked like a strong wind could blow her over, and her translucent complexion, not to mention her repeated evasiveness. "Look, if you were doing a deal, buying some stuff, I don't care about that, okay? I'm more concerned with who did this . . ." He jerked his thumb over to where the photographer was taking shots of the victim, a white male in his twenties, entirely drained of all his body fluids. "I don't care who sells you your smack. I just want to hear what you know, what you heard, what you saw, the whole truth, do you understand?"

For the first time since he'd been directed to her upon arriving at the scene, she lost her nervous demeanor. "I wasn't here to buy drugs!"

She sounded downright indignant. Utterly offended.

"Then what were you here for? Is your hook-up guy married?" Maybe she was having an affair or into anonymous sex for kicks. She didn't look like the type, but Nate had learned they rarely did.

"Oh, I don't know. Do you think he's married?" That seemed to flummox her.

Nate tried not to sigh. "I don't know. Tell me how you know him and why you were meeting him, and maybe we can figure out if that has anything to do with the poor guy wadded up like dirty laundry and crammed behind a ticket machine. I don't know about you, but I'd like to catch a killer here."

She winced and rubbed her arms absently. "That was rather appalling, wasn't it? Poor sot. Do you know who he is?"

She had quite the little focus problem and it was starting to bug the hell out of him. "Who were you meeting?" Nate glanced down at the notebook in front of him. Her name was Gwenna according to the uniform who had initially arrived on the scene. Gwenna Carrick. "Look, Gwenna, just tell me what you know about the guy you were meeting."

"I just know the user name he goes by. It's Slash87."

"User name? Online?"

"Yes." Her cheeks got a little pink.

"You were meeting a guy you met on the Internet?"

She nodded.

Christ. Why did everyone suddenly think it was a good idea to hook up online with total strangers and meet them in unsafe locales without knowing jack shit about them other than the fact that they used freakin' smileys in their damn e-mails? Yeah, Nate was officially out of patience.

"Okay. So you don't know his real name?"

"No."

"Have you met him in person before?"

"No."

"Where did you meet him online?"

"A special-interest loop. We were supposed to meet here at ten."

"Whose idea was that?"

"Well, meeting in person was mine. To meet here was his idea."

What guy suggests meeting on a monorail platform when there were nine thousand bars, restaurants, and casinos in spitting distance? One up to no freakin' good, that's who. The blonde was definitely stereotypically dumb to have agreed to do something so dangerous. "And you didn't see him when you got off the train?"

"I don't think so. But really, how would I know? I've never seen him before."

Nate let loose with the sigh he'd been stifling. "I mean, did you make contact with him?"

"Oh. No."

"So how do you know Slash87 isn't the guy posing for his final portrait over there?" Nate jerked his thumb toward the crime tape and the flash from the camera over the body.

She blanched. "Oh, God, I don't know. I never thought of that. Do you think *that's* Slash? How horrible."

Nate studied her expression. The horror looked genuine enough. But something about this woman didn't add up for him. "Were you here for a date? What were your plans for after you met up tonight?"

"We didn't exactly have plans. He just said he was going to be in town, and I suggested meeting up to chat. He gave the time and place. I guess I figured we would go grab coffee or something."

Human beings were so damn exhausting. Nate glared at her, hoping she would understand the severity of what she'd done. "Do me a favor. Don't agree to meet strange men you don't know from Adam in dark monorail stations by yourself, alright? It's just a bad idea all around."

"I didn't think . . ." She frowned a little. "I mean, I'm really quite good at taking care of myself."

"I can tell." Nate rolled his eyes. "What if you'd been a few minutes early? That might be you behind the ticket machine."

Her chin tilted up and he could tell he'd offended her. "I don't think so."

"Yeah, whatever, keep telling yourself that. You're damn lucky, Gwenna Carrick, that you're standing there curling your lip at me instead of on your way to the morgue." It infuriated him that she was being stubborn, that she'd been so stupid. She looked about as strong as his grandmother, an easy target, and yet was so nonchalant about risking her own safety. Didn't she get that there was one chance in life? That it could be gone instantly and that one little mistake could waste you?

Selfish, that's what it was, when people just strolled around acting invincible, taking risks for no reason.

"I'm fine."

He scoffed. "So what is this online special-interest group? Who joined first, you or Slash?"

"Slash. And it's a paranormal group."

"What the hell does that mean? Like you believe in ghosts and crap?"

"Not exactly. More like . . ." She glanced away. "Vampires."

"Excuse me?" He'd heard her, he was just hoping he was wrong.

"It's a group that believes in vampires. And well, likes to pretend they're vampire slayers."

"Nice. So you and Slash are pretend slayers? Were you meeting to stake someone?" More likely Slash was hoping to impale Gwenna with his personal stake. Any guy who spent all his time online pretending to be Buffy's male counterpart was probably not getting a whole lot of action.

"We were meeting because the slayers are going to be getting together in Vegas and I wanted to help Slash plan it."

"Oh, like a slayers' convention? Fun. So you're on the planning and decorating committee?"

"You don't have to make fun of me." She rubbed her arms a little and looked over his shoulder. "And if that is Slash over there it's highly insensitive of you to mock what is a harmless hobby."

"You're right. I apologize." While it still sounded seriously geeky to him, he had to remember that she wasn't exposed to violence the way he was. He could compartmentalize, dissociate from the victim, but it would be different for her. That was possibly a guy she'd chatted with, felt some affinity for. "We'll try to ID him as soon as possible and we'll let you know what we find. I need you to get me all the info on that Internet group."

Gwenna made a face, her chin set. "Fine."

The phone in his pocket buzzed. Nate glanced at it and cursed. It was the hospital.

"Excuse me, I need to take this." He started to turn away.

"Can I go home?" she asked hopefully.

"Yes, but I'll need you at the police station tomorrow for further questions."

As Nate pressed the talk button on his phone and answered, he caught one last glimpse of Gwenna Carrick. She was making a ridiculous face, lip curled back, eyes rolling, tongue sticking out, clearly expressing her feelings about having to show up at the police station.

It was kind of funny to see such an attractive woman resorting to the childish mechanism, and normally Nate might have laughed. Except that the voice on the other end told him exactly what he didn't want to hear. And he suspected it would be a long time before he ever laughed again.

Two

Gwenna should have skipped the hospital visit.

Finding that man's body had been disturbing and surreal, and she felt like she still had death's scent lingering in her nostrils. Not a good time to pop into the maternity ward.

But part of her had thought that seeing something so normal, so joyful as Brittany and her baby would ground her, settle her rattled nerves. Yet Gwenna was unprepared for the mixed feelings that hit her smack in the face when she watched Brittany and her baby. Nine hundred years had dulled her ache at the death of her daughter, but the pain would never go away entirely. That loss, that devastation, was part of Gwenna now, a permanent wound in her heart that would never close, and Brittany's joy pricked at her own pain. But at the same time she was ate up with happiness for Brittany.

Sucker Bet

"She's beautiful. Congratulations, Brittany, Corbin." Gwenna smiled at the couple, trying to be normal, act natural, shuffle through her conflicting feelings. She found it sweet that Brittany's new husband, Corbin Atelier, a French vampire re-turned mortal, was sitting on the hospital bed as Brittany held the baby, a possessive hand on both his wife and daughter.

"Thank you, Gwenna. She ez the most beautiful baby ever born. I am convinced of it," Corbin said, his French modesty on display.

Brittany laughed, glowing with pride and happiness despite the dark circles of fatigue under her eyes. "All babies are beautiful."

"Not zis beautiful," Corbin insisted. "Ava is stunning."

"Do you want to hold her, Gwenna?" Brittany asked, lifting her arms and the baby out.

Gwenna felt a panic rising in her throat. It had been years—centuries—since she had held an infant. But it would be rude to say no, and surely, now that she was in Las Vegas, far away from England, she could hold a baby in her arms without having a ridiculous mental breakdown. And maybe touching Ava would wipe out that ominous foreboding she'd been feeling since she'd known instinctively on the train platform that there was a dead body stashed nearby.

"I'd love to." Wiping her palms on her jeans, she forced a smile and moved forward for the transfer. They were all nervous—Corbin holding his hands under his daughter to catch her if the pass went bad, Gwenna feeling her already cool skin grow clammy with anxiety, Brittany fussing with the baby's blanket.

But the exchange went off without incident, and Gwenna found herself holding that tiny scrap of nothing babe in her arms. The soft, new smell of freshly washed skin and breast milk filtered up into Gwenna's nostrils, her vampire senses acutely aware of how tiny and human and alive Ava was.

Her weight was nothing, not compared to the strength in Gwenna's nine-hundred-year-old immortal arms. Yet staring down at that tiny face, Ava's eyes fluttering open and closing again, her cheeks smooth and shiny, Gwenna felt as vulnerable as she ever had. Here was responsibility. Here was the essence of true, pure love, and the source of eternal, agonizing pain.

"Your father is right," she whispered to Ava, settling her closer to her chest. "You're quite gorgeous."

Ava was also starting to whimper, a little squall erupting from her mouth.

"What's the matter, precious?" Gwenna rocked her and made soothing sounds, but Ava moved quickly from mild annoyance to full-fledged crying. She clearly needed to nurse, her tiny mouth rooting around Gwenna's tight T-shirt, searching for a source of relief. She wasn't going to get it from her.

"Why is she crying?" Alexis asked from the other side of the room, where she'd been talking to Ethan.

"She's hungry." Gwenna felt her face go hot as she had a sudden memory sensation from the baby rubbing across her chest. She would swear she could almost feel the tingling rush of her milk letting down, the way it had when her own daughter was an infant.

Disturbed, she tried to hand Ava back to Brittany, but the new mum was busy popping open her hospital gown, clearly to Corbin's horror.

"What are you doing?" he asked her, grabbing the gown before it could fall open and expose Brittany's chest.

His wife raised her eyebrows. "I'm going to feed our daughter."

Gwenna rocked Ava, whose little face was turning red. Corbin's eighteenth-century modesty annoyed her. In Gwenna's mortal youth, survival was more important than manners.

"Not with a crowd of people in the room. I do not think so."

Brittany rolled her eyes. "No one here gives a crap if they see my breast, Corbin. Breastfeeding is a natural, nonsexual action, and this is our family in front of us." She yanked her gown out of his grip, exposing the peak of her left breast.

Apparently not everyone agreed, because Ethan blanched. "Oh, now hang on there, Brit. Good God. We'll just leave. No need to argue, you two." He averted his eyes to the floor. "We'll be out in the hall if you need us . . . not that you'll need us to do what you're going to do, but you know, if you need . . ."

He bolted out the door. Alexis turned to Gwenna and rolled her eyes. "Okay, that was pathetic. The man runs the entire Vampire Nation, yet the thought of breast-feeding freaks him out. I'll never understand men."

"Me, either. But I don't really want to."

Alexis laughed.

Actually, that wasn't true. Gwenna knew these men entirely too well. They were overbearing, stubborn, egotistical, unable to express their emotions, and power hungry.

On cue, her mobile phone rang. Since just about everyone she communicated with was in the room—or hiding in the hall—Gwenna had the sneaking suspicion she knew who it was. Especially since Roberto had called her at least sixteen times since she'd slammed the door in his face.

Handing Ava gently to Corbin, Gwenna smiled at Brittany. "Congratulations again. I'm going to head on out. We'll chat soon."

"Thanks for coming by, Gwenna. I appreciate it." Brittany gave her a look, a shared understanding.

Brittany knew how Gwenna had worried about her daughter, could sympathize with the fear, because now she was living it, too. They both had given birth to daughters with more vampire blood than mortal running through their veins, and a mother's fear was a powerful thing. Gwenna only hoped Ava would come to a better end than Isabel had.

Feeling tears unexpectedly pricking her eyes, the baby's crying and the ringing of her mobile in her handbag shrill and harsh on her raw nerves, Gwenna just squeezed Brittany's hand and followed Alexis out of the room.

Her brother was frowning at her the minute she stepped out. "What's the matter? Who's calling you?"

"I don't know," she snapped at him. "I can read minds, but I'm not bloody omniscient."

Ethan held up his hand. "No need to get your knickers in a knot. I was just asking."

"Is it any of your business?" she asked, knowing she sounded defensive. But hell, she felt on the verge of tears, and she despised that feeling. It meant she hadn't made any progress at all, that she was still vulnerable and emotional. And it seemed she was going to pay for her standoff with her ex. Roberto was going to harass her mercilessly, another charming tactic of his.

It was the worst thing she could say, though, because Ethan had been about to let it go until she spoke. But he was a naturally suspicious person and her words made his eyes narrow. "What does that mean? Give me your cell phone." He held out his hand.

"No." Gwenna clutched her purse tighter to her chest.

"Who would call you, Gwenna?"

Her sister-in-law made a sound of impatience. "Leave it alone, Ethan. Gwenna's right, it's none of your business."

When Gwenna had traveled to Vegas for Ethan's wedding, she had been surprised at her brother's choice of a wife, because Alexis was very twenty-first century with her attitude. But the more Gwenna got to know her, the more she liked Alexis, and the more she realized that Alexis was actually strong in the way women of their eleventh-century mortal youth had been. Alexis did what she needed to do and got the job done without needing or expecting help from a man, and Gwenna suspected that was what appealed to Ethan about her.

"It is most certainly my business." Those blue eyes pierced her, studying her, calculating, accusing. "You're talking to Donatelli again, aren't you?"

Her brother knew just how to get to her, how to make her feel small and naughty, childish.

But she wasn't going to let him intimidate her. "So what if I am?" She wasn't, not technically in the way he meant, but even if she was, it wasn't Ethan's right to criticize.

Ethan didn't like her nonanswer. He took it as confirmation and exploded. "Christ, Gwenna! You haven't learned one goddamn thing in the last three hundred years, have you?"

That hurt. But it infuriated her more. She had learned more than Ethan would ever know. She had learned her lesson the hard way, over and over again, and had continued to have to swallow the lecture long after she had memorized it. "Go to hell, Ethan."

She spun on her heel and started down the hall.

He grabbed her arm and jerked her to a stop. "Gwenna . . . wait. You know I'm just worried about you."

"Give me a little credit for having *some* sense. I'm not some unruly teenager who's letting the town cad up her skirts."

"But that's exactly what you did! Twice. Why do you think I worry about you?"

For the first time in her life, Gwenna wanted to knock her brother unconscious.

Alexis made a sound of shock. "Uh, Ethan . . . not a cool thing to say, babe."

Gwenna vowed to be mature. "My relationship with Roberto is none of your business. It never has been. And I would appreciate it if you would respect my decisions." Gwenna straightened her back and took a deep breath, controlling her anger. "I know what I'm doing."

Ethan snorted. "Obviously not if you're sheet diving with Donatelli."

So much for maturity. She clenched her fists and gave a sound of exasperation. "Bugger off."

Her brother's jaw dropped. "Gwenna!" He turned to his wife. "Did you hear what my sister just said to me?"

"Yeah, and you really deserved it," Alexis said. "I would have said it to you years ago, but Gwenna's much nicer than me."

Gwenna was actually not feeling nice at all. It had been rather easy to blurt out that rude command to her brother. Ignoring

Ethan's protests, she yanked her arm out of his grip and headed toward the elevator.

Apparently deciding she wasn't worth pursuing, Ethan still yelled after her, "You'll just be sorry all over again for getting involved with Donatelli. You know I'm right."

Rolling her eyes, Gwenna waited for the elevator and tapped her foot impatiently. Just to annoy Ethan, she pulled out her phone and checked the missed calls. It was Roberto's number. Of course. She had changed the rules on him and he didn't like it. Despite what she led Ethan to believe, she wasn't planning to take any of Roberto's calls, and she'd rather die of starvation in the burning desert sun after a failed decapitation attempt than have sex with her ex.

She knew where his penis had been in the three hundred years since their divorce. Everywhere. Around the block several dozen times. Stopping at every strip club and brothel along the way.

If she were going to have sex ever again, which was doubtful, it wouldn't be with Roberto.

The elevator opened.

Gwenna stepped on.

Her eyes landed on a ruggedly handsome man leaning against the back wall, his eyes red and his expression stricken. Smashing. Just when she'd almost forgotten for a whole two minutes that instead of meeting Slash she'd found a murder victim, the cop who had so clearly thought she was an idiot popped up to remind her. "Detective Thomas?"

The phone in her hand rang again.

Damn it. Roberto again.

"Gwenna Carrick." Detective Thomas made a sound of exasperation, his voice angry and raw.

He had been impatient with her at the crime scene, she had been aware of that, but this tone was harder, different. Gwenna saw unshed tears in his eyes, saw his face was a mask of shock and pain, his shoulders tense.

"Are you okay?" she asked. Her phone rang incessantly, loud and obnoxious in the quiet elevator.

Despite the fact that he looked like he was going to crack, he just shrugged. "I've been better. How about you? Find any more dead bodies since we last met?"

Gwenna frowned. So he didn't want her compassion. He was on the emotional edge, obviously, and maybe embarrassed by that. Instinct told her to squelch the maternal urge to touch him.

If he needed flippant, she could do that. "No, no more bodies. But it wasn't for lack of trying."

Three

Nate Thomas let out a ragged laugh, dragging his hand over his mouth. God, like his day didn't suck enough already, now he was almost caught crying like a baby by the blonde from the train station.

But at least she'd picked up on his discomfort and had let it drop. It didn't sound like she was going to ask why he was just about blubbering on the elevator.

"Why didn't you answer your phone?" he asked, noting the way she gripped it so tightly her knuckles were white.

It calmed him down to study her, to assess her behavior, to wonder what she was doing at the hospital, and how she might be connected to the victim at the train station. Something about her was off, and he didn't understand what it was. And puzzling her out could help him to forget why he was at the hospital himself.

She glanced down at her cell phone and shook her head. "It's someone I don't want to talk to."

Someone she was angry with, if the pink spots of color on her cheeks were any indication. Her long wavy hair was also mussed, like she had tucked it back in irritation.

"Who? Your mother?" That was usually the person who pissed him off.

She gave a small shake of her head. "I wish." She hesitated for a fraction of a second, then said, "It's my ex-husband."

"Ah." That would explain her defensive posture—straight back, chin high, shoulders squared.

The door opened on the ground floor, but she didn't get off the elevator. "We're here," he told her, gesturing to the lobby, not liking the way she was looking at him.

Like she no longer saw him as intimidating, an authority figure, but instead with pity.

"I'm sorry," she said. "Whatever it is, I'm sorry for it."

He didn't pretend to misunderstand. He was too raw, too close to the edge. "Yeah, me, too."

She hesitated again, but then just stepped out of the elevator, turning her back to him. Her phone rang again in her hand. "Shit," she whispered, as her shoulders suddenly crumpled forward.

Nate moved up next to her. "What does he want?" he asked, not quite ready to leave. When he walked out that door, it would be real, and he didn't want to deal with reality just yet. And he could argue with himself that the blonde could help him solve a murder. Hell, the blonde just might be the murderer, though every gut instinct he had screamed that wasn't even close to the truth.

"He wants me back." She glanced over at him, her blue eyes sad, troubled. "He's never been good at taking no for an answer."

There was a mix of both exasperation and fear in her voice. It bothered him. She was a very petite, fragile-looking woman, young. Mid-twenties at most. A part of her worried that her ex could hurt her, he could sense that. And he was good at assessing people. It was half his job as a homicide detective with the Las Vegas Metro Police. An overzealous ex might also explain why she'd taken to the fantasy of a vampire slayers' group on the Internet. It was a way to exercise her version of control.

"How long since you split up?"

She squeezed the phone again and glanced at the display screen, frowning at whatever was there. "Three years." Flipping the phone open, she pushed some buttons. "He texted me a message this time."

Three years was a long time after a divorce for a guy to still be pursuing his ex. "What does he say?"

Shrugging, she closed the phone and put it in her purse. "It's nothing. He just wants me to call him."

"He just wrote 'call me'?"

"Yes. Well, he added a *now* to it, because it irritates him that I ignore him. Why?"

"It sounds like he's a problem." A problem that Nate understood. One he could deal with. What he couldn't deal with was the image embedded in his brain of his baby sister lying in that hospital bed, all the life, vitality, and essence gone from her.

"He is what he is. I'm used to it."

"But you're afraid of him, aren't you?" Nate shoved his hands in the pockets of his jeans and watched for her reaction to his question. She actually looked startled.

"No, I don't think so. Roberto would never hurt me, not physically, if that's what you mean." She tucked a strand of that pale wheat hair behind her ear. "But . . . he's very controlling. And what I think I'm afraid of is that when we're together, when we were married, I was willing to compromise what I thought was right because of him. He made me stretch my moral boundaries. Do you know what I mean?" She looked at him earnestly. "I don't want to be like that ever again."

Nate nodded, feeling his nerves settle, his near panic abating. He wasn't going to lose it, not right then anyway. He had a handle on it. "I know what you mean. We walk the line, and some people help us pull one way or the other."

"And we can't blame them really, we have to be responsible for ourselves, but we know it's wrong, and so it's better to stay away entirely."

Before he was even aware of what the hell he was doing, Nate said, "I'm headed to the coffee shop over there . . . care to join me?"

It wasn't the need for caffeine that had him craving coffee, but the desperate desire to stay away from his house, where Kyra's hospital bed loomed and the pervasive sick smell clung to the carpet. He didn't want to go home and he didn't want to be alone. Gwenna Carrick looked like she needed company as much as he did. Despite her earlier words, he doubted she'd encountered a whole lot of dead bodies in her life, especially not one done up like a pretzel and crammed behind a ticket dispenser.

"Okay," she said without hesitation. But then she bit her lip and darted her eyes to the elevator.

"Are you here with someone?" He could read the signs, and he didn't want to cause her complications. His own selfish need for distraction wasn't justification for getting her in trouble with a boyfriend. Though he had to admit he was curious as to why she was at the hospital in the first place.

"No. My brother and I were both visiting a friend, but he came with his wife. He's just very protective of me."

Not protective enough, given her night's activities. "That's good and not so good, I bet. It's nice that he cares so much, but it probably cramps your style. Maybe he would have a point if he objected to you hanging out with a total stranger. You know, say at a coffee shop, or meeting up with someone you don't know in a random place like a monorail station."

She made that face again, that ridiculous-looking pout that showed her distaste. "True," she said with a smile. "But I'd love a cup of coffee anyway, so shall we?"

Nate had originally thought her accent was British, but the way she spoke her vowels made him question his original guess. There was something about her that Nate couldn't put his finger on . . . like all the pieces to her puzzle just didn't add up. His sense of logic, the detective part of his personality, wanted to figure out who exactly she was beyond his first assessment of dumb blonde.

"Sure." He gestured down the hall and she started walking next to him. "So, you have a friend who's sick?"

"No. Our friend, well, actually she's my brother's wife's sister, so my brother's sister-in-law, but definitely my friend . . ." She stopped talking and flushed a little. "God, I'm babbling. All I'm trying to say is that Brittany had a baby tonight and we were visiting her. There were some health concerns, so we're very excited that everything is fine. She had a girl."

For some reason, Nate actually felt a smile tug at his mouth at her explanation. "That's wonderful." And amazing that he could actually freaking mean it. There was something soothing in knowing that while his sister had been leaving the world, a baby had been entering it. Kyra would have appreciated that.

"It was a little odd, too, though, considering what I saw earlier . . . I felt, I don't know, unclean. Like I shouldn't touch that sweet little baby. God, that makes no sense, does it? Just ignore me." She rubbed her lip and studied a painting on the wall as they walked.

"Hey, I understand. I see a lot of death. Sometimes it's hard to cross back over." God knew he was having a hard time crawling back at that very moment.

"Why are you here?" Stopping outside the coffee shop, she studied him. Nate wanted to squirm under that scrutiny. He knew what he looked like, because he felt like it, too—total hell. It made him feel exposed to have her blue eyes probing over him, compassion on her face.

"It isn't for a good reason, is it?"

"No." Nate pulled in a breath and made himself say it. "My sister just died." His voice cracked but he held on, fighting off the tears, the feeling that if he let loose that tidal wave of grief, he would just go right under and drown.

Gwenna's eyes went wide. "Oh. I'm so, so sorry." She reached out and took his hand in hers. "They're empty words and they don't fix anything, but I mean it sincerely."

Her touch was comforting, firm, despite the fact that her fingers were small and thin. She was close to him, their clasped hands brushing his thigh, and her pale blue eyes stared up at him with compassion. "Thanks." He should say something else, do better than that, but he wasn't capable of anything more.

She squeezed his hand. "Maybe we should skip the coffee . . . maybe you should head home."

"No. I don't want to. I can't, you know what I'm saying?" Nate stroked his thumb over the back of her hand. It was smooth and very cool. There was something reassuring about her, her obvious femininity, delicateness soothing. "Have you ever lost someone you love?"

There was a slight nod, than she whispered, "Yes. I know exactly how you feel."

"Who did you lose?" he asked, which was rude, but he wanted to hear, wanted to know that someone understood the pain he felt, the grief he was trying so hard to control. It wasn't the kind of thing you vented with your buddies over a beer about. There wasn't anyone he could really talk to, just say what he felt with total honesty. But for some whacked-out reason, he was spilling it to this woman and wanting answers.

"A sister. A brother. My mother." Then her eyes went wide, tears suddenly there, shiny and wet and agonized. "My daughter."

She might as well have kicked him in the gut. Nate felt horrible for asking, at the same time he felt a shocking sense of relief that she would, did understand. That he wasn't alone in his grief. But he couldn't fathom, absolutely couldn't get his head around losing so many people he cared about. And a child, a baby. His gut twisted at the thought.

"God, I'm sorry, I shouldn't have asked." With his free hand, he swiped at the tear that had fallen down her cheek with his thumb. "I can't imagine going through . . ." Nate looked at his thumb, suddenly distracted. Her tear wasn't clear, but a ruddy rust color, staining his skin. "Are you bleeding?"

"What?" Her expression was confused and she looked down at her arms and hands. "Where do you see blood?"

"On your face." He pulled his finger back so she could see. "It's like your tears are bloody." Which didn't sound healthy.

"Oh." She relaxed and waved her hand. "That's just normal for me. It's a genetic medical condition, nothing dangerous. But it's like when people have extreme sun sensitivity . . . I've been teased that I'm a vampire." She shrugged. "I know it's kind of nauseating, but it is what it is."

"A vampire, huh? Yet you're in the slayers' group." Nate wiped her cheek again, to show her it didn't bother him. He was just glad she wasn't injured in some way. Bleeding out your eyes sure in the hell didn't sound like a good thing. "So you must be a vampire playing both sides then. Have you come to suck my blood?"

Her head tilted and she gave him an intriguing, sly smile. "Only with your permission."

Ethan knew before he even got off the elevator that his sister was still in the hospital. He could sense her presence. And when the doors open, he smelled her vampire scent.

An apology was probably in order. Alexis had already told him as much, and he had a feeling his wife was right. For nine hundred years he had been criticizing Gwenna's involvement with

Donatelli, and it had never done anything but drive her faster into his weasel arms. So maybe it was time for a new tactic.

He was scanning the lobby for her, preparing to be sheepish, when he spotted his little sister with a man he'd never seen before in his life. And Gwenna was holding hands with him.

"Who the hell is that?" he asked Alexis. Gwenna didn't hang out with mortal men, which this one clearly was. Gwenna didn't hang out with anyone. She stayed in her hotel room and did . . . Gwenna things. Ethan was never really sure what his sister did with her time.

"I don't know," Alexis said, craning her neck to get a better view around him.

Ethan shifted so she could see, feeling outraged. "They're practically on top of each other."

"Wow, check that out. He's touching her face. Go, Gwenna."

"No." Ethan glared at his wife. "No 'go, Gwenna.' We don't even know who this guy is."

"What we do know is that he's not Donatelli. And if she's seeing this guy, I seriously doubt she's making it with the Italian, too. That's not Gwenna's style."

That was a good point. Gwenna was sedate. Steady. Reliable. Even in her stupid insane devotion to Donatelli she was predictable. She had always loved him and no one else. But if she was with another man . . .

"They look rather intimate, don't they?" Ethan asked, studying his sister's posture. She was leaning toward the man slightly. He wouldn't have expected Gwenna to take a mortal lover, but as long as she was staying away from Donatelli, Ethan was happy. Of course, that didn't mean he trusted anyone around his sister until he was certain of his intent. "Can you get this guy's name from Gwenna? I'll have Seamus run a background check on him."

Ethan didn't even have to look at his wife to know she was rolling her eyes. It was her favorite response to him, one he had to admit turned him on. Virtually everything Alexis did turned him on, which made for a very satisfying marriage.

"Here's an idea," Alexis said sarcastically. "Let's leave Gwenna alone and let her date whoever she wants. In peace. Without interference. You know, like let her make her own choices, whether they're mistakes or not. I like that better."

Gwenna and the mortal man moved off in the direction of the hospital coffee shop a few feet away. Ethan glanced down at his wife and scoffed. "Like you did with your sister? You've been telling Brittany what to do for twenty-six years."

Alexis, sexy little spitfire that she was, bristled. "That's totally different."

"How? We both love our sisters and we both stick our noses in their business. Just admit it."

"I won't."

"Which makes you a bigger hypocrite than me." Ethan saw the guy put his hand on the small of Gwenna's back as they got in line for coffee. "At least I'm honest about my protectiveness."

And as they soon as they got back to his casino, he was going to put in a call and have Gwenna's new little friend checked out.

God, they were both fucking morons. That's all Donatelli could think as he stared at his two principal bodyguards, Smith and Williams. Maybe he should just kill them both and start over from scratch. Surely he could find better staff if he discreetly advertised.

"Explain to me again how it was possible for Ringo to enter a locked room that the two of you were standing in front of?" Donatelli sipped blood from a wine goblet on the sofa in his hotel suite and glanced down at his cell phone. No missed calls. He was starting to get impatient with his ex-wife, Gwenna. She should at least have the courtesy to call him back. Where the hell were people's manners these days? And he was still absolutely stunned that she had used such a foul curse word with him. That was completely unlike Gwenna and, he had to say, rather unbecoming.

Smith cleared his throat. "Well. We thought he was allowed to go in there. He said he was. So we sort of let him in."

"And just stood there while he walked off with a week's supply of heroin?"

"I guess so."

"That was several grand worth of drugs." Like money grew on goddamn palm trees. Donatelli strove for patience. Not his strong suit. Never had been. He checked his phone screen again before he even realized what he was doing. Damn it. He felt his temper rising and surging, settling to pound at his temple. Where the fuck was Gwenna and why wouldn't she talk to him?

"We didn't . . ."

That set him over the edge. "You didn't know. I know. Because you're both fucking idiots." He pinned them with a hard stare. "Go tell Ringo I want my supply back. Break a few bones, show him I'm serious. And if he won't be reasonable, bring his wife to me. I'm sure I can convince her to exert her influence on her junkie husband. And he's fond of the silly bitch for whatever reason."

He waved them off. "Now get the hell out of here and send Katie to me."

His mortal lover would distract him. Ease the hard ache that had settled in his cock. Make him forget for twenty minutes that he missed his wife, that he burned for Gwenna still, that after nine hundred years of knowing each other, she was tightly entwined around his heart, his life, his very existence.

He would convince her that it was time to reconcile. That was what he wanted, almost more than the political power he had achieved in the Vampire Nation, and he would have Gwenna. Again.

Gwenna wasn't sure why she had agreed to go get coffee with a total stranger, but there was something about the way he was looking at her that had made her say yes. She didn't even like coffee, and though vampires could drink liquids, she didn't really enjoy it. It tended to sit in her stomach like a boulder. Yet Detective Thomas's eyes—a rich, deep chocolate brown—stared right into her. There was total focus on her, despite his obvious tragic loss. There was no shifting of his gaze around, no cajoling words or dissembling. Maybe it was because he had just walked away from death, but he came across as straightforward, honest, still and steady.

That was very appealing, and the complete opposite of Roberto.

So much so that she had gone into the coffee shop even when she'd known that her brother and her sister-in-law were standing in the lobby watching them. She was also curious about what the detective thought of the murder and was aware of his pain, sympathetic at the loss of his sister. If he wanted company, she was willing. She could use some herself frankly.

"What's your first name?" she asked as they sat down at a tiny table by the window. It was dark outside and the crowd in the shop was thin. "It's too cumbersome to keep calling you Detective Thomas."

"Nate." He gave a brief smile. "Not as cool of a name as yours, but it works. It's short for Nathaniel, though no one calls me that but my mother."

"Does your mother live here in Vegas?"

"Yeah, but she's in Australia right now. My parents . . ." He paused and cleared his throat. "They thought my sister was going to be okay. She was in remission, so they went to Australia for a month to visit my mom's family. I called them yesterday, but with making arrangements and the long flight, they won't be here until tomorrow."

Gwenna's heart squeezed. "Oh, your mother must be so devastated that she couldn't be here."

He gave a brief nod, then leaned back in his chair. "Sure. But I don't want to talk about it. Tell me about your friend's baby."

Nate might as well have said, "Distract me." Gwenna could understand that, the feeling that the grief was so huge and monstrous that you could only process it a tiny piece at a time or it would consume you. She could chat with him . . . she wanted to chat with him. Here was someone who didn't know her, didn't think of her as that poor sop Gwenna, Donatelli's passive ex-wife. There was nothing back at the casino that she needed to rush home to, and part of her was dreading going to her suite and finding Roberto standing on the doorstep waiting for her.

"Brittany had a girl. Ava Coco Renee Atelier."

"Now that's a hell of a name."

Gwenna laughed. She couldn't tell from Nate's still expression if he liked it or not, but she suspected he thought it was a bit much. "Brittany's husband is French." And a couple of hundred years old, but Nate didn't need to know that.

"But they live here?"

"Yes. Like I said, my brother is married to Brittany's sister, Alexis. My brother owns a casino here."

"Which one?"

"The Ava."

"Wow." Nate looked impressed. "He owns it?"

"Yes." Gwenna hoped he didn't think she was bragging. But Ethan had always been successful because he worked hard. Beyond hard. He was exhausting in his productivity.

"But you're not American."

It wasn't a question. She shrugged. "No. I'm British. I've been living in York, but I came here for my brother's wedding last August, then came back in December and decided to stay."

"Is your ex Roberto in England?"

Gwenna glanced at him in surprise. Had she said Roberto's name? She suddenly realized she couldn't read Nate's mind. Most humans came across easily to her, their thoughts floating across her consciousness like white noise until she tuned in, but with Nate there was only silence. Maybe that was because he was a detective, and used to shuttering and shielding his emotions.

"No, Roberto lives here."

"So why would you want to be where he is if he's harassing you?"

It felt like an accusation. Gwenna was tired as hell of having to explain herself, of having to work her life around Roberto and all her mistakes. "Why should I let him keep me from living by my family?" she asked, hearing the defensiveness in her voice.

He lifted his coffee cup and drank from it. Those eyes watched her, and she realized there was no judgment there. "You shouldn't, unless your personal safety is at risk."

Sighing, she ran her fingernail across the cocktail napkin her coffee was resting on. She'd painted her nails a rather bright red the day before, which was uncharacteristic for her. But she'd suddenly felt the urge to be bold. "My personal safety isn't at risk. Honestly, Roberto would never hurt me. And he can't really get close to me anyway, not if I don't want him to." Of course, he had just knocked on her suite door earlier that night. But she could have called security if necessary. "Ethan has staff that keeps an eye on Roberto. And me for that matter." Ethan thought she had no idea that he had her followed on occasion, but she was well aware of it.

She knew everything.

And she was a bird in a cage. Or to be more accurate, a bat confined to her cave.

"Staff? Like bodyguards?"

Nodding, Gwenna realized this probably wasn't the best topic for conversation with the detective who was investigating the murder she had discovered. Lunatic ex-husbands and personal security . . . she was bound to either convince him she was guilty of something, or send him screaming away from her and the mess her life was.

The first would be disastrous, the second disappointing.

Because the truth was, even at the crime scene, she had been aware that Detective Thomas was a very attractive man, in a rough sort of way. Sipping the coffee carefully, she checked out Nate's muscular arms and chiseled face. Definitely good-looking, and she could absolutely appreciate that. It had been a long three centuries in York, and it occurred to her that his muscular build could very possibly keep up with her immortal strength. Or at least close enough to satisfy her. Hell, she suspected it wouldn't require much to take care of her at this point . . . some days it felt like a warm breeze might do the trick, and Nate looked like a very sexual man. He could give her a run—or a ride—for her money. Not that she would actually do anything about it, but it was a pleasant fantasy in the quiet, warm shop.

"You're lucky you can have security like that. Hopefully it will keep your ex from ever getting physical with you." Nate held up his hand when she started to protest. "Look, I know you don't think he ever would. And maybe he wouldn't. But I'm a detective. I've seen the result of domestic violence, and sometimes these guys snap when you least expect it. Just be careful, okay?"

"Sure." She couldn't get offended because she saw Nate's sincerity, and he had the kind of job that would expose him repeatedly to violence. Violence like she had discovered that night. "How long have you been a detective?"

"Five years. Beat cop for eight years before that."

That would put him in his early to mid-thirties. "You don't look that old."

He laughed. "I feel old enough to retire tomorrow."

Gwenna smiled. "But you wouldn't. You enjoy it, don't you?"

"Yeah. I do. It's rewarding." He picked up his coffee and drank.

"My sister-in-law used to be a county prosecutor. Alexis Baldizzi. Maybe you know her?"

His eyebrow went up. "Sure, I know her. Great prosecutor. Cutthroat. I heard she married that crazy rich British casino owner . . ." He winced. "Oh, shit, that's your brother, isn't it?"

That struck her as amusing. Ethan really would hate to be labeled as crazy, but to mortals, he was simply an eccentric rich casino owner. To vampires, he was president of the Vampire Nation and a political powerhouse. She laughed. "Yes, that's my brother, Ethan. He is all of the above, and he and Alexis got married last August. I came here for the wedding, like I said, and decided to stay."

"I bet your brother and your sister-in-law had no idea you were planning to meet some guy in a train station, did they?"

"Why would they need to?" Gwenna lifted her chin up, hearing the censure in his voice. She had to remember that if she were mortal, agreeing to meet Slash like that would have been incredibly stupid. But what Nate didn't know was that she was a vampire, and hard as hell to kill. Nor could any mortal injure her or touch her against her will. Her strength, speed, and reflexes gave her a thorough advantage.

"I guess they wouldn't. Because if they had known, I'm sure they would have stopped you, like any sane person." Nate shook his head, like he still couldn't believe she had done something so ridiculous.

"No one can stop me if I make my mind up."

"Well, that's narrow-minded and dangerous."

"I didn't think it was a big deal. It was a public place."

"And probably just a place to meet you, so he could take you somewhere else in private to rape and kill you, and no one would even know where to start looking when you turned up missing."

That was a rather grim view of it. "Well, that's not what happened, is it?"

"Only because your boy either got whacked or did the whacking."

"Or it's a coincidence."

"I don't believe in coincidence. Slash wanted you in that spot." Nate crumpled up his paper napkin. "The question is why. What made you look back there, by the way?"

"I thought I heard something." Gwenna was lying. There hadn't been any sound at all. In fact, after the rush of passengers had departed, heading down the escalators to the street had been unnaturally quiet. She had instinctively taken the down escalator herself because she had smelled death. A deceased body had a very peculiar fungal and putrid odor that was unmistakable for anything else. She'd known someone was dead. It had been a matter of just figuring out where the body was, not that it existed. "And the machine was turned a little. I actually thought a cat or something was back there."

"That must have been a grim surprise." Nate shook his head again.

"It was." Gwenna wrapped her arms around her chest. Despite being nine hundred years old, she had never seen a murder victim before. She hoped she never did again. The man—boy really—had been almost unrecognizable because of the way he'd been stuffed back there, his skin waxy and pale. She shuddered involuntarily.

"Hey." Nate's voice softened. "It's okay."

"No, it's not." Gwenna sat back in her rickety chair. "It's not alright at all, because whoever that poor man is, or was, he's dead, and whoever did that to him is just walking around feeling pleased with himself for getting away with it. I feel responsible in some way . . . like if I'd gotten there sooner . . ."

"You'd be dead, too."

Highly unlikely, but she wasn't going to argue. "I know it sounds irrational, but I feel just awful."

"I wouldn't like you if you didn't." He popped the lid off his coffee cup and dumped two packets of sugar substitute into it. "Death makes us feel bad. That's normal. When it stops feeling bad, that's when we know we're in trouble."

Maybe that was what had happened to Roberto. He had lost his compassion for the suffering of others. He had learned to take his immortality for granted and fallen under the mistaken notion that having been granted eternity, he was entitled to use it as he chose.

"So your sister had cancer? How old was she?" she asked softly.

Nate didn't answer right away. He took a sip of his coffee and set it down. Then he met her gaze. The pain there was palpable.

"Kyra was twenty-five. She had leukemia."

"So young? That's just awful." And suddenly it made Gwenna profoundly ashamed. She'd had almost a thousand years of life and what had she done with them? Nothing. She had embroidered and played the harp and pianoforte, hosted dinners for Roberto, and read a vast quantity of books. But she hadn't done anything useful, not like her brother and Alexis. Not like Corbin, who had spent his vampire life engaged in genetic research.

"Yeah, it is awful. It totally sucks, really."

Nate's sister had lived but a whisper in comparison to her, yet Gwenna was ungrateful for her immortality. Or at least she had been. That had changed in recent months, and she should allow herself credit for that.

"I hope you were able to be with her at the end." Gwenna had wanted that with Isabel, had wished she'd had the chance to tell her daughter good-bye.

"Yeah, I was. Kyra, she is . . . was an amazing girl. She really did go through this whole thing with dignity and grace. I'm in awe of how brave she was. Right until the end."

The tears hung in his eyes again, and he fought them back brutally, clearly determined not to let them fall.

"It's okay to cry, you know," she whispered.

"No, it's not. Not here in the freaking coffee shop." Nate pressed on his forehead. "God, I'm sorry."

"Don't be." Gwenna reached for his free hand and slipped it in hers. "And if this isn't the place to let it go, let's find somewhere where you can."

"Like where?"

"My brother's casino. We can find a quiet corner."

"A quiet corner in a casino?" He looked skeptical.

"If you know where to go, absolutely."

She started to stand up but he resisted. "Gwenna, this isn't a good idea."

"Why not?"

"Because the department is going to have to ask you questions still about the online group you belong to. And if that victim is really Slash, there will be more questions. This isn't really even appropriate for us to be talking."

"So you came to the casino to interview me further. That's all. And we have been discussing it. I'm not a suspect, so why does it matter?"

"Everyone is technically a suspect. Especially if you knew the victim."

That honestly hadn't occurred to her. "I was in my hotel suite until nine forty-five. I took the train to the station, and then found him. I can prove I was at home until then because I had a fight with my ex-husband in the hallway right before I left. I'm sure at least someone had to have heard us."

"No one said you had to prove an alibi right now. We're a long way from that. We're just gathering facts right now." He stood up and gathered his trash. "You're right, let's go back to your casino."

"It's not mine." Gwenna picked up her coffee cup and followed him to the garbage, pitching hers after his. "It's Ethan's."

"But you live there, right?"

"Yes." Gwenna stuck her hands in her front pockets, suddenly wondering why it bothered her to admit that. "For now."

"So you moved from England a few months ago?"

"Five months ago."

"And what do you do for a living, Gwenna?"

That was a loaded question, though Nate couldn't possibly know that. "Not a damn thing."

Four

Nate Thomas had parked his car in the casino garage next to Gwenna's reserved spot, and now he was following her into the building, wondering if the reason he'd originally thought she wasn't all that smart was because she was actually incredibly sheltered. Naïve as opposed to dimwitted. While she had refused to elaborate, Gwenna had made it sound like she didn't work. She had clearly gotten married at a young age, if she had already been divorced for three years. And she was living inside her brother's pimped-out casino, which was about as far from reality as you could get.

A doorman gave Gwenna a big smile as he swung open the door for her. "Good evening, Ms. Carrick, how are you?"

"Fine, thanks, Reginald. How are you tonight?"

"Oh, can't complain." The doorman was tall and broad and held the door cheerfully for Gwenna. Then he seemed to realize Nate was actually with her as opposed to just randomly walking behind her. "Who's your friend?" he asked, voice dripping with suspicion.

"This is Detective Thomas. He's here to ask me some questions." Gwenna stopped and put her hand on the doorman's sleeve. "I was at the train station and I found some poor man's body. He'd been killed, Reginald. It was horrific."

"What!" Reginald looked outraged. "That's no good, Ms. Carrick. That's just wrong."

"You've hit it exactly."

"Does Mr. Carrick know?"

"No, thank God. And let's not tell him just yet, okay?"

"Sure, whatever you say."

"Thank you, dear."

Maybe it was being British, but sometimes Nate thought Gwenna sounded a hell of a lot like his grandmother. Yet she was young and beautiful, not a wrinkle or orthopedic shoe in sight. The contrast was a curiosity he wanted to explore. There was something totally enigmatic about her. The pieces to the puzzle seemed to jumble more, and none of them fit anywhere that he could find.

"There's a restaurant over here that is only open for breakfast. It's just a little diner thing. We can go in here if you like." She paused in the entrance to the grand lobby, skirting a glass end table. "Oh, wait, I have a better idea. We'll go in the spa. It's closed for the night and it has really lovely velvet couches."

He wanted to suggest they just go up to her place, but he knew that was wrong on a whole lot of levels. One, it would sound like a come-on, which he didn't mean. Not really. Two, he had just lectured her on dangerous behavior. Encouraging her to take a strange guy up to her room—even if was him—would encourage her carelessness. He had to take the high road, even if sitting in a darkened spa sounded way less appealing than just hanging out in her place. She'd said she had a suite, and he was betting it had a killer view of the Strip. But the truth was, the whole fact that he'd followed her in his car to the casino in the first place showed his judgment wasn't all that rock solid at the moment, so he should just let her call the shots. He wasn't even sure what the hell he was doing there.

Maybe that wasn't true. It had to do with Kyra, and the fact that he felt a little sick to his stomach, lonely, sad, and angry. He hadn't wanted to go home, but neither did he want to hang out in the lobby of a busy, crowded casino. Going to Gwenna's suite would probably be a mistake, though, given his shaky frame of mind, so the spa was really the best all-around idea.

And shit, if he lost it and blubbered, at least the lights would be dim.

"Sounds like a plan."

She smiled at him, and Nate felt something he sure in the hell shouldn't. It was a kick of lust, right where it counted. Which scared the crap out of him. The mind was weak at the moment, yet the body still was totally functioning, which made this a bad thing. A stupid idea. This was him with his head up his ass if he went up that elevator with her.

He went.

Which meant he was a total idiot.

But he was on the edge, and he knew it. Everything he felt, everything he'd lost, the hurt, the fear, the bitterness, swirled around inside him and threatened to take him down. He was going to crack, soon, the pressure pulling inside his skull, the lack of sleep, that last phone call to his parents, the indignity of yet another mindless murder on tonight of all nights, pushing and tugging at him.

It was Gwenna Carrick or a bottle of Jack, and she was a hell of lot more attractive than him drunk.

"What floor?" he asked as they stepped into an elevator with a thirtysomething couple who were leaning dangerously close to each other.

"Sixteen."

Gwenna glanced over at the pair dressed in cocktail party clothes. Nate watched her eyes widen a little at the fact that the couple were now making out vigorously. With lots of hand, tongue, and leg movement. Well, that was special. Shifting a little to block her view, aware that the guy's hand had just gone up the woman's skirt, Nate tried to think of something inane and conversational to say. "So . . ."

He had nothing. Especially since Gwenna had moved a little to see around him.

Instead of being appalled at the public fondling, she looked curious. Intrigued. She wet her lips. His own immediate and painful reaction to that was an instant boner. No hesitation, no slow inflate, just up, hard, and ready to go.

Which was more disgusting than the happy gropers behind him. He couldn't understand how he could get an erection on the same night he'd been to a crime scene and watched his sister die. It was like confirmation of everything he'd ever been told by his grandmother—his animalistic male body was totally disconnected from his emotions.

On the other hand, maybe it was just a coping mechanism of some kind. Distract him from the rough stuff with a simple physical response. That sounded right-on with what a therapist would tell him.

But he was starting to think maybe he should have stuck to the Jack Daniel's idea, because the last thing he or Gwenna Carrick needed was a one-night stand.

The elevator dinged right as the woman let out an encouraging moan in the small space, and her back slammed against the wall from a particularly aggressive lunge at her breasts by her guy.

"This is our floor," Gwenna said.

Thank God.

They stepped off as Gwenna murmured, "Well, those two are in for a fun night."

"Doesn't feel very fair, does it?" he said, glancing into the empty spa as she used a key card to open the locked door. "They're going up without a care in the world to bang each other's brains out, and here we are. Day from hell for both of us."

She glanced back at him, blue eyes filled with compassion. "I think it's safe to say yours has been worse than mine."

Damn, she really was beautiful. Just pale and soft, all pink lips and shiny hair.

What would she do if he just reached over and kissed her? If he just grabbed on, held tight, and buried himself and all his thoughts inside her?

She'd probably kill him or file a rape report.

God, he was wrecked. He needed to go home. "Maybe I should just go, Gwenna. I'm fucking walking the edge here . . . I don't think I'm very good company."

"Don't go." Moving in closer to him, her hair brushed along his jaw, her petite hands touching his chest. "I want you to stay."

Then she tilted her head up to look at him, her fair skin stark in the muted glow from the overnight lights.

"Why?" he asked, standing stiffly, aware of how soft she felt, how delicate and feminine, and how much bigger he was than her. The scent of her was delicious—fruity and womanly, with a hint of coffee—and Nate wanted to run his fingers through her pale, silken hair and just let it go, let it all go.

"Because I don't want to be alone," she said simply. "And neither do you."

Then she lifted her mouth and kissed him.

Nate hadn't expected her to do it, not really, even when he'd been considering the same damn thing, but Gwenna didn't hesitate. She just covered his mouth with hers and kissed him with a hell of a lot of passion. She tasted as good as she smelled, and her lips were tiny and soft, maybe a little lacking in finesse, but taking him with confidence and enthusiasm. It was a damn good kiss, one that ended too soon.

When she pulled back, he lifted an eyebrow. "What exactly are we doing here?"

"We're being alive, that's what we're doing."

A part of his brain, the small bit that was still functioning, wondered if she were conning him. If she knew more about the murder than she'd let on, this could be just a way to distract him. Nate thought he was damn good at reading people, though, and he got a different vibe from Gwenna. She didn't come off as savvy enough to be a con or a liar, and that pain in her eyes when she talked about her daughter had been real, and so had her horror when discussing the victim's condition. He'd stake his badge on it that she was legit.

Not that he really cared much at the moment. He suspected he'd take what she was offering anyway, even if she was a bold-faced lying user. It felt too damn good to have her body up against his.

Let it go. That's what he really needed. He just had to let it all go so he didn't completely and totally lose it, and that's what Gwenna was offering him.

Nate buried his hands in her hair on either side of her temples, letting the silky wheat-colored strands slip over his rough, callused skin. "Are you sure?" he asked, giving her a chance to back out. Because he wasn't playing around. If they started, they were damn well going to finish.

Her hands slid around his neck, and she shifted her leg so they had below-the-belt contact. "Absolutely positive."

Good enough for him. Nate gripped her hair tighter and drew her face to him, letting his lips collide with hers in a crushing, take-it-or-leave-it kind of kiss, wanting to touch and taste her with a pounding urgency. Her breath came hot and fast, mouth opening for him with little coaxing. His tongue slid inside, thrusting and dominating, and he pushed his swollen dick against her, frustrated that the awkward shove only made her bounce away from him, breaking contact.

They needed a bed. Or a couch. The wall was closer still, so Nate turned Gwenna and walked her back three feet, pinning her against the wall next to the reception desk. Better. He could get a firm hold on her hair, and grind his hips against hers while he kissed the daylights out of her. It occurred to him that maybe he should ease up, since she was petite, kind of delicate-looking, and a total stranger, but he dismissed that idea. He wasn't being rough, just aggressive, and she was taking it. Her eyes were rolled back, fingernails digging into his back, hips rising up to collide with his in a hard, desperate thrust.

Which was fucking hot. Nate disregarded all thoughts that had logic or caution attached to them and dove in, yanking Gwenna's T-shirt off over her head, messing her hair up. The shirt hit the floor and she made a futile effort to swipe stray hanks of hair off her face before giving up with a moan, while he bent over and sucked the peak of her breast. Her flesh was smooth and firm, her chest small and proportionate to the rest of her body, and Nate wanted all of it. With grappling fingers, he undid the clasp on her back and just ripped the bra off, barely noting that it was red as it followed her shirt to the carpet.

"Oh, yes," she said in a ragged voice when his mouth closed over her tight nipple. "Wow. That's really very pleasant."

He was thinking the same thing. She tasted delicious. He moved all over, from one nipple to the other and back again, loving the way his tongue slid easily across her smooth skin. Shifting downward, he traced over her ribs, dipped his tongue into her belly button, which made her jump, and since her jeans were so loose, managed to probe beneath the waistband in a brutal tease for both of them. Nate wanted at all of her, patience for the day completely wiped out.

Everything felt sharp and fast and hot, and he popped her snap with his right hand, while reaching into his back pocket with his left. He was almost positive he had a condom in his wallet since he'd made a habit of always keeping one on hand after a pregnancy scare with a girlfriend in college. He was good about replacing it when he used one, and he pulled the wallet out with jerky motions, determined to shoot himself if there wasn't one in there.

But there was, and he worked it out, letting the wallet fall from his fingers as he brought his attention back to Gwenna. She was holding on to the belt loops of his jeans, her chest heaving up and down in arousal, her cheeks pink, hair tousled. Her pants had slid down a little, undone and half-zipped, and there were red panties peeking up at him. She had her eyes closed, looking like without the support of the wall she'd be on the floor in a puddle.

Good.

Nate went down on his knees and tugged her jeans and panties down with one swift motion. A glance up showed her eyes flying open in surprise. He didn't give her time to speak, just closed the distance between them and kissed between her thighs, coaxing her legs apart with his thumbs. She was a true blond, skin flawless, body arching toward him. Nate buried his tongue into her, finding her clitoris and tasting it with bold, demanding strokes.

Gwenna was making rapid sounds of distress, her moans growing louder, frantic, hands burrowing into his hair and clamping down. Her arousal turned him on, made him so hard he ached with it, his whole body hot and tight, ready for release. He was light-headed, like he wasn't taking in enough oxygen, the room silent and dark around them, his control skittering and escaping. He stroked harder, deeper, possessively, wanting to taste her everywhere, sucking on the flesh of her thighs, and scraping his teeth across her swollen and slick clitoris.

Her legs trembled beneath his fingers and she went up on her toes, shifting away from him, trying to escape his touch. Nate knew she was going to have an orgasm, could feel the tenseness in her muscles, feel it in the way she yanked on his hair. He didn't want her there yet, not without him inside her.

So Nate stood up quickly, ignoring the pop in his left knee, and flattened his hand against the wall.

"Don't stop," she demanded, smacking his arm, which struck him as both hilarious and hotter than hell.

"I'm not stopping," he murmured, lips against hers, rubbing his erection between her thighs, encouraging her to spread further.

"It feels stopped to me," she panted.

Nate buried his head into her hair and thrust inside her with both abandonment and gratitude, a biting urgency, and hot, glorious desperation.

The tightness of her wrapped around him, stroking and milking his cock, the acute pleasure even better than he could have ever imagined.

It took all of thirty seconds to realize he wasn't going to make this time last very long. He was gone.

Gwenna couldn't believe she was standing against a wall in the chichi spa with a penis deep inside her. She wasn't exactly sure how it had happened, and if anyone had suggested to her three hours earlier that she would have sex vertically with a police detective before the night was out, she would have declared that person utterly insane. But it seemed the insane one was her, because she was in fact having sex with a virtual stranger after three hundred years of celibacy.

At least it was holding up to the wait. Nate was frantic in his attentions, aggressive and hungry, and she had to admit, she rather liked that. She wasn't sure she could have handled the intimacy of slow and explorative, but this fast and furious she was absolutely fine with. It matched her mood, her sense of hysteria at finding that man's body, at her frustration over still grieving for her daughter after so many years, her irritating helplessness that she would never, ever be able to fully disconnect herself from Roberto.

All of that mattered less when she was feeling the brutal slap and push of Nate Thomas thrusting into her. It did make her feel alive, made her vibrantly aware of her body, of the strength and power she had as a vampire. On her tiptoes, pants around her ankles, cool air and Nate's mouth sliding over her bare skin, she should have been embarrassed, should have felt self-conscious that she was for all practical purposes naked, while he was still fully dressed in his jeans and T-shirt.

But she didn't. She embraced the sensation of her bum scraping against the wall, her sandal straps digging into the tops of her feet, his fingers gripping at her waist, his penis hard and full inside her wetness, coaxing to life wants and needs she had thought were long gone.

Gwenna had never considered herself a particularly sexual person. She hadn't missed sex since her divorce, had never bothered to seek it out. But this was new and different and all-consuming. This was intense, and desperate, and overwhelming.

"Nate," she said raggedly, suddenly unsure, overpowered by all the sensations in her body, in her heart, at the feeling that she'd completely and totally lost all control. That the world as she knew it, had lived it, understood it, was shifting and cracking.

"Yeah?" He nipped at her jaw, her lips.

"I . . ." She shifted restlessly, mouth hot, throat tight, legs tensed. "I . . . don't know."

"Don't fight it, Gwenna, let it happen." Nate slowed down his pace, pulled way out, making her feel denied, and then slid back into her fully, deep.

The ability to speak, however incoherently, completely shattered. That movement, that whatever the hell he was doing, robbed her of words, thoughts. She just grabbed on to his arms and gave in to the orgasm, letting it sweep over her, a hot, shuddering rush of ecstasy.

She was aware of Nate moving faster again, of his breathing growing deeper, low grunts coming from him as he went over the edge himself, pounding hard through his orgasm, but she didn't react. Couldn't react. She just clung to him, speechless and insensible from pleasure.

Bloody hell.

The man knew how to shag.

And she had forgotten how to breathe.

They both stood shuddering and sucking in air for a minute, neither inclined to move. Then Nate was gathering her in his arms and peeling her off the wall when the phone rang, startling them both. Gwenna glanced over at it, feeling a little guilty. They were still in the spa's lobby, which was remarkably tacky. This had not been at all what she'd had in mind when she'd suggested a chat on the spa sofa. She could only imagine what Nate was thinking of her. Sense of relaxation and wonder already evaporating, Gwenna felt anxiety crash back in on her as the phone continued to ring incessantly. Anyone could have just strolled off the elevator and seen them. That would have made a pretty shot.

Obviously not having the same concerns, Nate gave a soft laugh, nuzzling her neck a little. "Sorry, I got a little carried away."

That was the thing about just giving in to passion and tossing over every inhibition she'd ever had. It was good while it lasted, but suddenly she felt awkward as hell. How in the world did she bend over gracefully to pull her pants back up?

The phone stopped ringing. Then immediately started again. As did her mobile phone in her pants pocket. That really destroyed her last shred of calm. "Oh, damn, maybe I should answer that."

"Why?" Nate asked, his expression indicating he thought the suggestion was absolutely ludicrous.

Resenting that he could just zip his fly up and be squared away and ready to head back out into the world, Gwenna tried to slide down the wall, bending her knees a little, to reach her dropped jeans. She missed gowns. This would have simply required dropping her skirts back over her legs in the nineteenth century. Not that she would know from actual experience. She hadn't taken to having sex with strangers standing up until just that very day.

"Because it could be important."

"Or more likely it's your ex trying to control you."

Well, there was that.

The spa phone began to ring yet a third time, and they both heard the elevator ding. Someone was getting off on their floor.

"Oh, damn," Gwenna said, panicking. No longer worried about how it would look from Nate's point of view, she bent over and yanked up her jeans, buttoning them posthaste despite the fact that her panties bunched painfully in parts that were sensitive and sore and didn't appreciate the rough treatment.

Nate grabbed her T-shirt off the floor and handed it to her before turning around and blocking her from view. She was yanking it over her head when she heard a voice say in surprise, "Ms. Carrick?"

Oh, lovely. It was Ethan's bodyguard and head of hotel security.

"Yes, Sam, it's me," she said, straightening her shirt and hair before peering around Nate's arm. "Can I help you?"

It really was unfortunate that even as a vampire she blushed. She could feel her cheeks burning. And there was no hope he wouldn't notice her blush or her state of disheveled dress, even though the room wasn't fully lit, because he was a vampire, too. With an acute sense of smell.

"I just wanted to make sure you're alright and that you don't need anything. We, uh, saw you come in here on the security cameras."

Oh, God. Mortification had a name and it was Gwenna Carrick. But at least she could reassure herself that they hadn't seen *her* on camera, just Nate. It would have been obvious to Sam that Nate was having sex with a vampire, given the lack of a visible partner on tape, and he had probably felt obligated for security reasons to at least investigate who that vampire might be. Ethan's former secretary, Kelsey Columbia, had been notorious for taking mortal men up to the office suite for quickies, but Kelsey wasn't allowed unsupervised in the building anymore since she had run off and married Ringo Columbia, an assassin and heroin addict.

"I'm fine, thanks so much. Sorry to cause trouble." Or more sorry she hadn't been smarter. Damn, she should have just taken Nate to her room. But she had been worried about how that would look to him or to any staff who might see her entering her room with an unidentified man. It was safe to say that this looked worse.

Sam hesitated, adjusting his cell phone headset on his ear. "Okay, then. Have a good night."

He turned around and headed back toward the elevator. Gwenna bit her lip. "Sam?"

"Yes?"

"You're going to tell Mr. Carrick about this, aren't you?" It was his job, she knew that, to inform Ethan of anything out of the ordinary. This certainly qualified as that.

But Sam shook his head. "Not if you don't want me to. If something has no bearing on hotel and casino security, I'm not obligated to tell Mr. Carrick about it."

He was letting her off the hook, sweet man. But Gwenna suddenly found that she was tired of worrying about her brother's reaction to her behavior. The goal she had set for herself was independence, and that had to start with being honest with her brother—telling him she loved him, but she needed to live her own life.

"No, that's fine, Sam. Feel free to tell Ethan. Or I can mention it to him myself. I shouldn't be up here. Though if you don't mind, I'd like the tape destroyed."

Sam almost grinned. She saw his mouth tilt up before he caught himself. "Sure thing." He nodded. "Good night."

As the elevator doors closed, Nate turned back to her. He looked amused himself. "Did we just make a sex tape?"

"It seems that way." At least he didn't appear angry with her.

"I wish I had known. I would have made sure my good side was facing the camera."

Gwenna laughed in spite of her lingering embarrassment. "Which side is your good side?"

"You tell me." His arm went around her waist, and he pulled her to him.

She liked the way he did that, so casually, so easily.

It seemed perfectly natural to say what she was thinking. "The front side. Bottom half."

"Yeah? Want to see it again? Somewhere without cameras?"

This was it. She could walk away now, astonished that she had felt such passion, but still slightly embarrassed that she had, or she could really thrust herself out of her comfort zone and explore the desire Nate inspired in her.

They had all night.

She had nowhere to be.

She'd had several pints of blood before heading out to meet Slash.

And her brother and ex-husband were somewhere else.

"I think I just might like that." Gwenna kissed him deeply. "The massage rooms don't have cameras."

"Lead the way."

She just loved the sound of that.

Five

Ringo Columbia sat in the ugly chair Kelsey had picked out for their new apartment and tried to focus on the two men in front of him.

Maybe he'd used a little too much this time, because he had the serious feeling that he was going to throw up. Just lean forward and hurl out all that blood, all that heroin, all his innards and breath and control. He hated this pain, this nausea, hated that no one would just leave him the fuck alone.

"Go away," he told Donatelli's bodyguards, Smith and Williams.

"You know we can't do that," Williams said, shaking his thick head back and forth. "You've got to return the stuff or pay for it."

"I can't return it." He'd shot up almost all of it, desperate enough that he'd skipped his preferred method of drinking his heroin in blood. This time he'd been so hungry for it, he'd just taken a needle and arm-popped it, not even looking for a vein. "And I don't have the money. So go away."

That would be the best thing, if they would just get out and leave him alone. He wanted to be alone. That seemed easy enough to him. Just open the door and disappear. But they wouldn't and it made him feel bitter as hell. What the fuck did he ever do to them?

Williams nailed him in the face with his fist, the force snapping Ringo's head back while Smith started a search of the apartment, ripping open their kitchen cabinets and desk drawers. Kelsey was going to be pissed. She worked her skinny ass off keeping their place clean and filled with weird little decorative shit, like pictures of apples and stands with scented candles. He could never figure out what was so great about having their house stink like cinnamon all the time, but she dug it.

Ringo should move out of the chair. He should stand up and kill both of the ugly motherfuckers, just take them out. He was faster and smarter and he should be able to fix this.

But he couldn't stand, not when he felt so sick and strung out, and the hazy sleepiness blanketed over the stomach rot and pounding skull. He took another hit to the head, and he groaned at the pain, leaning over the side of the chair and puking on the carpet.

Williams made a sound of disgust and stepped back. Good. Ringo hoped he'd leave, but the front door opened and he heard Kelsey's voice.

"What's going on here?"

"Hey, baby," he said, struggling to keep his eyes open. It would be so much easier to just let them close, to fall asleep and have the voices and the pain disappear.

Cold water hit him in the face. "Shit!" He jerked upright in the chair. His wife had thrown a glass of water all over him. "What the hell was that for?"

She stood there, her skinny legs apart, full lips pursed, the empty glass in her hand. "While you're just sitting there sleeping, they're wrecking our apartment."

"I wasn't sleeping." Was he? He wasn't sure. Now that he looked around, it seemed like Smith had made a lot of progress on destroying the room. There were cushions, papers, drawers pulled out everywhere.

"Okay, so you've been resting your eyes for the last ten minutes. Whatever. Call it what you want. Now get these guys out of here, Ringo." Her voice veered into whining. He really hated when she whined.

"I'd love to, but I don't think they're going to leave without their money, babe. Got any cash?"

Her shoulders slumped, her sexy little black shirt shifting over and exposing her shoulder. Ringo thought Kelsey was just the prettiest little stupid woman he'd ever met, though her brand of stupid was different than true dumbness. Kelsey was more random than idiotic, and she had some really killer qualities that he liked. He really did love her. He liked the way she giggled. But damn it, she wasn't giggling much anymore. That was a big-ass shame. She was a good giggler.

"No, I don't have any money." Kelsey turned to Smith. "How much?"

"Two grand."

"Ringo!" Her horrified expression made him ashamed, which made him angry.

"What? I just needed a little, Kels. That's all. You know what that's like." Hell, she'd been a user herself when she was a mortal. So fuck her. She wasn't any better than he was.

"Can you give us some time?" she asked Williams. "A couple of weeks?"

"I don't think so." The asshole shook his head and took one of Kelsey's scented candles and tossed it up in the air with his thick hands. "You'd have to really motivate me to risk Donatelli getting pissed at me for failing to deliver right away."

"What? A cut for you?"

"Maybe."

Ringo realized that Williams was leering at his wife, rolling his eyes up and down over her body. He sat up straighter. Maybe they could take advantage of that, keep the monkey off their back for a few weeks. "So what if Kelsey did a favor for both of you?"

"What kind of favor?"

There were limits on what he'd let these losers do to his wife, but a little oral sex had never killed anyone, and it would give them some time to find the money. Then he wouldn't have to give back the little bit of heroin he still had left. "Kelsey's a fun girl. Fucking amazing on her knees, as she can demonstrate for you if you're interested."

Smith smiled. "I might consider that. You'd like that, wouldn't you, Kelsey?"

But Kelsey didn't say anything. She just turned on her heel and went into their bedroom.

"I didn't mean right now, babe," Ringo called to her. Damn, her negotiation skills sucked. "Wait until they say yes first."

"Yes," Smith said.

Williams shook his head. "No."

Frustrated, Ringo was about to argue with him, try to persuade him to take a good deal, when he realized that Kelsey had come back out of the bedroom with a suitcase rolling behind her. That didn't make any sense to him. "What the fuck are you doing?"

"I'm leaving you."

It took him a full ten seconds to process her words. "What?" She didn't mean like leave him for good, did she? She couldn't mean that. Kelsey loved him.

"I'm moving out. You can deal with your addiction, these guys, Donatelli, all by yourself. I'm done."

Well, that sucked. "Come on. Let's talk about this." Ringo fought to keep his eyelids open. Shit, he was sleepy, and he just wanted to sink back and enjoy the haze. But he didn't want his wife to leave him. He didn't. "What's the problem?"

Her lip trembled as she grabbed her purse off the kitchen table. "Oh, I don't know, the fact that you offered to prostitute me for your drugs. That kind of says something about our relationship. You don't respect me. I'm not a priority to you."

Great, she was going into psychobabble land on him. "Oh, my God, come on. I'm sorry, shit, it just seemed like a fast fix. Don't get all worked up, it's just a blow job. You should want to help me, you know. You should support me."

She opened her mouth, than snapped it shut again. She turned to Williams. "Do what you have to do. But I'm just asking you, as a favor to me, not to kill him."

And with that his wife left. Just walked out, rolling her little prissy pink suitcase behind him, like she didn't have a fucking care in the world. Leaving him with Dumb and Dumber and a sick stomach and no money.

So much for loyalty. Love.

Ringo didn't even bother to duck the next blow. He just let it nail him dead on, rattling his teeth and bursting the skin on his cheek open. Wishing Kelsey had told them to kill him, he closed his eyes. He was already in hell. Might as well make it official.

And when he got there, he was going to make damn sure Donatelli followed right after him.

Nate was actually surprised that Gwenna hadn't just sent him packing with a thanks and a "don't call me, I'll call you." That hadn't exactly been his smoothest sexual encounter, and while he knew she'd had an orgasm, it had all been a little fast and furious. In the midst of it, he had been positive she'd been digging it, had felt her enthusiasm and her wild abandonment. But it seemed like the second he pulled it out, she was having regrets, trying to cover her nakedness up, and worrying about her phone ringing. Then she had been embarrassed as hell by the security guard and Nate had figured the night was over and he should be grateful for what he'd gotten.

But Gwenna had come back with the idea of slipping into a massage room and he was smart enough not to question fortune when it shined on him. Now he was kissing the bejeezus out of her on a massage table and feeling damn grateful she was giving him a chance to go back into the game. This time he was going to draw things out, build a little suspense, make her completely satisfied and glad she'd spent the night with him, not waking up in the morning wondering why the hell she'd had sex with a stranger.

To that end, he was employing a good old-fashioned make-out session, no rushing, no groping, just kissing slow and easy, like they were a raw sixteen and lip-locking was enough to satisfy. He could feel her relaxing beneath him, her knees sinking back down to the table, her hands letting go of the death grip she'd had on the front of his shirt. When he'd laid her down, she hadn't resisted, but she hadn't exactly embraced the idea, either. She had stiffened, knees up in the air, hands pressing against him like she was holding him at bay, her head slightly up off the pillow.

But now she was sort of melting onto the bed, all of her body relaxing and opening for him, her hair spread out around her head, her breathing soft and languid. Nate ran his tongue across her bottom lip, enjoying the sound she made. It was a tiny sigh, a release, a letting go. That was what he wanted, what they both needed. Here in the narrow semidark room, with a lingering scent of earthy candle and lotions, there was nothing to worry about. No reality. Just each other and pleasure, for a short space of time, before it would all crash back in on them.

Nate wasn't all that comfortable half standing, half leaning over her on the bed, but he was capable of compartmentalizing. He could ignore his calf muscle burning for the privilege of running his finger over her smooth cheek, down her neck, across her shoulder. Gwenna had amazing skin, with absolutely no imperfections anywhere. It was like brushing his lips over satin sheets, cool and sleek and expensive. He was very conscious of how big and rough and *guy* he was next to her, and he liked that. She was delicate and slight and all things soft and feminine.

"This is very nice," she murmured, breaking their kiss. "Did you notice the bed is heated? It feels delicious."

He had noticed because it was the last thing in the world he needed. He was generating plenty of heat on his own and knew if he lay down on the massage table with her, he was going to break out into a massive sweat. But he had noticed that Gwenna's skin tended to be always cold. She must have a slow metabolism or something. "Glad you like it. I bet it would feel even better under the blanket." With her clothes off.

"We're not going to fit in here together, you do know that, don't you?" She looked up at him with a slight smile.

God, her blue eyes were so gorgeous he could just about eat them. When he stared into their depths, when he saw all that pain, all that melancholy, all that determination, he wanted to bury himself in her and never, ever leave. It was scary as hell, but very compelling. Irresistible.

"We'll fit. We just have to do a little prep work." Nate ripped his shirt off over his head. "Your turn."

A spot of color appeared in her cheeks, but she sat up and removed her T-shirt, too, though she kept it bunched in front of her.

"You know what's coming next, don't you?" he asked, for some reason hoping he wouldn't actually have to say they needed to both take their pants off before he climbed under that blanket with her. Otherwise, once they were under, one of them was going to topple to the floor if they tried to undress on the narrow bed.

Expecting her to dance around what he was saying, she stunned him by saying, "Well, I'm hoping gobs of brilliant sex is coming next. Please tell me I'm right."

Nate let out a laugh. Gwenna was full of surprises. Good ones. "You are absolutely one hundred percent correct. But we have to ditch the jeans to make this work." To put action to his words, Nate undid his pants and got rid of them in two seconds. The boxer briefs followed suit.

Gwenna wasn't taking her jeans off, which was disappointing. She was too busy ogling him to undress, which he had to admit was hot. It made his cock jump a little at the clear appreciation she was showing. Her eyes went wide, and her pink lips formed an "O" at his movement, and her tongue flicked out to lick her lip. Nate forgave her for still having clothes on. Especially when she rolled on her side and wrapped a hand around him, stroking lightly up and down.

"Do you mind?" she asked.

Give him a minute to think about that. *Hell, no.* "Not at all."

"You're bigger than I expected," she murmured, using both hands to glide up and down on his shaft, fingers tickling over his balls.

Wait a minute. Even through the grip of pleasure, Nate wondered what that statement implied. "Bigger than you expected *before* or *after* I was actually inside you?"

Her fingers stilled. She gave a soft laugh. "Sorry. I meant before. You know, in general. Bigger."

Alright then. "I've never made a study out of it, but I'm glad I don't fall short in your eyes." And when was she going to start moving again? Nate thrust his erection into her cupped hand, trying to encourage her to stroke again.

She took the hint. "No, you definitely don't fall short."

Then she leaned forward and wrapped her lips around him. Nate closed his eyes and groaned. Wow. That was a beautiful thing.

Gwenna was shocking herself, but only in the best of ways. She couldn't believe she'd just taken it upon herself to pull Nate's erection into her mouth. But when she had turned on her side, it had been right there, and she had been curious. His whole body was muscular and firm, with hair in various places, lending to his overall rugged and masculine appearance, and his erection had added to the singularly attractive picture. Everything about him shouted male, and she had wanted to touch him, explore the way his flesh felt.

She also had the urge to taste his blood, to sink her fangs into his erection and suck on that pulsing hot liquid, but she knew the only way to do that was to put Nate under a glamour, and that wouldn't be right. He should have the option to say yes or no to her nipping some blood off him, which would require explaining that yes, in fact, she truly was a vampire. Which wasn't a conversation for the moment. They had more important things to take care of right now.

Like the fact that she was desperately aroused yet again, and amazed at that feeling. But as she slid her mouth up and down over Nate's flesh, she had a sexual epiphany. This actually felt astonishingly good. Tasted delicious. Felt powerful. Like she held the key to his control in her movements. A shift here, a lick there, and she could change the tenor of his pleasure, increase his moans, feel his body tense in ecstasy. It was exciting to register that kind of equality, that kind of give-and-take between them, that it wasn't him dominating the experience. The way she was used to with Roberto.

This was completely different, this was mutual pleasure, and she wanted to explore it fully. She took Nate into her mouth over and over until he was slick with her saliva, his hands gripping the back of her head, his heart pounding loudly in her vampire ears, and her own body was hot and tight and aching with desire. Finally, she broke off, breathing hard, her lips wet and swollen.

"Holy crap, Gwenna." Nate sucked in some air and shuddered. "You're killing me."

"But in a good way, right?" she asked, lying on her back and shrugging out of her jeans, making sure she did it slowly, human style, as opposed to with vampire speed, which she would prefer. Yet whisking her pants off before he could blink was sure to raise questions at a time when she didn't feel like talking.

"Absolutely in a good way." Nate bent over, dug around in his pants.

"What are you doing?" Back on her side, she leaned over and studied his bum. Very nice. Tight.

"I'm looking for a condom."

Knowing there was no way to convey to him that she could neither get pregnant nor give or receive a sexually transmitted disease, she kept quiet.

"Shit! I only had one." Nate's face was scrunched up in frustration, his voice angry.

Gwenna felt the need to soothe him, despite her own very real disappointment. She had truly wanted him inside her a second time. But she was willing to get over it and focus on oral sex. That's how big about it she was prepared to be. She reached out and traced her fingers over his abdomen. "No matter. We'll still find things to do, I'm sure." Dropping her wrist, she enclosed his erection with her palm. "Now just relax. You've gotten tense."

His teeth were gritted. "That makes me tense. In a good way. I could run downstairs and get some condoms . . . there's got to be a store open somewhere in this place. It's a casino. You can buy everything twenty-four/seven in a casino."

But Gwenna was feeling too in the moment to bother. She just shook her head. "Don't worry about it. Come onto this bed with me, Nate." Letting go of him, she kicked the blanket off her body with her feet.

It was a moment of pure and total liberation, watching his face go dark with desire, hearing his breath hitch. No man but her ex had ever seen her completely unclothed like that, and she wanted to revel in the feeling, savor the sensation that Nate found her attractive.

"You're amazingly beautiful," he said, eyes sweeping from head to toe and back again. "I'm a cop and not good at saying pretty things, but it's true. You're just . . . perfect."

Her instinct was to point out all the things that were wrong with her, categorize all the flaws, both physical and emotional. To tell him that she was too pale, too short, too sickly looking, and that she wasn't perfect because she had wasted nine hundred years of life doing virtually nothing of importance. But the point was to stop recriminating, to live in the moment, to accept each day as is and enjoy it, so she held on to that, smiled, believing Nate. "Thank you."

"Scoot over."

She expected him to climb on the bed with her, snuggle up alongside her, kiss her. But of course that would essentially be foreplay to penetration, and they couldn't do that. It was logical, the action he took, but she was still wholly unprepared for him to get on the bed on his side. In the opposite direction of her, legs by her face, so that his head was right down by her . . . "Oh!"

Embarrassed by both the action and her verbal reaction, Gwenna bit her lip as his tongue slid across her clitoris. She honestly had not been at all prepared for that. Nor had she anticipated his penis would be lingering in front of her face in a not so subtle invitation.

They were on their sides. They were head to feet, both ends, on a massage table. And he was a casual acquaintance, if you could even call it that. She should be astonished at herself. Absolutely and utterly ashamed.

Gwenna licked the head of his shaft with her tongue, tasting the sweet sticky fluid there. No, she wasn't feeling particularly guilty, regretful, or cautious. If she'd got this far, she was damn well going to experience all the night had to offer.

He made sounds of encouragement between his own ministrations. Gwenna was a little overwhelmed by the simultaneous sensations of him stroking between her thighs with his tongue while she took the length of him past her lips. It was delicious, heated, frantic. They quickly found a rhythm, him sliding inside her at the same time his cock went deep into her mouth, and Gwenna lost the ability to think rationally. Bloody hell, he was everywhere, filling every part of her, tripping off little pings of ecstasy all over her skin, her clitoris, her vaginal muscles. She could feel the tightness building, enjoying the echo between mouth and inner thighs. It was so good, it was almost too much, everything everywhere all at once, and she pulled back, knowing she was going to careen over the edge and lose control.

Nate's thighs were hard and muscular and she focused on them, reaching forward and giving in to the urge to nip at his warm flesh. Her fangs penetrated, tiny beads of his thick, rich blood dripping over her tongue. Nate jerked a little, his tongue pausing on her, but she squeezed his cock with her fingers, relaxing him back into motion, loving the intimacy of his flavor, his essence rolling back into her throat. It gave her a hint of his thoughts, too, a small mingling of his emotion with hers, the acute sensation of his pleasure blending and flowing over into her as she sucked, not drinking, just tasting. While his tongue stroked her, she broke contact with his thigh, licking her lips to take in the last lingering drops of his blood. At the moment she let him go, he plunged deep inside her and Gwenna gave in to her need and exploded.

It was an amazing feeling, that sensation of leaving her body entirely, of losing all muscular control and flipping around recklessly, wanting to back away from the acute pleasure and at the same time to sink more completely into it. He clamped on to her thigh to keep her from catapulting off the table as he stroked and tasted, and she wanted to scream with the delicious pleasure of it all.

This was what it was to feel alive.

And as her convulsions slowed down, she leaned over and took Nate back into her mouth to give him the same feeling. Gwenna could admit she wasn't the most skilled with this form of sex, especially not lying on her side on a massage table, but

Nate seemed to appreciate what she was doing with tongue and lips, so she kept at it, indulging her own curiosity by wrapping her hand around him and sliding up and down as a follow-up to her mouth. He felt wonderful, hard and tight with strength, and when he tried to pull back, she held on, not wanting to let go.

Her eyes were closed, but she knew when he was about to come, felt the tenseness in his body, heard his strangled groan. Then he was there, and Gwenna held on, enjoying the thrill of knowing she'd pushed him to that point, feeling the power of the pleasure between them, appreciating the taste and feel of him.

After a solid sixty seconds of them both just lying on the bed panting, Gwenna's mind a blissful blank, her body undergoing happy little aftershocks, Nate stumbled off the table. By the time Gwenna could formulate the question to ask what he was doing, he had climbed back on, this time his head by hers, and pulled the blanket over them. There was no hesitation on his part, he just moved in right next to her, pulling her tight against him, his arm securely across her chest, stroking the side of her breast.

He kissed her hair, above her temple, which suddenly made her want to cry.

"It's good to be alive, isn't it?" he said.

Gwenna knew what he meant. Knew that he saw death on a regular basis, knew he had to struggle with the finite nature of people, the constant sense of loss. She suspected that he didn't understand how to deal with a personal loss, like that of his sister, when he was so used to emotionally distancing himself with homicide victims.

"Yes, it is." She wiggled backward, getting closer to him, wanting that warmth, wanting that feel of his naked flesh pressed against hers.

They lay in silence for a minute, Nate's mortal heart beating even and steady, his chest brushing hers as it rose and fell with his breathing.

"A few months ago, I had this guy use me as a hostage." Gwenna wasn't sure why she spoke, but it seemed like if anyone would understand what she had been feeling, it was Nate.

"What? Are you serious?" Nate gripped her a little tighter. "What happened?"

It was easy to remember that moment when Gregor, a Russian vampire, had used her as a bargaining chip with Roberto. What wasn't easy was admitting how it had made her feel. "I stood there when he grabbed me, and he put this knife to my throat . . . and I have to tell you, at that minute I wanted to die. I wanted to just let him take my life and take this pain and guilt and boredom and make me go away. And I am so very ashamed of that."

Gwenna wasn't sure what she expected or wanted Nate to say, maybe acknowledge she was a horrible person for having such thoughts, but he actually said, "I doubt that's how you really felt."

"Excuse me?" Gwenna tried to move out of his grip, but he held on tighter. How could he dismiss what she had just said? It was a deep confession and he had the utter nerve to say she didn't mean it? "I absolutely did feel that way."

"You don't want to die, Gwenna . . . if you did, you would be dead already. But he played into your guilt, your sadness, and for a minute, maybe, you thought it would be easier to just let it happen, let it all go, leave this world. But he didn't and you were glad, weren't you?"

She sighed. "Yes. I'm glad to be alive."

"You've been through a lot." It wasn't a question, but a statement, his lips brushing over the top of her head.

"No more than anyone else." That was where her shame came from. She had held on to her grief, her pain. "After it happened, I realized how very selfish and shortsighted I've been . . . I can't and shouldn't control the length of my life, but I can control what I do in the time that I'm here."

Nate gave her a small squeeze. "Amen to that, Gwenna."

Gwenna stared at the wall, reflecting how odd, yet how right, it felt to be there, to have taken an opportunity and seized it, how interesting and intriguing it was to talk to someone she hadn't known for five hundred years. How pleasant it was to let her sexuality back out to play after keeping it in check for three centuries.

She wanted to say something, to think of some way to say thank you to Nate without sounding like a complete idiot, but she suddenly realized something else.

Nate was asleep.

And her phone was ringing again.

Gwenna listened to the phone ring and wrestled with her conscience. It had to be Roberto. Which meant she wasn't obligated to answer it. But she should turn it to vibrate so it didn't disturb Nate.

Reluctantly leaving the warm bed, and the warmer man, Gwenna slid out from under the blanket and searched for her purse, which was somewhere on the floor. Feeling a little odd scrambling around in the nude, she grabbed on to her panties and wiggled back into them. Then she added her T-shirt for good measure.

Her phone stopped ringing, then started again. She found it and was about to switch it to vibrate when she saw on the screen that it was Alexis calling. Her sister-in-law didn't ring her all that often, so Gwenna found it odd. She answered, horrible visions of something tragic having happened to Brittany, the baby, or Ethan.

"Yes?" She kept her voice low, very conscious of Nate two feet away. But he was sleeping hard, not stirring at all.

"Okay, we have a girl crisis. Are you busy or can you come over?"

Alexis always cut right to the heart of things. "What crisis?"

"Kelsey is here, crying her eyes out, and babbling about her marriage being over . . . she's totally destroyed, her mascara is all bleeding down her face, and I don't know what the hell to do with her. You know I suck at comforting people. Cara's back in Ireland, Brit's in the hospital, so you're all I've got. I need you to come and say the right things."

Walking out into the hall so she didn't disturb Nate, Gwenna wanted to both roll her eyes and laugh simultaneously. "I hardly know Kelsey. I doubt she'd appreciate me showing up right now."

"But you're very maternal. Please?"

Gwenna made a face. That was absolutely the way to make her feel guilty. Grateful she couldn't show up on the security cameras since she was rumpled in nothing but her T-shirt and panties, Gwenna paced back and forth. "Okay, fine, but I can't really see what I can do."

"Well, it will definitely be better than my handling of the situation. I told her she was better off without that junkie sack of shit husband of hers, and now she's locked in my bathroom bawling."

"You called her husband a junkie sack of shit?" Gwenna sometimes suspected Alexis was missing the gene for tact.

"It's the truth." Alexis sounded defensive. "You've met Ringo. He's a waste of space."

Gwenna had met Ringo only once at Roberto's when she had gone to discuss her ex-husband's stubborn insistence on continuing to pay her alimony she neither needed nor wanted. Kelsey's husband had been quiet, clearly a drug abuser, though Gwenna had felt more desperation from him than anything else. He'd looked like he was in a silent agony, begging for a way out. She hadn't sensed any violence from him, and she believed everyone deserved a second chance, despite what Alexis was always saying about every offender being a repeat offender waiting to happen.

Which was probably all the more reason that she couldn't justify sitting in a massage room watching Nate sleep when Kelsey was hurting. "Alright, give me a few minutes. I need to pop by my room first."

"Why, where are you?"

Damn. She was terrible at discretion. "Just running a few errands."

"With that hunky guy we saw you with at the hospital?" Alexis's voice sounded downright gleeful. "Shit, if you're with that hottie, don't worry about me and Kels. We'll work through it. I'll get her drunk or something."

"No, it's fine. I'll be there." Then some little devil inside her prompted her to say, "He's actually sleeping now, so it's good timing."

"Oooohhhh. That sounds promising."

Gwenna could feel her cheeks going hot, and not just from embarrassment. She was actually feeling a bit boastful. Yes, she had a naked man sleeping a few feet away from her. And since she didn't intend to inform the world at large, the least she could do was brag on it to her sister-in-law. Because there really was something fun and exciting and delicious about what she had done. "He's mortal. He'll be out for hours."

She didn't mean that quite the way it sounded—like she'd thoroughly wore him out—but Alexis just laughed.

"You go, girl."

"I'll see you in a few minutes." Gwenna quickly hung up, not wanting to give Alexis time to dig further into her relationship with Nate. Because she had no idea where they went from here, if at all, and she didn't want to speculate out loud about it. That would ruin the pleasant satisfaction she felt.

Going back into the room, she finished getting dressed. Nate was still out cold. She figured she had hours before he even roused. He'd had a very rough couple of days, and he probably hadn't slept well. Given what he was still facing with making arrangements for his sister's funeral, it was a good thing for him to be sleeping so deeply. She'd chat with Kelsey and be back in an hour, and he'd never know she'd been gone. It wasn't like she could sleep anyway. After nine hundred years of night walking, nothing could force her to sleep at only three in the morning.

It seemed like she should leave him a note or something and let him know what she was about, but at the same time that struck her as odd. She could call him and leave a message on his cell, but she didn't have the number and she couldn't very well dig through his pants looking for it. Besides, she'd be back in a flash.

Sucker Bet

Nate woke up to the sound of screaming. Intense, feral, female screaming. It yanked him straight out of a deep sleep, almost sending him rolling off the bed onto the floor. Heart pounding, head thick and disoriented, he sat up and tried to figure out where the hell the noise was coming from.

A woman he'd never seen before in his life was standing in the doorway staring at him in utter horror, hysterical shrieking coming from her mouth. Then as equally baffling as the screaming, she suddenly turned and ran, taking that hideous sound with her. Thank God.

Nate swallowed hard and tried to settle his heart rate back to normal. She'd taken five years off his life, easily, and no one had the right to produce volume like that before he'd had his coffee. Rubbing his eyes, he wondered where the hell Gwenna had gone. She must have slipped out to use the restroom or something, and lucky her, had missed getting caught in the buff by a spa employee.

Glancing down, he saw the blanket was history. At some point, probably because of Gwenna's body tucked up next to his and the heated bed, he had completely kicked the blanket off. It was on the floor. And he was totally naked.

The woman reappeared in the doorway, with a coworker. The first woman was young and thin, the second was older, and heavily padded. Interestingly enough, it was the younger woman who looked horrified, like she was certain he was a gigantic pervert who had slunk into the massage room to flash her. The older woman looked more curious than anything else, her eyes sweeping over him nice and slow-like.

She said, "You're either really early for your appointment or really late."

"I don't have an appointment."

"We don't do walk-ins." Disapproval crossed her face. "And how did you get in here in the first place?"

"Just call security!" the younger one said, her ponytail bouncing as she backed up, clearly ready to run again.

"No, don't do that." Nate held his hand out reassuringly. "Look, I'm a friend of Gwenna Carrick's. I'm actually a detective with the Las Vegas Police, and Gwenna let me spend the night here." That was the truth, in essence. But he knew she wouldn't want everyone to figure out they'd actually spent the night together.

"Gwenna Carrick?" They glanced at each other, obviously unsure.

"Do you know Gwenna?" Nate tried to discreetly shift the pillow in front of him. He was comfortable naked, but this conversation was getting kind of extensive.

"Sure, she comes in here once a week for a massage, our last appointment of the day."

"Well, she's a friend and she let me crash here. But if you ladies would give me a minute, I'll, uh, get dressed and be out of your way."

"Oh!" The young one blushed.

The older one took another lingering look, not even trying to hide the fact. Nate plopped the pillow firmly on his unit. Geez, he wasn't some stud horse. She didn't need to check him out so intently.

"Did you see Gwenna on your way in here by chance?" he asked, when it became obvious they weren't leaving.

"Nope."

Ponytail shook her head as well.

Nate started to wonder where exactly Gwenna had run off to. And why she'd left him alone, naked, in the massage room. The warmth, the intimacy, of the night before felt suddenly and inexplicably gone without Gwenna in his arms.

And on the heels of that loss, he felt the weight of responsibility crashing in on him, heavy, brutal, and raw. Today he had to make arrangements for Kyra's funeral. Today he couldn't avoid the truth—his sister was dead and it sucked.

There was also a killer to catch.

And a blond Brit beauty to track down.

Tired of waiting for the women to leave, and resigned to a day almost as hellish as the one before, Nate climbed off the table and went for his clothes. He wasn't looking forward to what he had to do.

Yet it was satisfying to hear the younger woman scream again when he stood back up, jeans in hand, and gave her a full frontal.

Gwenna made inane sounds of comfort, patting Kelsey's head, and looked to Alexis for assistance. She wasn't exactly sure what to do with the woman sprawled across her, head in her lap like Kelsey was a three-year-old and Gwenna her mother.

Alexis just shrugged and held her hands out. No help there. No wonder Alexis had called her—Gwenna couldn't see Alex tolerating Kelsey's clinging for more than thirty seconds.

"Kelsey, dear, you have to realize that Ringo just isn't himself right now." Feeling terrible for the pain Kelsey was suffering, Gwenna stroked her long dark hair and tried to use logic. "You're not dealing with Ringo, your husband, but Ringo, the drug addict. When someone is caught in the grip of a drug like that, it becomes their entire priority. They're no longer the person you knew, and you can't take his behavior as an insult."

Kelsey lifted her head off Gwenna's lap and sniffled, her face a swollen, splotchy, mascara-streaked mess. "He told two guys I would give them a blow job if they ignored the fact that he stole drugs from them!"

Okay, so that was rather appalling. "But if he was in his right mind, he wouldn't have done that."

"I know. I like him so much better when he's being Kyle." On her side now, Kelsey wiped her cheeks on the thighs of Gwenna's jeans.

A little unnerved by the invasion of her personal space, Gwenna tried not to squirm. And she always thought it was weird as hell that Kelsey called Ringo by the name *Kyle*. She didn't understand how that was a nickname, but then again, Kelsey wasn't always easily understandable.

"So you have a decision to make . . . you either have to be patient and hope Ringo will get off the heroin, or you can cut ties once and for all and get on with your life."

"Those choices suck." Kelsey's lip trembled aggressively. It astonished Gwenna that Kelsey had been crying for literally hours on end, but her lipstick had neither smeared nor faded. She'd have to ask for the brand when Kelsey had calmed down a bit.

"Yes, they do."

"There really is no choice," Alexis said, crossing her arms in front of her chest. "You can't go back to that loser."

Really, Alex needed a class. Sympathy 101.

Kelsey's eyes shimmered with blood tears. Gwenna had been intrigued by that fact for the last hour as she'd watched Kelsey cry. She'd met only a few vampires over the years who cried blood tears like she herself did, and it was interesting that Kelsey was one of them.

"Boys are stupid," Kelsey said with vehemence.

That was no news bulletin. "You won't get an argument from me. I was married to Roberto Donatelli, remember? I'm not exactly a poster vampire for Good Choices."

Kelsey sat up, much to Gwenna's relief. Her legs were going numb.

Wiping her nose with her wrist, Kelsey said, "It's Donatelli's fault that Ringo is an addict."

That irritated Gwenna slightly. "So maybe Roberto makes drugs accessible to men like Ringo, but that doesn't make him responsible. Ringo is an adult and he made the choice to start using."

"No, he didn't. Donatelli slipped the heroin in Ringo's blood and got him addicted before he even knew what was happening, when he was still just a fledgling."

"Somehow I highly doubt that." What purpose would that serve? And Gwenna knew Roberto had his flaws, but willful drug addict creator didn't fit his personality. Too messy. Too malicious.

Her voice had got sharper than she intended. But sometimes she was tired of everyone implying Roberto was pure, unadulterated evil. There were lots of positive points to Roberto's personality. He was generous and loyal and charming. She never would have married him in the first place if he were Satan in Italian shoes.

"It's true!" Kelsey insisted.

Alexis jumped in. "Hey, now, no catfights over worthless men in my house. We can all agree that every man is responsible for his own behavior, and that neither guy is exactly a saint or guilt-free here. What's more practical and more important is what Kelsey is going to do now. You need a place to stay. And a job."

Gwenna flushed a little. Alexis was right. They needed to focus on practicalities. And why was she defending Roberto anyway? God knew he'd probably throw her to the wolves. But even as she thought it, she knew it wasn't true. Roberto would try to control her, dominate her, subjugate her, but he would never allow anyone to actually physically harm her.

Damn, it was complicated when you shared the kind of history they did. Though not even Roberto knew Gwenna's deepest secret, and that worried her lately. Half a dozen people now knew about Isabel, her daughter. But Roberto didn't. And she suspected for the first time in their long lives, he would want to kill her when he found out she'd had his child and had never told him, not even during the three hundred years of their marriage.

"I'm sure Ethan will let Kelsey stay in the hotel."

But Alexis shook her head. "I don't know about that. It's a security issue, and you know how Ethan is about security lately. Kelsey didn't exactly endear herself to Ethan when she helped Ringo escape from his house arrest."

Kelsey didn't say anything, just bit her pouty lip as she sat on the couch next to Gwenna.

"And Ringo did try to kill Ethan, after all." Alexis looked rather put out by that fact.

"On Donatelli's orders," Kelsey said.

They were getting nowhere. "Okay, we've disintegrated into defending our respective men again. And frankly, I'm not sure any of them deserve our loyalty."

Both Alexis and Kelsey's mouths shot open.

Gwenna held up her hand. "It doesn't matter! The question is, are you leaving Ringo for good or just taking a little marital break?"

"I don't know." Kelsey rubbed her hands on the knees of her tight jeans. "I really, really love him. I want him back to *him*. I want him better."

"Babe, you can want it all you want for him, but Ringo has to decide he's ready to be clean and stay clean. You can't make it all okay for him," Alexis said in a soft voice.

Gwenna heard the genuine sympathy from her sister-in-law, and she knew she was right. Kelsey couldn't fix her husband. Any more than Gwenna could alter the inherent flaws in Roberto. You could care about someone until you were blue in the face, but that didn't solve real, concrete problems.

"But it's because of Kyle," Kelsey said.

The tone of Kelsey's voice had Gwenna swinging her head around to stare at her. Kelsey sounded odd, eerie, unnaturally high, and suddenly very calm.

"Who the hell is Kyle?" Gwenna asked.

She glanced over at her sister-in-law, who was shaking her head. But she wasn't sure if Alexis didn't know the answer, or if she was indicating that Gwenna shouldn't go there with Kelsey.

Kelsey suddenly stood up and tossed her hair over her shoulder. "I shouldn't have come here. I don't want you to get into trouble with Mr. Carrick. He hates me now."

"Where are you going to go? Don't worry about Ethan." Alexis ran her hand through her short blond hair. "We'll work something out. Why don't you go check into another hotel? Get a good day's sleep and we'll see about finding you a job tomorrow night."

"Tomorrow night I'm going to The Impalers concert," Kelsey said, adjusting her bra and V-neck T-shirt so her nonexistent cleavage was visible.

Gwenna was struggling to follow the thread of Kelsey's thoughts. Obviously so was Alexis because she flexed her fists and took a deep breath.

"Okay . . . so after the concert we can discuss finding you a place to stay permanently, and a job. And by the way, who the hell are The Impalers?"

"They used to be The Suckers. They play classic rock. I know the bass player. We used to party in New York in the sixties when my name was Summer."

Honestly, Gwenna just had to give up. She had no idea whatsoever what Kelsey was talking about.

"Who are you going with?"

"No one."

"You're going alone?"

Obviously attending a rock concert solo sounded as batty to Alexis as it did to Gwenna, but then she'd been a virtual recluse for three hundred years. She'd never set foot in a bar or concert, and the thought of doing it alone was literally incomprehensible.

"Sure."

"I know I'm going to regret this," Alexis said, "but maybe I should go with you. We haven't had a girls' night out in a while."

"Cool." Kelsey smiled at Alexis. "Wear something sexy. There will probably be cute guys there. And the boys in the band are all single."

Gwenna wished she could flip a switch and turn off her angst as easily as Kelsey did. She could have spared herself a few centuries of worry.

"Want to come with us, Gwenna?" Kelsey asked. "I could do your hair."

As tempting as that offer was, she had to pass. "I think I'll skip this time . . . I might have plans for tomorrow night."

Maybe it was presumptuous, but she was rather hoping Nate would be interested in another go at it. Especially as he was sure to have another painful day ahead of him.

Alexis grinned. "Gwenna has a mortal boyfriend."

Damn it, she was blushing. "He's not a boyfriend. He's just a friend." Who she happened to have shagged. She thought they called that friends with benefits, which absolutely worked for her. "And if my plans don't work out, I'll ring you. Maybe I will go to the concert."

Anything to avoid questions about Nate. Speaking of which, she needed to scoot back to the spa before the day staff strolled in and found him.

Before he thought she'd ditched out on him.

Of course, maybe he wouldn't want to see her. Maybe he regretted what had happened.

Maybe he was too busy to worry about where she was.

Maybe he would never think twice about her again.

And maybe she was a highly neurotic vampire who needed to get out of the house more often.

Why did it feel like once a penis was thrown into the mix, she was utterly incapable of handling herself? Roberto had made her ridiculous, left her feeling completely out of control. And she was determined no man would ever have control of her again.

If Nate wanted to see her, he knew where to find her. He was probably too busy with his sister's funeral arrangements to give her a second thought anyway. She didn't want to intrude on his grief, or put herself where she wasn't wanted. And she had got neurotic again. Damn it.

No dangling after men, no wallowing, no worrying. She was independent now.

"Actually, I'll go with you. It should be fun." Fun wasn't the point, though. The principle was.

Kelsey let out a whoop. "Cool! And you have to wear something blue. You look hot in blue."

That was all that mattered then.

Seven

Normally, Nate knew how to take a hint.

But he wasn't feeling particularly normal.

He stood in the lobby at the Ava, feeling exhausted, gritty, stubborn. The lingering taste of bad coffee was in his mouth, and his shoulder muscles were screaming from being taut with stress all day.

So Gwenna Carrick had slipped out on him. He should leave it at that. Let it go.

But he didn't want to. He wasn't in the mood to put up with a disappearing act. If she didn't want to see him again, fine, whatever, but she should have said it to his face. There should have been a good-bye. What was so fucking hard about that?

And he had some questions for her regarding the dead guy in the train station. Some interesting little facts had popped up during the course of the day and he was curious as to what her reaction would be to the news.

Nate went up to the front desk. "I need to speak to Gwenna Carrick. What room is she in?"

"I'm sorry." The desk clerk gave him a generic smile, her blond hair sliding over her boxy uniform jacket. "I can't give out that kind of information."

Extracting his badge from his pocket and holding it up in front of her, Nate said, "I'm Detective Thomas with the Las Vegas Metro Police. I need to speak to Ms. Carrick about an ongoing murder investigation."

The girl blanched. "Oh, um. Hold on. Let me get my supervisor." She turned and ran off.

Nate was tempted to just reach over the counter and type Gwenna's name into the computer, but he restrained himself. Five minutes later he had the information he needed and he was in the elevator heading to the twenty-first floor.

He had questions and he was going to get answers.

Gwenna scanned through her e-mail, checking both her private account and the slayers' loop for signs of Slash.

There were posts from him the night before, but that was unreliable as far as she was concerned. Sometimes e-mails hit the loop immediately, sometimes there were random and unpredictable delays. It didn't prove that Slash wasn't the guy now lying in the morgue.

The possibility of his death made her shiver. Not that she had any reason to feel guilty. He had suggested the meeting location, and in his many posts, Slash hadn't come off as a particularly nice guy, but still. It wasn't like being a bit of a shit in e-mail justified popping someone off.

But she actually discovered a personal e-mail from Slash to her that appeared to have been sent that morning, given the time listed in the header. That was promising and she went to click on it when the doorbell rang.

"Damn." She really wanted to see what Slash had to say. Scanning it quickly as she stood up, she read a quick apology from him for missing their scheduled meeting. He'd had to work, he said, and couldn't get away in time.

The doorbell rang again and Gwenna jogged over, vampire speed, her mind processing Slash's e-mail. If he was at work the night before, surely he couldn't have been killed and stuffed behind a ticket dispenser then. That meant it was all a coincidence. The murder victim had nothing to do with Slash or the slayers' loop. And she'd just been stood up.

It was a total relief.

She opened the door without checking the peephole, expecting to see Alexis or Kelsey, early for their concert outing. Kelsey had threatened to bring a big giant bag of makeup to play with on Gwenna. Already intent on protesting, she yanked the door open and opened her mouth, an adage about "less is more" on her lips.

The words died when she realized it was Nate at her door. Looking tired, angry, and impatient, if his raised hand was any indication. He was going for a third knock with a taut fist.

"Hi!" she said inanely, wishing like hell she wasn't wearing yoga pants. But she'd just thrown them on after a shower, knowing Kelsey would insist on going through her closet and picking out an outfit anyway. Kelsey was just that type, and Gwenna was actually lousy at dressing herself, so she was willing to give it a go. As long as it didn't involve anything see-through or so short that sitting wasn't an option.

But now she was in stretchy, second-skin gray pants that screamed Friday Night Without a Date, and Nate was staring at her without saying a word. Feeling that annoying and telltale burn creeping up her cheeks, Gwenna forced a bright smile. "What brings you by?"

"Can I come in?" he asked, gesturing to her suite. Not smiling.

"Oh! Of course." She had spent too much time in York. She's forgotten how to deal with other human beings on a day-to-day basis. The bulk of her contact with people was online, which wasn't exactly social skill building. "I'm sorry . . . come in. Please."

He followed her into her apartment and she gave a quick glance around, making sure nothing inappropriate was lying around like a basket of dirty knickers or bags of blood. Of course, he'd seen her knickers when he'd ripped them off the night before, so it was not like a little personal laundry would distress him, but still. And bags of blood would just be bad. Bad blood. Bad, bad, bad. She'd have to mess with his memory, do a little erasing, if he saw anything vampiric, and that just felt wrong. Violating, really, after what they had shared.

"Have a seat," she said, gesturing to her sofa. Ethan's design staff had done a respectable job of ensuring the suites were more apartment than hotel room, and they were done in rich textures and quality furnishings. It was tasteful, yet Gwenna realized she'd never quite bothered to make it her own. It was still just a hotel suite in her brother's casino. Not home. No more than Roberto's Italian villa had been her home. She'd always known his staff had little respect for her, and Roberto himself had never given her any authority over decorating or their living arrangements.

Making a home of her own was yet again another thing she had never got around to. Or maybe she just hadn't known how.

"Thanks." Nate sat down and gave a sigh, like his body and bones were weary.

He still hadn't given a reason for his appearance, nor did he look like he was in a loving, touching, squeezing mood. Gwenna was absolutely unsure how to proceed. She had no previous one-night-stand experience and hadn't been given any illicit sex etiquette tips at the girls' school she had attended in her youth.

Of course, here she was stupidly worried about how to handle a postorgasm encounter, and he had probably spent the day contacting family and the funeral home. She was an insensitive cad, thinking of sex when he was grieving.

"Are you doing okay? Did you have a chance to speak to your parents today?" she asked, taking the chair across from him. She wanted to touch him, to just reassure him, offer a bit of comfort, but he looked very hard, very closed off.

"Yes. They got stuck in L.A., but they should be here by morning." His fingers drummed across his knees, over and over, and he was sitting forward, stiff. "I wanted to let you know that the victim wasn't your pal Slash."

Gwenna was surprised at how relieved she truly was. And yet how sorry that someone else's life had ended in such a vulgar fashion. "Oh, good. Thanks for telling me. I thought it couldn't be him, because I got an e-mail from him saying he had to miss our meeting because he was working late, but it's good to hear it officially, because you know how e-mail can be . . . it's totally unreliable in terms of time, etc."

Nate just shook his head. "It wasn't him."

"I'm so sorry for whoever it was. Were you able to identify him?"

"Yes. His name is Andrew Fletcher. Twenty-one years old. Does that ring any bells for you?"

"No. Should it?" Why was Nate looking at her like that?

"Andrew Fletcher spent a lot of time online, including a vampire slayers' loop that also has a member named Slash87. You can confirm this for us, but I'm going on the assumption this is the same loop you're on and we've been discussing. Andrew's online name was Buzzdrew."

"Bloody hell." Gwenna recognized the name immediately. Buzz was constantly posting to the loop. He had a sharp sense of humor and an impressive vocabulary. And he made her extremely happy by always using capitalization and punctuation. "You can't be serious."

"Oh, I'm afraid I'm very serious. So how much of a coincidence do you think it is, Gwenna, that one loop member suggests you meet at the very location where another one has just been brutally murdered? Drained of all his blood, in fact. Like a vampire."

Gwenna had suspected that had been the case. She had seen the victim's pallor, and normally she could smell blood, all the time. While she had heightened smell and could decipher shampoo, skin lotions, toothpaste, and various other scents on mortals, blood was always the easiest to pick out. It hovered around mortals, their blood scent like an aura. It had been absent in Andrew's body. But she hadn't really put it together, had been so shocked, and very aware of a strong fleshy odor. She'd just attributed the lack of blood scent to his death. Now she was appalled to realize that Nate was right. This couldn't be a coincidence. It was too odd. Too planned. Yet it made no sense against the backdrop of knowledge she had—that the slayers were planning a large-scale attack on vampires in Vegas. So how would murdering one of their own fit into that?

"That's awful. Absolutely horrible."

"Yes, it is. And there are over four hundred members on that slayers' loop. We have to go through every single one, matching online name to real name, and we don't have the staff or the computer expertise to do this kind of crap. But you can save us a few minutes by telling me which cutsie little fake name is yours."

It was a bit mortifying, but Gwenna cleared her throat and went out with it. "QueenieG." No more apologizing to men.

That actually brought the closest thing to a smile on Nate's face since he'd walked in the door. "QueenieG? Okay, then, thanks."

Gwenna realized she could help him save a bundle of time and labor. "I know who about half the loop members are, and I can give that to you for the investigation. I've been playing around a little and seeing who is who. The ones who registered with real names are in a spreadsheet I created, and the ones who used fake names or registered anonymously are in a separate spreadsheet. In my spare time I've been picking through those, searching for their real identities. I've found about a fourth of those."

She was trying to be helpful, but he gave her an odd look. "Why were you collecting that kind of information?"

The truth was incomprehensible, so she just shrugged. "I was curious. I get bored easily and I like to do online searches. It's like a puzzle to find someone's real identity."

"But you don't know Slash's real name?"

"No, I haven't found his yet." Much to her annoyance.

Nate just looked at her, clearly thinking. He had this way of staring right into her, immovable, just like he had in the elevator. Like he had during sex. He could simply look at her, and it was like he was seeing everything—the real her, the inner thoughts, the secrets, the true Gwenna no one else understood.

"What do you do for a living?"

She'd given a vague response the first time he'd asked her that and he hadn't pursued it, which was amazing given how much they'd talked the night before. At least initially. Then they'd been too busy moaning to form words. But he was waiting for her answer now to his utterly loaded question, though Nate couldn't know that.

"I don't do anything."

"You don't work?" Nate didn't move or change postures, but she could sense his discontent with her answer. He had excellent control over his expressions, and he could sit as still as the dead, but she was starting to clue in to the way his thumb went up and down, up and down when he was studying her.

"No, I don't work." That wasn't a lie, though not the whole truth, either. "I never did." She took a deep breath and forced the rest out. "And after my daughter died and my marriage ended, I had something of a breakdown. So I've just been sponging off my brother."

For the first time since he'd arrived, she saw a crack in his control. His fingers stopped moving, his eyes looked troubled. "Gwenna. I'm sure your brother doesn't see it that way. I'm sure he wants to help you."

"He does." She couldn't argue that Ethan had been good to her, despite his annoying tendencies, because he had. She had never lacked for money, housing, material luxuries. He gave her whatever she wanted and way more than she'd ever ask for. But lately it had begun to rub that Ethan controlled her finances. He was so generous—more than he should be really—but it meant that yet again Gwenna wasn't independent. "But I keep thinking that I really need to learn how to take care of myself. One sort of needs a job skill to do that, though."

"You didn't work before you got married?"

"No." That was simpler than explaining she had been the pampered daughter of a Norman lord, and she'd spent her days sewing and practicing the harp in the eleventh century. "I was a bit sheltered coming up."

"Well, what would you like to do? If you could do anything." Nate sank back into the sofa and waved his hand at her, like a career might pop up out of thin air.

His was a question no one had ever asked her before. Gwenna wrinkled her nose. "I don't know." She closed her mouth. Opened it. Closed it. "Well. I . . . don't know."

Nate raised an eyebrow. "Well, maybe you should think about it."

Maybe. But it sounded rather overwhelming. She had never considered that she could have a career. That she could be a modern woman like Alexis and Brittany. The thought was a little dizzying.

"I'm not sure I'm really good at anything." Gwenna bit her fingernail, than stared at her hand in confusion. She hadn't done that in centuries. Since those early days of her marriage to Roberto when he used to disappear for weeks at a time and she had worried incessantly. "Not really."

"What do you do every day?"

"I sleep a lot," she said, because that was true. "I tend to stay up really late at night. Last night was normal for me."

He shot her a look of irritation, not even remarking on her unintended sexual innuendo. "So what do you do at night then?"

Besides shag strange men in empty spas on massage tables. The unspoken words just hung there in the air between them, and Gwenna wanted to crawl under the table and die. Except going under the table would have her at crotch level with Nate, and she couldn't die anyway. It was hell to be wading through this with no clue how to have a normal relationship with a man.

Though obviously any sort of so-called relationship she had or might have with Nate had not exactly got off on a normal foot, either. She'd had sex with him after discovering a murder victim, which possibly proved her brother's accusation to be true—she was not to be trusted when it came to men.

He was waiting for her answer. "I read. I do things . . . on the computer. I play the piano." Infiltrate vampire slayer loops and drink copious amounts of blood.

"What things on the computer?"

She should have known that he would call her on that one. He was still in detective mode. "I just like to explore, to read things, to do research. I'm a repeat poster on Wikipedia. Especially the section on Norman history. I do a lot of genealogy."

"And hang out in online vampire slayer groups."

"Just the one." So there.

Nate let that go. His fingers started drumming again. "So you're smart. Well read. You have extensive computer research skills. And you play the piano. It sounds like you could do a lot of things."

Gwenna shrugged noncommittally, not really wanting to discuss this with him. It made her feel inadequate. Lazy. Self-indulgent. "No one is going to pay me to play the piano."

"Why not? This is Vegas. There's a piano in every other lobby."

"But I'm not that good."

"Then why did you mention it?"

"Because you asked what I do."

"So clearly you enjoy it. No one is expecting a genius at these joints, you just have to be able to play without hitting a bad note."

"I don't hit bad notes." She'd had nine centuries to practice the blasted thing, she'd better not hit bad notes. But that didn't mean she was capable of entertaining anyone with her playing.

"Then what's the problem? If performing in front of people makes you uncomfortable, you could record music."

She made a face without really meaning to.

He raised an eyebrow. "Okay, that's out. How about a librarian?"

Did she look like a librarian? That was startling. Though probably true. "They have degrees."

Now Nate seemed determined to forge her a career path. Like if he could just hit on the right idea, she'd get a job and get her act together. Hell, maybe there was something to that.

"So then something with your computer skills . . . you could start one of those services where you find people online for clients. That's huge right now and it sounds like you know exactly how to do that."

Now that idea actually intrigued her. Gwenna sat back in her chair and crossed her ankles.

"What, no excuse for this one?" He gave her a wry look.

Since she had been making excuses, she just gave him a smile back. "Now that could be interesting. I have a lot to learn, but I do enjoy the challenge of ferreting out info online."

"Maybe you can practice by helping the department match the rest of those e-mail addresses to real names."

Gwenna nodded. She'd been thinking the same thing herself. "Sure, of course I can do that. Whatever you need to help figure out what the hell is going on and who's responsible for Andrew's death. I can e-mail you the list I already have so you can get started."

First on her list was going to be Slash and FoxyKyle. They dominated the loop. And they had both taken measures to secure their identity. Gwenna wanted to know why.

"You got any paper? I'll give you my e-mail address."

Gwenna retrieved a pad of paper from the kitchenette area and watched Nate scrawl something on it with the pen she'd handed him. He was left-handed, and his elbow tilted out at a funny angle when he wrote. But his strokes were confident, sharp. Just watching him reminded her of the night before, of his hands moving over her with that same matter-of-fact approach. He took, but he didn't own, didn't try to possess or dominate. He was just positive his touch would be well received and he was right. She had welcomed every lick, every suck, every touch.

And now they weren't going to speak about it, and she was going to let him walk out the door and deny herself the chance to explore his body further all because she was a lifelong introvert.

It was beyond stupid.

He stood up. Sexy as hell, with caramel-colored hair; broad shoulders; face, demeanor, and expression as rugged and impenetrable as the north moors; a man's man, with a penis large enough that he was entitled to brag about it.

If she wanted a crack at same said penis yet again, she was going to have to be bold. She fought for the nerve, for a little backbone. To be QueenieG, in real life, as well as online.

"I'll be in touch." He passed the paper to her with zero hand-to-hand contact and headed for the door.

Gwenna stared at his back. He really and truly was going to walk out and never even discuss the fact that his cock had been in her mouth not eighteen hours earlier. And she'd done a pretty fine job of working him over, if she did say so herself, and he wasn't even going to acknowledge any of that? It irritated her enough that she steeled herself. Damn it, she did not like being ignored.

"Are you honestly just going to leave without even mentioning that we had hot sex last night?"

Nate came to an abrupt stop. Gwenna's heart was pounding as he turned around, but it was more from anger than nerves. If he just did that thing where he stared at her and didn't speak, she was going to throw something at him. Like her sofa.

But his eyes narrowed and he said in a very low, tight voice, "You're the one who left without a word. I figured that meant you didn't want to discuss the fact that we had hot sex. On a massage table. Where you came three times."

Oh, my. Gwenna felt heat flare up spontaneously between her thighs. Had it only been three times? She'd been fairly certain she'd spent the whole time in a sort of continuous orgasm.

If the fact that she had left was the only thing bothering him, then she could resolve that straight away. "Sorry about that. I got a call from my sister-in-law that a friend has left her husband—a real rotten sort—and she was crying . . . it was a girl thing. I had to go over there and offer some comfort."

"You're just a comforting kind of gal, aren't you?"

"What the hell does that mean?" It almost sounded insulting.

"Nothing." Nate rubbed his head with his hand and made a sound of frustration. "You could have woken me up. I felt like a jackass waking up in that room by myself while the staff checked me out."

Yikes. The staff had found him? That must have been an eyeful. "I thought you could really use the sleep . . . I know you'd had a hard couple of days and it seemed important that you get some deep sleep."

He stared at her. She stared back.

Nate sighed. "Fuck."

That's what she had in mind, but she didn't think that's what Nate meant.

"Gwenna. I have had a hard couple of days and I don't have it in me to be playing guessing games. If you didn't mean to ditch out on me, what are we doing here? What do you want from this? Just last night?"

She shook her head. It felt like they'd just got started and she was attracted to him, physically and otherwise. "No. I would like to see you again. What do you want?"

What Nate wanted was a big old tropical island far away from death with Gwenna naked on it, but seeing as that wasn't a real likely possibility anytime soon, he gave her the simplified version of the truth. "I want you." Painfully. Immediately.

Her blue eyes widened, sparking with desire. "It's good to hear we're in agreement then."

Nate closed the distance between them. Gwenna was wearing the tightest stretchy pants he'd ever seen, and he loved the way they hugged her ass, and even better, the way they clung in front, outlining her sex for him. He cupped the back of her head and kissed her, hot and hard, forcing her lips open with his tongue, while his free hand stroked over the front of her pants, and his cock went hard on cue.

Her gasp against him satisfied him. Gwenna's knees bent, and she leaned forward, her soft fingers wrapping around his wrist like she meant to stop his touch. The hell with that. Nate pressed his thumb against her clit, nudging her legs apart. Then he stroked and petted her over the soft stretchy pants, loving the way the fabric cupped her mound, enjoying the sound of her breathing in his ear, her tiny little gasps and sighs. Gwenna was petite and proportionate, but while he'd originally thought she was fragile, lithe, skinny, he now knew her body was all woman, with curves and a healthy muscle tone. She was thin, but firm, curvy, but toned. Perfect. Absolutely fucking perfect.

Driving her wild without undressing her was really damn hot, and Nate saw no reason to stop. He kissed and licked her mouth, his fingers moving over and over her, brushing her nipples, smoothing over her tight ass, sliding up and down in the indentation in her pants he'd created by stroking her, pressing a little deeper and deeper as she moved restlessly, knees bending further.

"Take my pants off," she murmured, her cheeks bright pink spots of color, and her eyes half closed, glazed with desire.

Nate bit her bottom lip. "Shh. You're fine like this."

Her gasp of indignation turned him on. "Take my pants off," she demanded, clamping her hand around his wrist and holding him still with a strength that surprised him at the same time it made him hotter than hell. Damn, the lady wanted her pants off. She looked so sweet and innocent, like she'd faint at the sight of a naked man, but looks were deceiving. Shit. Gwenna gave as good as she got.

"Yes, ma'am." He ripped her pants down to her knees and slid two fingers inside her wet, eager body.

"Oh, hell, Nate." She closed her eyes, and still gripping his wrist, she came, with graceful shudders, head falling back, back arching, hips thrusting to meet his touch.

It was beautiful. And suddenly, in the midst of the lust, the hot, wet desire to grab her hips and fuck the life out of her, Nate felt something else. Maybe a kind of gratitude to her for sharing herself with him at the right time, maybe an attraction for her as a woman, a human being, or maybe a kind of interest stirring to life that went beyond sex, and the instinctive urge to protect her, in all her intriguing mix of strong yet incredibly vulnerable. Whatever the hell it was, it was there, and Nate was caught off guard. It wasn't a bad feeling, but it was unnerving, and he needed to regroup, get a grip on his life before he dove in and did something stupid as hell.

So after she came back to earth and smiled at him, making little sighs of delight, Nate gave her a soft kiss, and pulled her pants back up.

That earned him a frown. "What are you doing?"

"I need to go back to work."

"You can't take five more minutes?" Her outrage nearly made him laugh.

"I don't want to settle for five minutes," he told her, which was true. It was also true he was feeling a little like he'd been nailed by a baseball in the gut, and he needed to figure out what the hell that meant. Or more importantly, what to do about it. "What are you doing tomorrow night? Can I see you?"

Tomorrow was Kyra's wake, which meant he should probably spare Gwenna the lousy company afterward. But then again he'd have to see his parents, which was always a total nightmare, and Gwenna Carrick was a wonderful distraction. She had a quiet comfort about her that appealed to him.

"Oh, shit, I can't tomorrow." She entwined her fingers with his. "My brother has this big corporate party thing and I promised I would go. I'm appalling at these functions—I can't think of a damn thing to say and I hide by the potted plants, but I told Ethan I'd be there. How about Sunday night?"

"Sure. I'll call you." He took another kiss, enjoying the way she responded so quickly to him, and the sensual feel of her mouth beneath his. "Can you send that slayers' loop info before you go to bed tonight?"

The doorbell rang behind him. "Expecting company?" If she had a date, he was pretty sure he was going to be ugly jealous. On the other hand, if it was her loser ex-husband, Nate was going to enjoy threatening him with a little force.

"I'm going out with my girlfriends." She moved around him, adjusting the waistband of her pants—which he had messed up—and opened the door.

Nate saw an amazingly thin woman with long dark hair dressed in the tiniest red outfit he'd ever seen in his life. It was like a headband masquerading as a dress. Next to her was a blonde who was a solid ten inches shorter, wearing jeans, high heels, and a sparkly blue shirt. Gwenna looked a little under-dressed for whatever night out they had planned.

"Who are you?" the brunette asked. She didn't sound accusatory, just sort of mildly curious.

"I'm Nate Thomas. Who are you?"

She walked into the apartment and blinked. "I'm Kelsey Columbia, but after my divorce, I'll have to decide if I want to go back to being Kelsey Dickens or not. I've never really liked that name. I was kind of thinking this is my chance to just pick whatever name I want. What do you think of Kelsey Kinko?"

Nate kept his voice even. "That works."

The blonde shook her head. "I told you that sounds like a stripper name."

His thoughts exactly.

While Kelsey pouted, the blonde stuck her hand out in his direction. "I'm Alexis Baldizzi-Carrick, Gwenna's sister-in-law."

He shook. Firm, confident grip. "Nice to meet you. I'm Nate Thomas, a detective with the Las Vegas Police."

At which point Gwenna grabbed his other hand and tugged on him. "Well, thanks for dropping by. I don't want to be late for the concert and I'm not even dressed, so sorry to rush you off, but we'll speak soon, and I'll see you on Sunday."

Gee, he could take a very subtle hint.

But while she could shove him out the door, he wasn't about to let her forget the unfinished business they had for Sunday.

Nate tugged Gwenna up against his chest. "Sounds good." Then he gave her a big-ass kiss, with tongue, sliding his hand all up and down her backside for good measure. "See ya, Gwenna."

Then he left, absolutely positive he had a shit-eating grin plastered across his face.

Eight

Ethan Carrick hated Roberto Donatelli with every fucking bone in his body. Once they had been friends, back when London was nothing but a mudhole and the Americas didn't exist to Europeans. But then Donatelli had seduced Gwenna and left her to die giving birth to his bastard child, and Ethan would never forgive him for that. Donatelli was a cruel, heartless son of a bitch who enjoyed playing people for power, and would trample anyone who got in the way of his self-serving plans.

Not to mention that he was just annoying as hell. A metrosexual moron.

God, Ethan hated him.

They stared across the conference table at each other.

Donatelli leaned back into his leather chair. "I can practically hear your teeth grinding, Carrick. You need to at least pretend to like me at the Inaugural Ball tomorrow night."

"I'll tolerate you, nothing more. Everyone knows this is a political alliance, not a friendship."

A smirk on his smarmy face, Donatelli said, "You mean I'm not invited to your ranch for fishing, hunting, and relaxing man talk away from the office?"

"I don't own a ranch. And if I did, I'd burn it down before I let you set foot in it." Ethan was still appalled that Donatelli was vice president of the Vampire Nation, while he was president. But there had been no choice. Ethan had been on the verge of losing the election because of the growing unrest of Impure vampires, born mortal with vampire genes, and later turned to vampire. They felt that vampires like Donatelli, who encourage vampire population growth, spoke to their rights more than a conservative like Ethan did. Then when Gregor Chechikov had entered the race, Ethan had known they would have a disaster on their hands if Chechikov won. He was a Russian lunatic, plain and simple, with plans for cloning vampires. Ethan had seen an opportunity to ensure Chechikov didn't come into power by aligning himself with Donatelli. Together they became a moderate, all-inclusive ticket, and it had won them the election, averting what amounted to vampire civil war.

But the immediate result was also that Ethan had to work together with Donatelli in some functioning capacity for the next forty years, and he needed to learn to control his dislike of the bastard or they would never accomplish anything. And unless he got a handle on his anger, Ethan would spend the next four decades walking around pissed off, which was bad for his mental health.

"Let's just get to the point here. Tomorrow we walk in together, get sworn in, and have drinks. It should go smoothly enough. Are you bringing a date or something? Because you can't be strolling into this with some bimbo mortal or eighteen-year-old vampire chick. We all know the truth about you, but you have to least pretend to have some sort of class." Maybe he was just getting a dig in, but hell, he wouldn't put it past Donatelli to do something as stupid as bring his mortal blood slave to the Inaugural Ball.

Donatelli didn't rise to the bait. He shrugged. "I didn't think having your sister as an escort would be in the least bit offensive. Gwenna has always conducted herself with perfect decorum."

The Italian was just so good at infuriating him. "Gwenna isn't your date." He didn't think. She had made it sound like she wasn't against speaking to her ex-husband, but surely that didn't extend to putting on a party dress and walking with Donatelli into a room filled with a thousand vampires. Gwenna didn't like attention, and the kind of buzz their being together would create was enough of a deterrent for his sister, he was sure.

Besides, she had been with a mortal and Alexis was right. Dating two men was not Gwenna's style. Hell, as far as he knew, she hadn't dated any man but Donatelli.

"She's not my date yet. But she will be. I'll drop by her suite after we're done here."

The bastard's self-assurance irritated Ethan. What gave the jerk-off the right to even ask Gwenna to be his date? She'd divorced his sorry ass three hundred years earlier, which meant she wasn't obligated to be seen in public with him. "She won't say yes."

"Yes, she will. She and I have been on much friendlier terms lately. She'll do it as a favor to me, and as a favor to you. She'll understand how important it is for our government to show unity."

There was truth to that, and Ethan didn't like it. But he still said, "I wouldn't expect her to bleed for me like that, and she knows it."

"Being my date is bleeding?"

"Hell, yes. I imagine it would be more fun fucking a frog than dancing with you."

"How colorful. Hopefully you'll never have to do either, because I'm not too keen on the concept of waltzing with you, either." Donatelli looked casually around. "Where's your secretary? I need a drink."

Ethan turned to his bodyguard, wanting this little meeting over. God, he was never going to survive forty years of this drivel. "Would you please find Brenda and see if she can find a drink for Mr. Donatelli? Thank you."

"Is Brenda your new secretary? I hope she's more efficient than that idiotic Kelsey you had previously. While Kelsey is attractive in a vapid, slutty sort of way, she's distressingly dumb. Though loyal. It's a beautiful thing to see her clinging to her junkie husband."

It was still a rather sore spot with him that Kelsey had essentially betrayed Ethan after he'd spent the last forty years providing her with gainful employment—despite her questionable secretarial skills. Hearing Donatelli rub it in wasn't conducive to a stress-free work environment. Nor had it made him the least bit happy to hear from his wife that she intended to spend the night hanging out at a rock concert with Kelsey. That screamed male strippers and possible jail time to him. Kelsey was a magnet for trouble.

"Kelsey left her husband, so just let her be, alright?" Though he had no intention of rehiring her. She had proven herself untrustworthy. "And by the way, you can't drop by to invite Gwenna to the ball, and have her laugh in your face and say no, because Alexis told me Gwenna has plans tonight."

Ethan paused to make sure he had Donatelli's full interest.

"Oh, really?" Donatelli didn't look like he believed him.

"Yes. She has a mortal boyfriend and they're out tonight." And Donatelli could put that in his fucking pipe and smoke it.

"You don't have any exciting clothes at all." Kelsey stood in front of Gwenna's closet, giving every appearance of being in mourning for slut outfits.

Gwenna hated to break it to her, but she wasn't an exciting woman. It was highly unlikely she would have a secret snappy or stylish dress hiding somewhere. "Sorry. I haven't needed a lot of going-out clothes living in an old castle by myself."

"But you're in Vegas now." Kelsey pointed out the obvious as she abandoned searching through Gwenna's many T-shirts, twin sets, and khaki slacks. "And I brought a few outfits in case we found ourselves in this very situation."

Alexis snorted, lying straight across Gwenna's bed on her side. "I can't wait to see this."

Gwenna wasn't nearly as enthusiastic. "Kelsey, what's wrong with me just wearing a pair of jeans? It's just a rock concert, right? Don't people wear jeans to concerts?" They always did in Disney movies. Gwenna liked the Disney channel because every problem was perfectly wrapped up in under two hours, all while the laugh track went off for every canned and trite joke. It made her happy. Being dressed in Kelsey's clothes did not make her happy, since Kelsey was five foot ten, weighed ninety pounds, and was notorious for exposing two thirds of her body at any given moment. She liked to tell herself it was because Kelsey had no reflection and couldn't see exactly what she looked like, but that was probably false hope.

"Sure, it's a rock concert, but you want to be pimped out a little. You don't want to look like you're headed to Wal-Mart. And these guys are vampires, remember, so they're going to notice us immediately."

She didn't know they were vampires because no one had bothered to explain that little factoid to her earlier. "No, I actually had no clue they were vampires. Are you telling me the entire band is undead? Is the whole audience full of vampires?"

"No." Kelsey looked at her like that was an idiotic suggestion. "Why would the audience be vampires? They're a vampire band pretending to be vampires so no one knows they're really vampires. But since we're vampires, we know they're vampires, of course."

Right. She should have guessed that. Gwenna sat down on her bed next to Alexis. "Maybe I should just stay home." She could call Nate and see if he was still available . . .

"No!" Kelsey shook her finger at her. "You're cheering me up, so you have to go."

Shit. When put like that, there was no way out of it. Gwenna was very good at feeling guilty. "Okay, fine."

"Thank you!" Kelsey beamed. "Now let me go get my bag. I left it in the other room. I have the cutest blue dress I brought for you to wear."

"Fine. But while you're getting that, I have an e-mail to send." She turned to her laptop, which she'd brought into the bedroom with her so she wouldn't forget to send the spreadsheet to Nate. Clicking on her mail, she was surprised to see another e-mail from Slash.

From: Slash87@gomail.com
To: QueenieG@aol.com
Subject: Tonight

Hey Queenie,
Everyone is going to The Impalers concert tonight. If you can get a ticket, meet me there. I'll find you in the crowd.

S

Now that was rather an odd coincidence. Yet another one. Slash and "everyone" were going to be at the concert that Kelsey had talked her into attending. And the band members were all vampires.

Plus if Slash was confident he could find her in the crowd, then he knew what she looked like. Which meant he had been at the train station and had seen her, because she'd only previously given him a very generic "short and blond" description of herself. He'd never be able to pick her out of a crowd based on that. She shivered. What if Slash was the killer of poor Buzzdrew? She couldn't even imagine what the motivation had been for that.

But Andrew had been mortal and vulnerable as such. Gwenna wasn't. And she was bound and determined to figure out what the hell was going on—especially if true slayers were planning an actual attack. Given the large number of vampires in Vegas for the Inauguration, it would be perfect timing for that sort of large-scale attack, and she had no intention of allowing such a thing to occur.

She clicked Reply.

I should be able to get a ticket. See you there. And don't stand me up this time.
;-)

Queenie

Might as well let him know she hadn't appreciated his not showing the night before. Then she pulled Nate's e-mail address out of her pocket and entered it in her address book. She clicked to send him an e-mail, attaching the slayers' loop spreadsheet. Then she typed quickly.

Hi Nate,
Here's the info attached as discussed. I also heard from Slash again . . . we are meeting at a concert tonight, The Impalers. They pretend to be vampires as part of their act. Will give you a description of Slash after I meet him. See you Sunday.

Best,
Gwenna

She was absolutely certain her e-mail sounded boring and ridiculous, but she wasn't sure what else to say. And it was Nate's work e-mail, so it wasn't like she could talk dirty to him even if she were so inclined to do so, which she wasn't. Well, she found the idea sort of intriguing actually, but wasn't exactly sure she'd know how to go about it.

"What are you doing?" Alexis asked.

Gwenna jumped, as if she had actually written a dirty e-mail to Nate and Alexis had seen it. Lord, she needed to get a grip on herself. "Just dashing off this thing to Nate." Alexis and Ethan still didn't know about the murder and she had no intention of telling them.

"You're really digging this guy, aren't you?" Alexis sounded downright gleeful about that.

Gwenna closed her e-mail and prepared to face her sister-in-law, and an endless round of teasing. Only to find herself being confronted by Kelsey with a fistful of blue fabric that wouldn't cover a Chihuahua, let alone a full-grown woman. "Whatever that is, I'm not wearing it."

Kelsey smiled. "Yes, you are. Please? It will make me feel so much better to see you looking hot."

Damn it. Gwenna sighed and took the dress—if that's what it was. It looked more like an odd pair of panties. "If it looks appalling, you have to be honest with me."

"Of course." Kelsey nodded.

"Scout's honor," Alexis said from the bed.

She didn't believe them, but she was also very impatient to get to the concert and find Slash, so she stomped off to the bathroom to try and interpret what constituted "hot" in Kelsey Columbia's world.

Donatelli hated Ethan Carrick. He'd spent a lifetime poisoning Gwenna against him, and Roberto had never been able to figure out why. He loved Gwenna, always had. He wanted nothing but happiness for her. So why in the world was Carrick always so determined to keep Gwenna from him?

He had wanted to smack the satisfaction off Carrick's face when he had mentioned that Gwenna had a mortal boyfriend, but he had restrained himself. There was a much more rational way to deal the situation.

"Williams." He snapped his fingers for his bodyguard, and tossed back a glass of blood. There was an excellent view of the Vegas Strip from his room at the Venetian, but he stared at it without appreciating it. The very idea of another man's hands on his wife had him in a foul mood, even though he knew it was a ridiculous attempt on Carrick's part to irritate him. Gwenna didn't date. She never had. In the three hundred years since their divorce, Donatelli couldn't even count the number of women he had bedded. But he was conversely positive that Gwenna had never let another man inside her body.

Because she still loved him and they belonged together.

"Follow Gwenna and tell me if you see her with a man. I want you to watch her and tell me everything she's doing for the next forty-eight hours."

Williams nodded and left.

Donatelli sighed. It was so highly inconvenient that Gwenna had developed such a stubborn streak. It was clearly a Carrick trait. One he despised.

And one he would break her of if it took all of eternity.

Nate allowed himself a two-hour nap before heading back to the station to see if the autopsy report on Andrew's body had arrived yet. It hadn't, but he did have the e-mail from Gwenna as promised providing him with half the list members' real names matched to their e-mail addresses.

"Hot damn." It was a lucky break, and a huge time saver. Now they could zip through the list and eliminate any names of those out of town with clear alibis. There was someone on the list who was the killer, Nate was convinced of it. He just needed to methodically determine who it *couldn't* be to figure out who it actually was.

His good humor disappeared when he actually read the body of Gwenna's e-mail. She was going to meet Slash. Who very possibly was a murderer. At a concert with fake vampires.

"Jesus Christ." The woman had absolutely no sense of self-preservation.

"What's up?" Jim Connors, the other detective on the case, glanced over at him from his paper-laden cubicle.

Nate explained the situation. "What makes sense to her about doing this? I swear, she'd walk in front of a fucking bus and never even notice it until it ran her over." It was that naïvety, that innocence, about Gwenna that appealed to him, while at the same time it frustrated him to no end.

"Yet given the looks of this spreadsheet, she's not stupid." Jim gestured to his computer screen, looking at the data Nate had just forwarded to him.

"No. But this still means I'm going to have to show up at this damn concert and see what the hell's going on." His temples throbbed. "Fake vampires. What is the matter with people? Can't people try a little reality once in a while?"

"Reality's no fun, Nate, my man." Jim leaned back in his wheeled chair, making the seat squeak from his ample weight. "People need a little escape. It's good, clean fun. You want me to go check out the concert? I'm about to head out of here anyway."

The rational thing to do would be to take Jim up on his offer. But Nate wasn't feeling anything close to rational. He was running on little sleep, his emotions were threatening to suck him under, and he had an intense, burning need to keep Gwenna Carrick safe all by himself. It wasn't the department checking up on her, it was him, the man, Nate Thomas.

"Nah, that's okay. I can handle it."

He thought he sounded casual as hell, but Jim barked out a laugh. "So that's the way the wind blows, huh? She was a pretty little thing, I'll give you that. A little too delicate for my taste, though." Jim patted his substantial gut. "I'd crush her. I like a woman I can really grab on to."

Now there was an image he didn't need. "She'd never go for you anyway," Nate drawled as he turned his computer off.

"Hey, thanks." Jim threw a pen at him.

Nate caught it and tossed it onto his desk. "I'm just telling you like it is. She's hot for me, and you wouldn't stand a chance."

He was bragging to throw Jim off the truth, but then he remembered the way Gwenna had responded to his fingers moving inside her, and he knew the truth was that Gwenna was hot for him. And he was hot as hell for her. It wasn't logical, but it was there, and it was intense.

Which might explain why he was heading to a concert by a fake vampire band with every intention of hauling her delicate ass out of there and kissing some sense into her.

Gwenna turned to Alexis. "I feel slightly uncomfortable." Which was her very British way of describing the fact that she wanted the earth to open and swallow her and the very tiny dress she was wearing.

"Why?" Alexis scanned the dark room. "You look fantastic. Just relax."

Easy for Alexis to say since she was wearing jeans. Gwenna was wearing an exercise in insanity. With a plunging neckline. Which she kept trying to tug closed, only to have Kelsey smack at her and spread it even farther apart than it was originally.

So she hovered as close to Alexis as possible without stealing her oxygen and held a little clutch purse in front of her chest. This had been a really poor lapse in judgment. And given the vast crowd of concertgoers, there was no way she was going to find Slash. All she knew was that he was male and in his twenties. That took her potential pool down to a mere thousand guys, many of whom were strolling around pierced, tattooed, and wearing chains off their clothes or body parts. She saw lots of people opening their mouths and exposing fake fangs to each other as well, which she found incredibly disturbing.

Why did they want to be vampires? What exactly was the lure? Immortality, she supposed. Power. And of course, the irony was that Gwenna had never asked for her vampirism, had been given it by Ethan to prevent her from bleeding to death after Isabel's birth nine centuries earlier. There had been many times where Gwenna would have gladly given the gift of eternity back.

No longer, though. She had a purpose now, and it was to ferret out the slayers and prevent an attack. And she needed to help Nate find Andrew's killer. His hobby, his playacting, like all these men around her pretending to be vampires, had gotten him killed, and somehow she felt inadvertently responsible for that.

"Hey." A guy with a shaved head and a black T-shirt that stated, "Get Impaled, You Know You Want It," smiled at her.

Yikes. He was flirting with her. He was big and scary and she was so not ready for this. Gwenna felt the urge to grab on to Alexis and pretend they were a couple, but that would be an avoidance technique. And she was resolved to be stronger, more confident, to meet problems head on and deal with them entirely on her own.

"Hi," she said. Wow, that was really handling things.

Of course—duh—maybe this was Slash. Which meant she had to talk with him long enough to determine if that was a possibility.

The guy had to yell, since the opening band was on stage making what sounded to Gwenna like a godawful amount of noise. "You been to see The Impalers before?" he asked her, leaning down to speak directly to her ear.

His breath tickled her cheek. Shifting slightly away and looking up at him, she shook her head and forced a smile. "No, this is my first."

"A virgin." He grinned. "You'll like it, they put on a good show."

She just smiled, wracking her brain for something flirtatious to say, or at least something conversational. "I, uh . . ." Nothing. Zero. She couldn't even complete the sentence because her mind was utterly empty of words. And he was starting to lose his grin, like he thought she was a half-wit. Which maybe she was.

Kelsey saved her by moving in between the two of them and putting her forearm on Gwenna's shoulder, using her as a support. "So what's your name, cutie?" she said to the very tall and tattooed man who was the polar opposite of the descriptive cutie in Gwenna's book.

"Jason. What's your name?"

"Kelsey." She nudged Gwenna. "And this is—"

Gwenna cut her off, bursting out with, "I'm Queenie. It's nice to meet you."

Alexis gave a snort of amusement. Kelsey said, "Wow, cool, I like it," as if they didn't know each other. But Gwenna should be grateful Kelsey didn't just flat out give her away. And the guy was looking a bit skeptical.

"Queenie?" he said.

"Yes. My parents were British and Mum had royalty envy." It was much easier to roll with a lie when it was ludicrous. She briefly wondered why that was as Jason started to back up. "Is Jason really your name?"

"Uh, yeah. Well, um, enjoy the concert. See you." He disappeared into the crowd.

"Shit, I think you scared him, Gwenna. And he was cute, too." Kelsey frowned at his retreating back.

"I scared him? I don't think so. I'm not the least bit scary." She rather resented that. And if he couldn't take an unusual name, then he wasn't worth her time anyway. Not that she was at all interested in Giant Jason, but it was a bit insulting to think that little bitty her had been so weird or uninteresting that he had felt the need to dash off. Wimp.

But the important fact she had gained from that encounter was that she was now down to nine hundred and ninety-nine potential Slashes, because Jason hadn't reacted at all to her online name.

"What's with the Queenie thing? If you're going to use a fake name—which I totally support—couldn't you come up with a better one?" Alexis asked. "Like I think maybe I'll be Mackenzie for the night. I've always liked that name because it's a power name."

"Oooh, fake names. Okay, I'll be Winnie," Kelsey said.

Gwenna tried to imagine how Kelsey had plucked the name *Winnie* from the vast stores of knowledge in her sixty-year-old brain. It was more random than Queenie, which was really saying a lot. "Winnie. That's an unusual name. What made you think of it?"

"I've always liked the Pooh Bear stories." Kelsey's lip started to tremble. "Ringo used to read me the Winnie the Pooh books."

Now there was an intriguing glimpse into Kelsey's marital life. Her heroin-addicted assassin husband had read her the silly old bear stories? "That's so very sweet, Kelsey." And odd as hell, but who was she to judge?

"I need a drink," Alexis said. "So Mackenzie is going to the bar. Can I leave Winnie and Queenie together without the two of you getting into serious trouble?"

"Why would we get in trouble?" The very concept seemed to puzzle Kelsey. "We'll be totally fine."

"Okay, but stay together. Got it?" Alexis shook her finger at them.

Gwenna nodded. "We'll be fine." Her sister-in-law was spending too much time with Ethan. She was getting to be almost as overprotective as he was.

"Does anyone else want a drink?"

"No, thanks." Unlike other vamps, Gwenna had never developed a taste for any drink besides blood. But then she was supposed to be opening herself to new experiences, embracing life. "Actually, I'll have whatever you're having."

"I'll take a martini. Something flavored," Kelsey said.

"Okay, I'll be back."

Alexis headed to the bar, and Kelsey grabbed Gwenna's hand. "I'm so totally depressed. We have to hit on guys, that always makes me feel better."

And she dragged Gwenna to the nearest quartet of men, who looked up with obvious lustful interest, which was to be expected given they were being assaulted by two women not wearing enough clothing. Gwenna felt her cheeks burning, but reminded herself the room was dark, with red strobe lights, and no one would notice in the slightest her blush. Besides, she was supposed to be looking for Slash. It was part of her new plan to be proactive. Waiting around for him to approach her was so last century.

"So which one of you has the biggest penis?" Kelsey said to the men.

Nine

Gwenna about laid an egg. *That* was Kelsey's preferred method of hitting on guys?

Of course, her rather private and very inappropriate question got a reaction from all the men, who actually weren't of the tattooed variety, but looked like they had gone from the fraternity house to the golf course and had somehow landed in the wrong concert hall. All four insisted they had the biggest dick ever known to man, bragging to such an extent that Gwenna would have thought they were carrying an anaconda around in their pants from their descriptions.

"I'm serious," the one said when Kelsey told him he had to be lying. "It's just a fact. I'm huge."

"Show us," Kelsey challenged.

Oh, no. Gwenna wanted out of the *us* in that statement. She said, "No, really, don't show us. We believe you."

"I don't. I bet you've got nothing." Kelsey waved her hand in the air and started to turn.

Big Dick grabbed her arm and said, "If you want to see it, I'll show you."

Kelsey gave him an incredibly sweet smile. Gwenna was astonished at how manipulative Kelsey was behind that ditzy grin. "Cool. All of you, bring them out on the count of three."

Which was how Gwenna found herself staring at four penises simultaneously, doubling her lifetime exposure to male members in a matter of five seconds.

It was astonishing how they could all look essentially the same, yet so very different. Big Dick had a right to his brag. He definitely looked supersized next to his companions. Beyond that, Gwenna was just really starting to get a good look when a club bouncer yelled, "Hey! Put that shit away. This ain't no strip club."

She confessed to be slightly disappointed when they all immediately complied, tucking and zipping and looking around as if they'd just recalled where exactly they were. Not because she had any interest in actually interacting with any of their penises, but out of pure curiosity. It was the anatomical part that drove so much of male action she found herself wondering what was the big deal exactly. But that brief exposure didn't answer her weighty question in the least.

"That was hot," Kelsey told them. "Thanks." She took Gwenna's arm and led her away, whispering, "Never overstay the welcome or they'll start to get pervy ideas."

While Gwenna didn't think it was the lingering that would give them pervy ideas, but you know, perhaps the request to see their penises, she wasn't going to object to leaving.

"What were you doing?" Alexis demanded, standing where they had been when she'd left them, glaring while juggling three drinks.

Kelsey giggled and took a martini glass from Alexis. "Nothing."

"We just saw those guys' penises," Gwenna confessed.

"Oh, Lord." Alexis rolled her eyes and swallowed half her drink, handing the remaining one over to Gwenna. "Oh, look, I think the band is coming on to play."

The noisemakers had left and there was some movement onstage. Gwenna couldn't see very well because she was short and it was a standing-room-only concert in a nightclub. There were some tables on the balcony to the side, but the majority of the room was just a vast crowd of heads blocking her view. She could see the drum set and a guy with dark hair behind it messing around adjusting things. The rest of the stage just looked crowded with instruments, mics, and amplifiers. Absently, she took a large sip of her drink and stood on her tiptoes.

Bloody hell, the martini Alexis had got her was strong. Her eyes were watering, which could be dangerous, given her predilection for blood tears. She swiped at her eyes and gave a little cough.

Someone jostled her elbow. "Hi."

It was a guy. Another version of the jeans, black t-shirt, skull-and-crossbones-necklace-wearing, shaved-head guy.

"Hey. Is your name Slash?" she asked, deciding to hell with subtle.

"No." He raised an eyebrow. "But it could be if you want it to."

"No, I don't. I hate that name. I despise it. If you were named Slash I was going to spit on you."

"Ooookay." He turned and left, practically running.

Gwenna couldn't believe she'd just done that. She burst out laughing. "I'm losing my mind," she told Alexis.

"No, you're just coming into your own, sister. Go with it."

Maybe that was it. She was coming into her own. It was a liberating feeling. She'd had sex on a massage table with a hottie cop, and now she was getting sloshed on a martini at a rock concert wearing a napkin for a dress. This beat the hell out of sitting by herself in York sewing fuzzy scarves.

"Hey." She grabbed the arm of a guy in his young twenties walking past her. "Are you Slash?"

"No," he answered directly to her cleavage, which she actually had, thanks to Kelsey's plunging dress.

"Oh, then you can keep walking."

"What if I don't want to keep walking?"

"You have to."

"Why?"

"Because I said so."

"Oh." He left with a disappointed look.

Either Gwenna was drunk with power or the martini that was essentially pure alcohol with a dash of apple flavoring had gone straight to her head. The room was getting quite warm and her fingertips felt slightly numb. By the time the band had taken the stage and performed their first set, Gwenna had plowed through two more martinis, had spoken to at least fifty guys, got propositioned multiple times, and was shown another three penises—confirming for her that all men were not created equal. She also had her ass fondled with no idea who the culprit was, and still had yet to find the infamous and ever elusive Slash.

He was starting to tick her off.

And she was definitely drunk. She was as drunk as her Uncle William when he'd fallen into the ale barrel and had drunk it down so he wouldn't drown without an adequate air supply.

"Who is Slash?" Alexis yelled into her ear, The Impalers blasting out a song that Gwenna thought she might recognize. Or maybe it was just that so many songs had the word *baby* in them.

"I don't know who Slash is." Which was the damn frustrating part of the whole thing.

"What? Then why the hell are you asking all these guys if they're Slash?"

It seemed obvious to her. "So I know if they're Slash or not."

Alexis frowned. "You've totally lost me. And you're drunk, by the way."

"I know. It's kind of nice." Fuzzy. Warm. Making her horny.

"Your brother is going to shoot me."

"So?" Gwenna drained her fourth martini, damn proud of herself for going to the bar and ordering it without help. "It's not like a bullet would kill you. And Ethan needs to stop treating me like a child. I'm a grown woman and I can make my own decisions."

Her *s* in decisions did a monstrous slur. Okay, so she couldn't manage to say *decisions* right at the moment, but she was still capable of *making* them.

"I totally applaud making your own decisions. If they're good ones."

"Don't be so critical, Alexis, that really makes me sad."

"I'm sorry, but please, can you just lay off the martinis and stop talking to strange men?"

That sounded boring, but she nodded, not wanting to argue.

"Hey, let's try to run up onstage," Kelsey said, her hips jiggling to the music.

"Okay." Gwenna handed her martini to Alexis. If she was up onstage, she could scan the crowd for Slash. Even though she had no clue what he looked like, somehow the logic made sense to her martini-soaked brain.

Her sister-in-law sputtered. "No! Bad decision. Bad, bad, bad. You're going to get thrown out!"

"Nah. I know half the guys in the band," Kelsey said. "And I had sex with the bass player back in the sixties. It's cool."

"See?" That sounded highly encouraging to Gwenna. "Kelsey knows the band."

And she proceeded to follow Kelsey through the crowd, weaving and smiling and dancing with concertgoers as they made their way to the front. Getting past the bouncers was a snap, since they were mortal. She and Kelsey just fast-walked, vampire speed, between two of them on the side, and then leaped onstage.

Wow. It was hot and bright up there. And loud.

Pulling Gwenna behind the guitar player and turning sideways, Kelsey swayed to the music and made a few "oh, yeah, oh, whoo, ooh" sounds at appropriate times in the music.

Backup singers in a rock band. Brilliant.

Gwenna turned and did the same. This was kind of fun. The guitar player glanced back and looked them up and down, amusement on his face.

The bouncers didn't have the same loving feeling toward them. Gwenna felt a meaty arm encircle her stomach and she was contemplating using her strength to break free when she glanced to the side and saw a very familiar face.

"Nate!" She waved as the bouncer lifted her completely off her feet. "What brings you by?" Not that he could hear her, but she was delighted to see him, and his very handsome face.

He looked a bit off put, though.

She wondered why that was.

Nate had been pretty damn sure he wasn't going to enjoy his little stroll into The Impalers concert, and that he was going to hate Slash on sight just for the simple fact that he was spending time with Gwenna. Nate wanted to spend time with Gwenna. Nate wanted Gwenna. He didn't want her trolling around town with other guys. It was that simple.

He was also worried about her and her lack of concern for her personal safety. She was knee-deep in a murder investigation and didn't even seem to realize that. It was obvious she had been telling the truth when she'd said she lived a sheltered life.

That particular fact was a little difficult to remember, though, when he stared up at the stage watching Gwenna gyrate and sing along to the music wearing a scrap-of-nothing blue dress.

For a brief second, he thought she was a legitimate backup singer because that was the only explanation his brain could conjure up. Until the bouncer grabbed on to her and hauled her lily-white ass off the stage. Gwenna Carrick had apparently charged the stage. Jesus, what the hell was she thinking?

She spotted him, giving him a big smile and a perky wave. "Nate!"

He thought she might have also said something else, but it got lost in the black T-shirt the beefy bouncer was wearing as he made fast work of flipping her over his shoulder and hopping off the stage. It was clear he was going to keep walking and toss her rear out of the club, so Nate stepped up.

"Hey, sorry about that, she's with me."

The guy stared him down, obviously trying to decide if he gave a shit or not. "Keep her drunk ass off the fucking stage," he said, dropping Gwenna to the floor without warning and giving a little nudge on her shoulder to send her in Nate's direction.

She stumbled backward and would have totally gone down except that Nate grabbed her arm and steadied her. She still tripped out of her shoe, though, giving a cry of pain, and that pissed him off.

"You got a problem?" he asked the bouncer, any patience he might have hauled out of reserve just used up. "You may be a badass bouncer, but I'm a fucking cop, and you're shoving around my girlfriend."

"Hey, I'm just doing my job, man. She went up onstage and I took her off. No big deal." The bouncer held out his hands. "Tell her to stay the fuck out of restricted areas and I won't have to touch her."

It wasn't exactly an apology but the guy didn't give him the fight he seemed to be looking for, so Nate took a deep breath and nodded. "Fine." Then he took Gwenna's hand, since she seemed to be struggling fruitlessly to bend over and put her shoe back on without toppling onto the floor. "Come on, babe, forget the goddamn shoe. You can put it on in the car."

"What about Kelsey?" Gwenna asked, turning around and pointing to her friend he'd met earlier in the evening, as she was likewise carted offstage by badass bouncer number two.

"Oh, Jesus. What the hell were you two doing up there?" And he wasn't sure why it shocked him, but Gwenna clearly was drunk. Her eyes looked glassy and she was wobbling precariously.

"Kelsey knows the band," she said, like that explained a damn thing.

"Don't move." He shifted closer to the stage and went through the same routine with the second guy, flashing his badge so he wouldn't throw Kelsey out of the building, either.

In two minutes he was standing in front of Gwenna and Kelsey, frowning at the party pair. "Don't do that again," he told them, then immediately felt like a jackass. He sounded like their father, and truthfully neither one of them looked the least bit repentant or grateful for his assistance.

"It wasn't a big deal," Gwenna said, her mouth opening very widely when she spoke, her words all rushing together like her tongue was out of commission.

"Are you drunk?" he asked, already knowing the answer.

"Shit-faced," she confirmed.

Alexis appeared next to him. "Hey, look, it's two thirds of the Supremes. You guys were pretty good up there."

"You encouraged them to do this?" he asked, feeling a little outraged.

She just shrugged. "I didn't encourage, but I couldn't stop them, either. They're grown women."

"Where's Slash?" Nate asked Gwenna, yelling to be heard over the pounding music.

"He stood me up again," Gwenna said. "The bloody rat bastard."

She looked pissed off, but Nate was actually relieved. There was no reason to assume Slash was guilty of murder, but there was no reason to believe he was innocent, either. And Nate didn't like the guy's little habit of making plans to meet Gwenna.

"I need to talk to you. Let's go somewhere quieter."

"Can we shag once we're there?"

Nate froze in the act of reaching for her hand. She *was* drunk. Jesus. Alexis snorted behind him. Nate studied Gwenna. Her hair was looking a little wild, blond fluffy curls falling in all directions, and her lipstick was wandering off her bottom lip. That blue dress that showed her entire freakin' navel was hiked up on her thigh, and falling off her right shoulder. Pink cheeked, glassy eyed, dead drunk, looking like a poster child for the morning after already, she wasn't exactly at her best. But Nate thought she was fucking gorgeous, and she was blinking up at him, her blue eyes wide, her lips parted and wet, her breathing a little faster than normal, and the flush of desire over her cheeks and neck.

She wanted him. He could see that.

And oh yeah, he wanted her, too.

No matter that his whole body felt like it could just drop to the ground in exhaustion, there was one part of him that had no problem staying up for her.

"After we have a little chat, I'm absolutely positive you can talk me into a shag," he told her. "Then when we're done being British and shagging, we can fuck like Americans."

Her little pink lips formed a perfect "O" as her eyes went wide in shock.

Nate didn't wait for an answer, nor did he wait to get reamed by Alexis, who looked disgusted and ready to go feminist on him.

He just hauled Gwenna by the hand until they were across the room, out the door of the club, and halfway down the block. He paused in front of a clothing store that was closed for the night, intent on lecturing her on the dangers of meeting anyone from the vampire slayers' loop until they had more concrete answers, when she shoved him backward against the glass window.

"What the . . ."

Gwenna snuggled up against him, her hand finding his dick on the first grab. "I can't wait another split second to do this," she said, and pulled his head down for a hot, wet kiss.

He had things to say. Important things. Shit that mattered. But hell if he could remember what a single one of those was. She had scattered his thoughts with the first warm taste of her mouth. The way she felt pressed against him, her fingers cupping his erection firmly and possessively while their tongues tangled, had him breathing hard and aching with the need to fill her body.

When she broke the kiss and started nibbling on his bottom lip, he moaned, "Gwenna. We need to go somewhere more private. Your place. My apartment is too . . ." He broke off when she bit his lip hard, then sucked on it. He felt that pull, felt that tug, all the way to his groin, and he slapped his hand onto her shoulder for support.

"Fuck, what are you doing?"

"I bit you," she said in a sweet, pretty little voice. "You taste good, Nate."

"Come on, babe, the hotel . . ." It was down the street. They just needed to walk. To get there. But instead of moving, Gwenna was yanking down his zipper and pulling his cock out. Right there on the street.

Nate glanced around. They were in a shadowy alcove, and while there were people milling around like always in Vegas, no one was paying attention to them. Yet. He tried to hang on to his resolve. But damn, it was hard when she was working over his cock like a pro. She had him by the balls, literally, and was stroking up and down his shaft, then around the tip with tight, confident motions, and it felt amazing.

But he still forced her to stop. And moved her a few feet over, and behind a scaffolding and tarp rigged up to paint the building's second floor. It wasn't a hotel room, but it was some form of cover, and should keep them out of jail for public exposure. The April night was cool, but Nate didn't even notice. He was on fire, and Gwenna didn't have a single goose bump, despite her skimpy outfit.

"Oh, goody, privacy," she said with a naughty smile.

It was in the back of his mind that this was taking advantage of her drunken state, and he almost pulled the plug, except that she prevented him from stopping, from any movement, speech, or rational thought of any kind, by gathering up the front of her dress and exposing her inner thighs to him. Where she was wearing no panties. Then taking his cock and sliding it over her clitoris, dipping it into her wetness, then back up again to rub her swollen clit.

Holy crap, that was hot. He leaned against the wall for support and concentrated on breathing and not ejaculating prematurely. Both of which seemed like monumental tasks at the moment.

Gwenna's knees bent as she began to move her own body in tandem with the up-and-down motion she created with her wrist on his cock. With her dress around her waist, he had one hell of a view, and when she used her free hand, and spread her blond curls apart, he about swallowed his tongue.

She sank down on the length of him and gave a hearty sigh of appreciation. "Bugger, that feels good."

That was the understatement of his lifetime. Nate gripped Gwenna's waist and savored the moment. "Yes, it does, babe. It feels better than good. It feels amazing. You're amazing."

Then he thrust upward, filling her, and sending her into a nice, low moan. Her head snapped back, and Nate flicked his tongue out and trailed it up and down the exposed part of her chest. It was definitely an intriguing dress, showing off her flesh in a narrow ribbon from neck to navel.

Gwenna met him thrust for thrust, her hands on his shoulders, her cries growing louder with each slap of their bodies together. It was fast and frenzied, and their bodies slipped and slid together, a hot, wet joining that shoved Gwenna into a quick orgasm, her nails digging into him, her tight opening squeezing onto him as she shuddered. He gave one last power thrust, then followed her, gritting his teeth as he came inside her with a tight pulsing orgasm.

Her moans slowed and she sank against his body as the last waves of ecstasy rolled over him. Then they were clinging to each other, sweaty and breathing hard, her face plastered against his chest, his heart pounding from the adrenaline rush. Nate kissed the side of her head, and loosened his grip on her waist. She sighed and snuggled a little closer, but made no attempt to disconnect their bodies. Neither did he.

They were still standing like that a solid minute later when his phone rang in his pants pocket.

"Shit." He didn't want to answer it, but he also couldn't turn off the detective in him. Part of him was wondering if it was the call telling him the autopsy report on Andrew Fletcher was in.

Gwenna dug into his pocket and retrieved his phone. He held his hand out but she just grinned and pushed the talk button. "Nate Thomas's office," she said in a clipped, secretarial voice. "May I help you?"

That made him grin, especially given that she was drunk and still sitting on his cock.

"One moment, please." She handed him the phone. "A Jim Connors wishes to speak to you."

Nate took the phone and disengaged himself from her, pulling her dress back down over her thighs. With the phone against his shirt, he gave her a soft kiss. "It's work. It will just take a second."

"I understand." She tucked him back into his pants and snuggled up against his chest.

Wrapping his free arm around her, Nate lifted the phone to his ear. "Yeah? What's up?"

"Where the fuck are you?"

"I'm on the boulevard, about a block from Caesar's." Behind a scaffolding tarp, but Jim didn't need to know that. Nate watched the black nylon flap in the breeze and tried to focus.

"You're supposed to be at that concert looking for Gwenna Carrick and her little online buddy."

"I'm actually with Gwenna Carrick at the moment."

"But you're not at the club."

"No." What the hell was Jim getting at? "Is there some kind of problem?"

"You bet your horny ass there is." The phone rustled as Jim shifted. "Get back to that club. The manager just found a dead body backstage. Victim is a white male, twenties, folded up like an origami crane in a storage closet. Scene team and the coroner on their way."

"Shit." Nate shoved off the wall. "You're kidding me."

"No, sir. Makes you wonder about your cutsie little blonde, doesn't it? What do you think she was up to tonight before you got in her pants?"

While it pissed Nate off, he knew he'd be thinking the same thing in Jim's shoes.

"I'll be there in five." He hung up and looked down at Gwenna. She had been with her friends all night. She was drunk. She was too sweet. There was no way she could be a cold-blooded killer. He'd stake his life on it.

But the facts told him that he couldn't rule Gwenna out as a suspect, no matter what his gut said. She was involved on the loop. She was at the scene both times. She could be faking her intoxication. And in a crowded concert, she could have slipped backstage and killed someone. There was no report yet on how Andrew had died, or how his blood had all been drained.

Nate knew Gwenna couldn't have done that. He could look into her eyes and know that she was a loving, compassionate person.

But he also suspected she had secrets she didn't share with him, and that she knew more than she was telling him about the slayers' loop.

"What's the matter?" she asked him now, her face showing concern, her hand reaching for his.

"We've got another body."

"Oh, no." Her face went white. "Where?"

"Backstage at The Impalers concert."

Ten

Alexis felt like a groupie. She couldn't believe she'd let Kelsey talk her into going backstage at The Impalers concert.

"Hey, Davey!" Kelsey was saying, throwing herself into the arms of the dark-haired bass player. "Long time no see."

"What's up, Summer? You're looking good." He gave her a big, friendly grin.

Summer? Lord, Alexis had forgotten that Kelsey had changed her name in the sixties from Nancy to Summer. In the eighties she'd made the switch to Kelsey.

"It's Kelsey now, remember?"

"Yeah, I know, but I can't get used to it . . . and I heard some crazy shit about you getting married, too. What's up with that?"

Kelsey made a face. "That was a mistake."

Sucker Bet

Alexis stood there feeling slightly impatient while Kelsey and Davey the bass player plopped down on a couch and played catch-up. Kelsey was pouting and trembling and he was patting her knee in reassurance. At least Kelsey hadn't exaggerated when she'd said they were friends, which was usually par for the course with Kelsey. She thought everyone was her best chum, right before they stabbed her in the back or ignored her. But Davey seemed to be actually glad to see her.

Glancing around the room, which was nothing to get excited over, just a couch and a few chairs done in fake leather, Alexis tried not to cough as the other guitar player's cigarette smoke drifted by. A couple of the guys were standing around talking, throwing darts at a board on the wall, and the one she thought was the drummer was sitting in a chair with a woman on his lap wearing black tights with tiny silver bats on them. The band had all introduced themselves, but she had promptly forgotten every single one of their names. Nor was she particularly interested in flirting with any of them, as Kelsey had suggested with a giggle when they had made their way backstage. Wow, she had become a boring old married woman. How weird was that?

"So this is going to sound like a line, but haven't I seen you somewhere?" the guy to her left asked. He was the one with the vast majority of his head shaved except for a long ponytail right at the crown, and some aggressive silver studs sticking out of his lip.

He was also tall, which irritated her on principle, given that she was size of an average American ten-year-old, and she had to tip her head half back to meet his eye. But he had great eyes, a light blue, and they were friendly, not the least bit smarmy.

"I think I would remember meeting you," she said with a wry smile. "But I do have to go to a lot of political parties, so maybe I bumped into you somewhere."

He stuck out his hand. "Drake."

"Alexis Baldizzi-Carrick." She shook his hand firmly.

Recognition crossed his face. "Oh, shit, I know who you are now. You're President Carrick's wife. No wonder you looked familiar. We played a fund-raising dinner for the president before you were married, but I'm almost positive you were there."

"If you saw a short blonde looking bored, then yeah, that was probably me."

He laughed. "Not digging being a political wife? Politics isn't for everyone."

"Oh, I like politics. I love politics. I like the strategizing and the planning and the execution of policies. I'm having an absolute blast overhauling the judicial system in the Nation, but being *just* a political wife at these functions? That I don't like."

"I don't think I would like being a political wife, either."

Alexis laughed. "You could probably really rock a cocktail dress, though."

"Only if it's black." He grinned. "Hey, do you want a drink or anything? We travel with our own special bar."

"Sure." She could use a little blood. All this worrying about Gwenna and Kelsey was exhausting. "And hey, sorry my friends got up onstage with you. That's what I get for ditching out on my Secret Service guards." She hated that she had to spend every minute of her life with bodyguards—sometimes a vampire just needed privacy—so she left them behind whenever she could, much to Ethan's frustration. But it had become a rather amusing game to see how many ways she could trick the guards.

"No big deal." He just shrugged. "We have women doing that all the time. The bouncers usually take care of them. And I knew David knows Kelsey, so it was cool. Who was the other chick, though?"

"That's my sister-in-law."

Drake called over to the stage manager. "Hey, Pete, what did we do with that cooler full of drinks?"

"I stuck it in a closet. I'll go find it."

"Thanks, man." He turned back to Alexis. "Your sister-in-law? Like your brother's sister, or the president's sister?"

"The president's sister." Whoops. It hadn't occurred to her when Gwenna had rushed the stage that Ethan would be none too happy with Alexis or Gwenna for her little stunt. That wild party behavior from his sister and wife would reflect badly on him on the eve of his Inauguration. Shit. She was really a lousy political wife.

"Alexis!" Kelsey called from the couch. "I had the coolest idea and Davey agrees with me."

Uh-oh. "What idea is that?"

"You know how I need a job and stuff now that I'm divorcing Ringo because he's a total asshole?"

"Yes."

"Well, I'm going to join the band! I can play tambourine and sing back up."

Alexis almost laughed. "Wow, that's an . . . interesting idea."

Given the appalled looks on the other guys' faces, it wasn't one they were really digging.

"We don't need a backup singer," Drake said, shooting David a pointed look.

But David just shrugged and made "let it go" faces at Drake behind Kelsey's head. "We can at least try it in a rehearsal or something."

Kelsey squealed and gave him a big kiss on the cheek, Davey's arms wrapping around her. Another second and their lips were locked in a kiss that was about two tongues beyond "we're just friends." Davey did a thumbs-up toward the guys as Kelsey's leg entwined with his.

Yeah, someone wanted to get laid.

Drake just snorted. "No shame. He has absolutely no shame."

Alexis was about to suggest that Kelsey fell in the same category, when the stage manager returned, sans a cooler of blood.

"What's the matter?" Drake asked.

The stage manager looked like he was going to pass out, his skin pasty and beads of sweat on his upper lip. "Dude, in the closet."

"What?"

"There's a dead guy, man."

Donatelli waited impatiently for Williams to say something. "So? What did you see tonight? Where the hell was Gwenna?" He shuffled a deck of cards forcefully on the dining table in his suite.

"She went to a concert with Alexis Carrick and Kelsey Columbia."

"Really?" It was odd that Alexis was hanging around Kelsey again. Carrick couldn't be thrilled about that. Donatelli didn't think he was all that enamored with Gwenna in Kelsey's company, either. That girl was a loose cannon and notorious for partying. Not a good influence on a woman like Gwenna, who was a lady in the truest sense of the word. "What concert?"

"The Impalers."

"Who the hell are they?" He expected Williams to say Celine Dion, Elton John, or a symphony, not someone he'd never heard of.

"They're a rock group—all the members are vampires and they pretend to be vampires onstage as a gimmick. Mortals love it."

"A rock group?" That didn't sound like Gwenna. She must not have realized what Kelsey was dragging her into. "Poor Gwenna. What did she do the whole time? She must have been bored."

"Well . . . she talked to a lot of people actually."

"What people?" Donatelli forgot his cards and glanced up sharply at Williams.

His bodyguard shifted uncomfortably. "Men. She talked to a lot of men. She was, uh, wearing this really pretty dress, and she well, looked good, and guys seemed to want to talk to her."

"Of course she looked good. She always looks good. But that doesn't mean she should have to tolerate men accosting her. I hope she told them all to go to hell."

"Sometimes. But sometimes, I think actually she was the one who started the conversation. Like the four guys who whipped out their . . ." Williams gestured to his crotch. "I'm pretty sure she and Kelsey went up to them first."

Donatelli felt the blood drain from his face. "Strange men showed my wife their cocks? In a public place? Why didn't you stop them?"

"You told me to watch her and tell you everything she did. So that's what I did. And she was really slinging back the martinis and running all over the place. I had a hard time keeping up with her. Then she jumped up onstage with the band."

Crumpling the card in his hand, Donatelli focused on not losing his temper. Gwenna didn't drink. None of this made sense. And never in a million years would his wife deign to crawl up onstage at a rock concert and express interest in some long-haired musician. "You can't be serious."

Williams swallowed audibly. "Yes, sir, I'm sorry to say I am. She went onstage and pretended to be a backup singer until the bouncers hauled her off. Then a mortal guy she seemed to know left with her."

"Where did they go?"

"Well. He put her in a cab, which took her straight back to the Ava. She went in and up to her room."

"Okay, then." That sounded more like Gwenna.

"But . . ." Williams looked like he was in pain.

"But what?"

"Before he put her in the cab, they, um, you know . . ." His hands came together, went apart, came together.

"What the fuck are you trying to say?" Like he was going to sit there and play charades. This wasn't a damn undead dinner party.

"They got, you know, they, well . . . had sex." Williams's face was bright red and he was sweating profusely.

The entire world went black in front of Donatelli's eyes as rage swelled up and consumed him. "How do you know that? Where exactly did this allegedly occur?"

"I saw them, sir." Williams dropped his head down and rubbed his upper lip. "It was on the street, beyond some construction scaffolding. I was following them, making sure I didn't lose them, wondering why they were going back there and I saw . . ." His hands came together again. "Against the wall. Then I just went on the other side of the tarp and waited for them to finish because I knew you wouldn't want me to watch."

He didn't want it to happen at all, let alone anyone to watch. Donatelli spoke very, very carefully. "So, you're telling me my wife had sex with a strange man standing up outside, against a wall?"

"Yes, sir."

Donatelli stood up slowly. Then flipped his dining table over onto its side with a burst of fury. "Kill him."

"Sir?"

"Find out who he is and kill him. The man she was with. I want him dead within seventy-two hours."

No one was going to touch Gwenna. And if she didn't want him, insisted on maintaining this ridiculous divorce, Donatelli would be damned if he'd let another man have her.

Gwenna had sobered up fairly quickly after the phone call that another body had been found. After Nate had flagged her down a cab, she had returned to her suite and headed right to her computer. It seemed really important to focus on finding the real names for the rest of the e-mail addresses on the slayers' loop.

It was the least she could do to help Nate and the investigation. She didn't care about clearing her name, though she knew that she had to actually be on the list of suspects. She had been in both places a body had been found, and she was on the slayers' loop. Plus she had the horrible suspicion that once this latest victim was identified, they were going to determine that he was on the loop, too.

While she had been drinking like a fish at The Impalers concert and having phenomenal sex with Nate on the sidewalk, the slayers' loop had exploded with the news of Buzzdrew's death. Gwenna was following the thread backward, trying to determine who had first posted the news of his death, and deciphering who knew exactly what, when her mobile phone rang.

A glance at it showed it was Roberto. She should just turn off her ringer, but then it would vibrate all night as he left nine hundred voice-mail messages. Better to just get it over with.

"Hello?" she said absently, studying her screen. The news about Buzzdrew didn't seem to originate from any of the principal players on the loop. It was from a lurker, whose e-mail address was dumbfuck69@dumbfuck.com. Obviously someone brimming with maturity.

"Gwenna, it's Roberto. How are you?"

Her ex-husband's voice was quite polite. No overt and oozing charm. No references to her being his wife or calling her darling, beautiful, gorgeous, or my love.

How odd. "I'm fine, how are you?" No reason to be rude when he was trying so hard.

"I'm quite well, thank you. Just undergoing some last-minute preparations for tomorrow's swearing-in and the ball. Your brother and I had a meeting this afternoon. Did you have a pleasant evening?"

Gwenna frowned. She and Roberto didn't do casual chitchat. He was starting to unnerve her. "I'm glad to hear you and Ethan are setting aside your personal differences for the sake of the Nation."

"We are both in agreement that it would make quite a positive statement to that effect if you consented to accompany me to the ball tomorrow night."

Shit. So that's where this was headed. "Roberto, that's just not a good idea." And she found it difficult to believe that her brother would applaud her spending a whole night with an arm through Roberto's, even if it was a smart political maneuver.

"Why not? Carrick and I both feel that it will show unity between us, and we'll present a strong and solid government to our constituents."

"I think it would just muddy the water with gossip." And be an unbearable and insufferable evening for her. She didn't want to go and make polite conversation as it was, and she couldn't fathom being paraded around by Roberto while everyone whispered about them. "Besides, I'm not an asset to you. I never was. I am a horrific hostess, which you know damn well, considering it was a flaw you constantly pointed out in me during our marriage."

"I did no such thing."

She couldn't prevent a snort from flying out of her mouth. "Oh, come on. Now you're being utterly absurd. You hated the way I was so shy and lousy at commanding the household staff and overseeing all your many parties and soirees. I distinctly recall the afternoon when you told me to get my fucking nose out of a book and go slap the housekeeper about, as was befitting a lady of my rank, and your wife."

The words still rankled, all these centuries later. Roberto had married her knowing full well what her temperament and personality were and had chosen to ignore that. He had always assumed she was or could be whatever he wanted, despite the truth irrefutably staring him in the face. While he had wanted a woman capable of ordering and commanding his household with an iron fist, she had been the polar opposite, happiest when reading in the privacy of her salon.

"I don't remember saying anything like that." His politeness was chipping away, and he was starting to sound irritated. "I can't believe that you could possibly remember that verbatim, either. But then, you were always intent on keeping a list of every misdeed of mine, from saying 'damn' at the dinner table to forgetting your birthday. Once. One lousy time I forgot and I was subjected to your tears for two days. All I ever wanted was for you to enjoy our life together . . . to take a little pride in yourself and your position, and to not let the staff and the other ladies run riot over you."

Gwenna felt the insult of his disapproval all over again. "You wanted me to get a backbone."

"Yes."

"But not with you. And now that I have, it drives you insane, doesn't it? Well, sorry, Roberto, but after all these years, I've finally found my backbone and it's not going to break anytime soon."

"I don't consider making a fool out of yourself by jumping onstage at a rock concert to be getting a backbone. That's just being a fool."

She gasped. The . . . the . . . she couldn't think of a word ugly enough to describe him. "God, I just hate you sometimes, Roberto. You weren't always such a gigantic bastard, were you? I swear I must have been blind and stupid to imagine we could both live in Vegas and coexist, if not as friends, at least in peace."

"I'm not the one starting an argument. I asked you to go to the ball with me! Doesn't that tell you I'd love to be friends?"

"Actually, no, it doesn't. It tells me either that you're using me to make a statement of power to my brother, that you're interested in having the attention tomorrow focused on you and not Ethan, that you heard I went to a rock concert tonight and it infuriated you enough to want to keep me by your side tomorrow so I don't do something you'd consider equally as idiotic, or you're just plain horny. Perhaps it's all of those." She pushed her chair back and stood up. "But I'm absolutely certain it's not because you want to be chums and hang out at the pub together."

"You wouldn't be this angry if you didn't love me."

That was the most ludicrous logic she'd ever heard. "You're impossible. And I need to go now before I try to strangle you through the telephone."

"Be ready at six. I'll swing by and pick you up."

He had to be ingesting drugs. "I'm not going to the ball with you!"

"Wear blue, please. You always look stunning in blue."

"I'm not going."

"See you then. Good-bye, love."

Gwenna hit the end button and tossed the phone across her desk. The man had the thickest head imaginable. He was as stubborn as ten bulls and she was always waving the red cape without meaning to. Okay, to be completely honest, sometimes she meant to, because he was infuriating.

But while she felt intense anger and frustration with him, the most overwhelming emotion she felt at the moment was resignation. Roberto would never go away. Ever. He would follow her through eternity, harassing and hounding her, until she retreated, back to York, or to somewhere else far away, where he would leave her alone for a century or two.

What had seemed so promising, so possible—a new life, independence, a career, some sort of relationship with Nate—now all seemed hopelessly naïve and optimistic. Whatever she tried to do, whoever she would like to date, wherever she might travel, Roberto would be there, in person, or with someone to watch her, and he would remind her of the simple, sweet girl she'd been, who had loved unconditionally and who had lost it all. She would try to forge ahead into the future, and he would always drag her back into the past, and that was immensely depressing.

Gwenna tucked her hair behind her ears, stood in the middle of the room, and stared blankly at her computer screen. So she was still paying for her mistake in marrying Roberto. Hell, for losing her virginity to him when she was a sheltered eighteen-year-old.

Roberto was going to plague her no matter what she did. She might as well take what she could out of life and enjoy herself along the way, doing her best to ignore him. Maybe eventually he would get tired of her lack of reaction, or find that she was no longer what he even wanted if she was too outspoken, too much of a modern woman. The point was, she couldn't let him dictate her future. She just refused to allow that.

Returning to her computer, Gwenna clicked on Dumb Fuck's e-mail.

> ***Hey, did you all hear? Buzzdrew from the loop is dead . . . got whacked in Vegas and word is he was drained of his blood. Can you believe that? Man, it sucks to be Buzz . . . DF***

His sensitivity was touching. It was also absolutely lacking in any facts or any hint of how he might have known about Buzz. Considering the police hadn't even identified Andrew until earlier that day, that was amazingly early for DF to have caught wind of it. Gwenna imagined it would be in the Saturday paper, but that wouldn't be out for another eight hours, and when she did a search on the news channels' web pages, they only listed the story as a murder in the train station, the victim a white male. No name. Certainly no mention of the slayers' loop. And no one else seemed to profess any prior knowledge of Buzz's death before DF's post.

Which made her very suspicious of Dumb Fuck.

FoxyKyle expressed concern in her post, and she was either an excellent liar or she was truly upset. She repeatedly said how awful it was and how funny and witty Buzzdrew was. She even suggested sending flowers to the funeral, which was either a lovely gesture, or the sign of a very calculating and manipulative woman.

Slash's response was along the lines of DF's. Sort of a wow, that's awful, but life goes on. Nothing to indicate he realized the crime had occurred where he had intended to meet Queenie. And no mention that he and Queenie had been talking privately, or that he was actually in Vegas, where the murder had taken place.

Methodically, Gwenna created a list of who posted in what order, who expressed distress, and who showed callous disinterest, and e-mailed it to Nate. Then she posted her own message about Buzz, expressing her sadness and disgust and her hope the killer would be caught, which was all very much legitimate. She did feel absolutely horrific that Andrew's life had been cut off at such a young age. As Queenie, she also offered to contribute to the flower fund. Then at the very bottom, she added, "Does anyone think it had something to do with this loop??"

That would get people talking.

Eleven

Nate stared at his mother and prayed he wouldn't call her a complete insensitive bitch at his sister's wake. He just bit his tongue and listened to her litany of complaints.

"I can't believe you chose this funeral home. It's in such a rough part of town. I swear I saw graffiti on the building across the street. I was afraid to leave my Mercedes in the parking lot."

He had chosen that particular place because it was close to his house and the police station, and no other reason. In his mind, funeral homes were all the same, and it wasn't exactly a crime-ridden neighborhood. It just wasn't plunked down in the middle of two-million-dollar homes, which was what his mother would have preferred.

"This isn't really a lot of flowers, either. And I can't say I care for the arrangement of lilies with baby's breath. This isn't prom."

Nate felt a dull pounding behind his eyes and an overwhelming stabbing pain in his chest. He had no explanation for how this woman had given birth to a person as amazing as Kyra had been, or how his mother could show so little grief at losing her daughter. She truly was more concerned with appearances than the fact that Kyra was gone forever. They would never hear her laugh, never see her get married, never have the joy of watching her raise her own children. She was gone. Dead.

And yet his mother still walked the earth, serving no purpose that he could tell other than to irritate the hell out of him. It was an injustice he didn't understand and was having a damn hard time swallowing.

As they greeted guests, accepted countless condolences, and stood for hours and hours, his mother sniped and pecked and clawed at him every chance she got, griping and complaining and criticizing, her sharp words scraping at his raw nerves until he thought he was either going to demand she shut the fuck up, or he was going to do the unthinkable and walk straight out of his sister's wake. He held on, pulling every ounce of patience to keep it together until he thought he absolutely couldn't stand another second.

That's when he looked up and saw Gwenna Carrick enter the room. She was wearing a simple black dress, her hair pulled back into a smooth knot, her gaze moving around the room. When she spotted him, she looked at him with such sympathy, such understanding, that he cleared his throat to get rid of the lump that was suddenly lodged there.

She walked straight over to him and took both of his hands and kissed his cheek. "How are you holding up?" she murmured.

"I've been better," he said truthfully, squeezing her hands. Seeing her helped, though, and he wasn't sure why. Maybe it was because her sympathy was legitimate, her own grief so palpable when she had discussed her daughter. Maybe it was also because she'd taken the time and trouble to find out where the wake was, when he hadn't told her, and she had stopped by even when Nate knew she had a big party at her brother's casino she had promised to attend.

Maybe it was because he liked Gwenna Carrick in ways he didn't exactly understand or totally trust. But the bottom line was that when he was with her, he just felt better.

"Who's your friend, Nathaniel?" his mother said, touching his elbow.

Nate sighed, letting go of one of Gwenna's hands, but keeping the other, and pulling her into his side. "This is Gwenna Carrick. Gwenna, this is my mother, Sylvia Thomas, and my father, Art Thomas."

"I'm so sorry for your loss, Mr. and Mrs. Thomas," Gwenna said.

"Thank you. How do you know Nathaniel?"

Not very subtle, but Gwenna didn't seem to notice. "We met through a mutual friend."

Intriguing way to put their first meeting at a murder scene. Gwenna was quite the diplomat. Knowing his mother would probe mercilessly until she got whatever she was looking for, Nate nudged Gwenna a little. "Can you excuse us, Mom? I need to speak to Gwenna privately."

His mother looked ready to protest, his father saying nothing as usual, his face an expressionless mask, but Nate just walked away, carting Gwenna with him.

"Thanks for coming," he said to her as they moved toward the back of the room.

"You're welcome. And you know how very sorry I am that you've lost your sister."

He did know that. Her eyes spoke it loud and clear. "Thanks. Can you stick around for fifteen minutes? I can leave then, thank God, and I'd like to see you, just for a few minutes. I know you have your party thing to go to, but maybe we could grab some coffee." He just wanted—needed—to be with her.

"Sure. Absolutely. I'll just take a seat in the back here and you can get me when you're ready."

Nate kissed her smooth forehead. "Thank you."

Half an hour later Nate was sitting on his back patio with Gwenna, stretching his legs out and yanking off his tie. "I won't keep you, I promise," he told her. "I know you need to go. I just need a minute to decompress."

"It's fine," she said, sitting in the chaise lounge next to him and crossing her feet at the ankles. "This party will go on all night long so no one will notice if I'm not there at eight on the dot."

He had nothing to say, really, but neither did he want to be alone. It was comforting to sit beside Gwenna, to let his body relax one tight muscle at a time, and know that she wouldn't chatter needlessly, wouldn't question him, wouldn't say stupid platitudes, or focus selfishly on herself.

The weather was cool but dry, and his backyard was quiet, peaceful, despite his mother's concerns about crime. It was a nice working-class neighborhood, and he had gotten into his house before real estate had exploded in Vegas.

"You might have noticed that my mother isn't exactly collapsing in grief," he said after a minute, because he needed to explain.

"Everyone expresses grief differently."

"True. But she doesn't really feel it. My mother is a piece of work. My father cares, he's just a workaholic who worships success and the almighty dollar. In his heart, he does care. But my mother . . . she honestly doesn't give a damn about Kyra or me. She cares about what people think of her, of her social status, but she is actually incapable of love. And she's a pathological liar." Nate suspected he sounded a little whiny, but he just needed to explain. Maybe needed someone to believe him, see what he saw so clearly. "She'll lie about anything to get what she wants. You know how I told you she went to Australia because she thought Kyra was in remission?"

Gwenna nodded.

"Well, I actually think she did it on purpose, knowing Kyra would die. That way she didn't have to deal with her actual passing, and she had the added bonus of extra sympathy from people that she wasn't here."

"That's horrible."

Nate tipped back his beer bottle and took a long swallow. "Yeah, well, she's not a nice lady, my mom. Sure you don't want a beer?"

"No, thanks."

"You don't eat or drink enough," Nate told Gwenna, looking at how thin she was as she stretched out. He didn't think he'd ever seen her put a bite of food in her mouth.

She gave him a rueful look. "I drank plenty last night."

He gave a soft laugh. "Yeah, you were a little shit-faced. I hope you don't think I was taking advantage of that fact on the street there."

"You absolutely were taking advantage and you know it."

Now he grinned. "You're right." But hell, she'd been so eager, and his resistance was seriously down when it came to her.

She reached over and whacked his arm. "Shame on you. But I'm glad you did. I totally wanted you, and it was very sexy."

"I like that you tell the truth, Gwenna. I despise liars . . . and people who manipulate, tell you one thing and mean another. Just tell the goddamn truth, you know?"

"You're a very black-and-white kind of man, aren't you?"

"I guess I am." Nate drained his beer. "It's easy to start picking each action apart and judging and suggesting that maybe this was wrong or wasn't wrong because of x, y, or z, but it's all just justification. There is right and there is wrong, and most of us just lie to ourselves when we do something that's wrong and try to claim there was a reason it was okay. But wrong is wrong."

"I know what you mean. So what happened last night? Who is the person they found at the concert?" she asked quietly.

There were things he shouldn't share, reasons he needed to play it straight, but he could give her the basic facts. The media was bound to pick up on it soon, since two murders with the same MO could be spun out in the news as a serial killer. "His name is Johnny Walker. And yes, I got a call about an hour ago that when his computer was recovered from his parents' house in Sacramento, it showed he was a member of the vampire slayers' loop as Death Angel, or something like that. I'm sorry, I don't remember exactly. My brain is fried."

Cracked, fried, and scrambled.

"Oh, this is just awful. I don't understand what the connection is . . . I mean why loop members? And if Johnny didn't live in Vegas, what was he doing here?"

"That is the million-dollar question. Don't worry, I have every intention of solving that little puzzle along with a few others. We'll catch our killer. He's on the loop. We just have to find him." He turned to her. "And thanks to you, we'll get there quicker. Thanks for forwarding all the names and your thoughts."

She bit her lip. "You're welcome. It's the very least I can do. And you know, Nate, I just find it very odd that Slash was at both locations—or at least mentioned both locations—where a body was discovered. I've got a bad feeling about him."

"Me, too."

They sat in silence for a minute, Nate wondering if it was wrong to see Gwenna again. He wanted to. Felt an intense, edgy desire to make sure she didn't leave without confirmation there would be a next time for them. Not as detective, citizen, but as a man and a woman. He was falling for her like a ton of fucking bricks. Maybe it was the timing, maybe it was the way she looked at him with those big blue eyes and oozed compassion, or maybe it was the fact that the sex was all-consuming, irresistible, but Nate knew he was going, going, gone.

But whether that was a good idea or not was a huge-ass mystery.

"I should let you go."

"Yeah, I guess I should." She sighed and made no motion to get up. "You know, I really like your house and yard. It's just right, isn't it?"

It was two bedrooms, one bath, and a tiny rectangle of a backyard. It was just right for him. Any more and he wouldn't be able to keep up with cleaning and maintenance. "It works for me."

"When I was married to Roberto, we had this big fancy villa in Italy and another house in London. They were pretentious, uncomfortable. I like this much better."

"Thanks." He thought it was bizarre that she came from the same world his mother had scratched and clawed to get into, and yet Gwenna seemed to want out. "The ex leaving you alone these last few days?"

She shrugged. "No. He'll be at this party tonight. He's rather put out that I refused to go with him."

"Maybe you should take legal action. Get a restraining order." Or maybe Nate should have a little man-to-man chat with him.

Gwenna stood up. "Oh, that's not necessary. I told you Roberto would never hurt me, and no sense in getting his back up. It is what it is."

"Can I see you again?" he blurted out, suddenly afraid this was it. She was walking out. "Tomorrow night, like we planned?"

But she smiled at him. "That would be brilliant. And I'll see you at the funeral. I wouldn't let you go through that alone, you know."

That kicked him where it counted. He started to stand up, but she stopped him by bending over and grabbing the end of his tie in her fist. "I'm rather fond of you," she said, before giving him a warm, lingering kiss.

Damn, was the feeling mutual.

It took all of three minutes for Roberto to spot her when she walked into the Inauguration Ball. Gwenna barely had a chance to buss her brother on the cheek and offer her official congratulations in public for his winning the election, when Roberto descended on her. He was furious and she knew it. He had expected her to be waiting for him at 6 p.m. sharp, wearing a blue dress.

It was nine thirty, she had managed to evade his escort, and she was dressed in black. And damned if she didn't feel a little gleeful about the whole thing.

"A word, if you please," he whispered after he gave her a polite, public greeting for anyone watching. "Let's head to the bar."

"No, thank you." She smiled vaguely at a middle-aged man she recognized from somewhere. Preservation of the Undead Council? She wasn't sure. Sad to say, but she didn't keep up on politics. "I don't need a drink."

Roberto made a sound of impatience. "Don't be impertinent."

"Who, me?" She met his gaze full on and gave him a large smile. "I wouldn't dream of doing such a thing."

"Why didn't you tell me Brittany had her baby?"

So that was what bug had got up his butt. "It wasn't my place to do so."

"She's my daughter. That baby is my grandchild."

"Poor thing."

Whoops. Had she said that out loud?

Roberto turned a nasty shade of red. "You're completely out of control."

"It's not your job to rein me in." But Roberto had redirected his attention toward the door.

"Of all the fucking nerve," he said, the irritation he had displayed toward her gone, replaced by cold, calculated hatred.

His words made her shiver. She was used to his impatience, his bossiness, his annoyance with her. But this expression on his face was different—harder, a true anger, and it was a little scary.

Roberto said, "I'll kill him."

"Who?" She turned toward the door, alarmed at his shift, wary of that disdain in his voice.

"Ringo Columbia. He made sloppy work of the last job I gave him, stole a couple grand in heroin from me, and now has the audacity to show up here? Security needs to escort him outside. And then I'll kill him."

It was a sign of how utterly furious Roberto was that he had just admitted out loud to her that he'd had heroin in his possession. Roberto was always vague about his business dealings and preferred to tell her when they were married that he was involved in trade, nothing more. What shamed her now was that she'd known intellectually he was a bootlegger, but had chosen to pretend it wasn't true. Now he had obviously moved on to drug dealing, which made Gwenna wonder if Ethan knew. Politics and illegal business practices weren't a good combination.

Security was already talking to Ringo, who looked strung out and half-asleep. There was a woman holding his hand, and it was most definitely not his wife, Kelsey. This woman was tall, intriguing, exotic as hell. The kind of woman who walks into the room wearing designer clothes and an aloof expression, while all the men drool, and all the women seethe and instantly despise her. Gwenna confessed she was a little irritated herself by that display of confidence, the way the woman just scanned the room calmly, unperturbed by the bodyguards swarming them.

"Who is that with Ringo?" Something about the couple made Gwenna's skin crawl, and it was a disturbing sign of just how much when she found herself reaching out and gripping Roberto's sleeve for some kind of bizarre protection.

He put his hand on the small of her back, and moved in front of her. "Go find your sister-in-law. I think it might be wise for you and she to retire to the ladies' room for a few minutes."

"Why?"

"That's Sasha Chechikov. Gregor's wife."

"The guy who lost the election to Ethan?"

"The very same one."

"Why is his wife here with Ringo? Isn't she mortal?"

"Yes, she is. And as to why she's here . . . that's a very interesting question, my dear, and I don't know the answer to it. Now leave, Gwenna." He gave her a hard, commanding look.

If she wasn't so disturbed for reasons she didn't understand, she would have told him where he could stick his commands, but she didn't bother. She found she had no desire whatsoever to hang about. In fact, she had done her duty. She had showed up, kissed her brother, and she desperately wanted to leave.

Turning, she nearly bumped into a couple of women who were watching the doorway and murmuring in low voices. "I can't believe Kelsey married him," the brunette was saying, shaking her head and fingering her diamond pendant.

"Well, you know ever since Kelsey had all her blood drained and was left for dead, she's been nuts. Not that she wasn't nuts before, because she was, but since she was drained, she's like incapacitated. You know they say that Donatelli did it . . ."

The woman with curly blond hair stopped speaking when she realized Gwenna was staring at her. "Are you okay? You look a little pale."

"Sorry . . . I've skipped feeding for the last few days. I feel a bit faint."

"There's an open bar. Go get something to drink."

"Thanks." Gwenna turned and walked quickly off. Roberto couldn't have drained Kelsey . . . she just couldn't believe he could be so cruel. Not to mention that surely Ethan would have told her his suspicions. Then again, Ethan preferred to think she was incapable of handling unpleasant truths and tended to shield her. So she supposed it was entirely possible that Roberto had been the one to leave Kelsey for dead.

But that aside, the conversation had also triggered a possible theory for the loop killings.

Heading straight for the balcony, Gwenna dodged and weaved in and out of vampires young and old, smiling and nodding and giving cursory greetings. When she stepped outside in the cool spring night, she pulled her phone out of her bag. Edging away from an amorous couple sharing a cigarette and heated looks, she dialed Nate, hoping like hell he wasn't in bed already.

"Hello?"

"It's Gwenna. Can I ask you a question?"

"Sure."

"How did those boys die? Do you know?"

"Strangulation. Then they were drained of blood, though we're not sure how. That's not a clean job normally."

"There were puncture wounds on their necks, weren't there?"

Nate was silent for a second. Then, he just said, "It's possible."

"Oh, God." Gwenna put her hand over her eyes and leaned against the wall for support.

There was only one explanation for what was going on.

She was not the only vampire on the slayers' loop pretending to be mortal.

And that other vampire was a killer.

Twelve

"What are you thinking, Gwenna?" Nate asked her, his voice sharp, curious.

She couldn't tell him the truth in its entirety but neither could she bring herself to lie to him. And they were on the same side—they wanted to catch a killer. "I think the killer is on the vampire slayers' loop." She was whispering, aware of the couple ten feet away from her.

"Yeah, we figure that's pretty much a given, since that's the only connection between the two victims, and they were killed by the same method."

"I think that whoever is doing it is trying to make it look like a vampire killed them."

"Okay." Nate was rustling around and she heard a soft drink can being opened. "So we have a delusional serial killer."

He wasn't getting the bigger picture. "No, what we have is a killer who understands that killing members of a slayers' group in a way that makes it look like a vampire did it, will have those slayers ready to take action and retaliate. Which means to kill a vampire before—in their minds—another slayer is taken out."

She should have seen it before. It was a brilliant strategy. Some of the slayers had been pushing for action, for a large-scale attack on vampires. This kind of violence would only give credence to their claims that vampires were dangerous and the time to eliminate them was now.

Nate was silent for a second. Then he said, "You've got to be kidding me. These people on this loop . . . they don't really take this shit seriously, do they?"

Gwenna stared out at the Strip, at the faux landscape that was Vegas, everything meant to look like something else, everyone intent on forgetting reality. "Some don't. But some do. They take it very seriously."

"Why are you on that loop anyway? You just a Buffy fan or what?" he asked her.

"I like observing people," she told him.

She heard Nate swallow as he took a drink. "You don't really believe in vampires, do you?"

If he only knew she was standing at the Inaugural Ball for the president of the Vampire Nation, with approximately a thousand undead voters behind her in the room celebrating. That would test the boundaries of his black-and-white world.

"It doesn't matter what I believe. What matters is that someone either believes it himself or knows others do."

"Why do you think Slash has been contacting you and wanting to meet you where bodies are turning up? If there's something you can tell me, any thoughts at all, I really need to know it."

"I have no idea why Slash is suggesting these meeting places. And I actually contacted him privately first." She looked back, saw the party going on full swing, the dancing, the flutes of blood being passed around on silver trays, the laughter. Those who were vampire understood who she was, and why they needed to stay together, organized for their protection and prosperity. "No, there's nothing I need to tell you. I've told you everything."

Everything she could. And that made her suddenly sad. She had been sharing such intimacy with Nate, their bodies, his grief, her frustration with Roberto. Yet it was cursory, elusive . . . Nate was mortal, and she would live forever. He would never believe what she was, and she didn't want to try to convince him. She didn't want to see the look in his eyes, the admiration and attraction for her, disappear.

He would either think she was a complete lunatic or he would actually believe her, and that would be even worse. Mortals had all manner of bizarre reaction to vampires, including a fiery moral obligation to kill them, intense fear, or the desire to share their immortal gift. Gwenna didn't want to see any of those from Nate. She wanted her relationship with him to stay as it was, a quiet, growing friendship and a steamy physical attraction.

"We need to get a court order to trace Slash's e-mail back to his true identity through his e-mail provider if we can't find it any other way. It could take weeks until we know who he really is."

"Maybe I can make plans to meet him again."

"No, it's dangerous as hell."

"I could meet him with you backing me up." Though she wasn't afraid, not of being killed. It would take a cunning and incredibly strong mortal to overpower her enough to take off her head.

"Except that every time you try to meet him he stands you up. I think he's playing you, Gwenna. And I don't like it."

Well, she wasn't too fond of it, either. "It's worth a go."

"No."

"Yes." Damn it, on television the police were always sending in civilians to act as sitting ducks. Why didn't he see the brilliance of this? And she suddenly realized that she was digging in, feeling stubborn and contrary, because Nate was assuming control, giving her orders, like Roberto. Like Ethan.

But he just sighed. "Can we not argue about this, please? I really need to get some sleep . . . why don't we talk about it tomorrow?"

Ouch. So maybe she was leaping to conclusions. He wasn't her brother or her ex, and he'd been having a couple of really brutal days. She didn't need to contribute to his stress.

"Sure. Of course. You get a good night's sleep and I'll see you in the morning."

He sighed. "Yeah. Thanks, Gwenna. Good night."

"Good night, Nate." Gwenna hung up and stared at the phone in her hand, her heart swelling with something that she was fairly certain she shouldn't allow.

Bloody hell, she was falling in love with him.

And Lord knew, she was absolutely old enough to know better, but it didn't seem to matter. She wanted to go to him, comfort him, hold him, make him a sandwich—which was laughable since she hadn't touched a cold cut in a solid nine hundred years—and love him.

Stuffing the phone back into her clutch, she turned to the door of the penthouse.

She needed a drink.

Nate had a whole new respect—and gratitude—for Gwenna Carrick. They'd known each other all of what, three days, and yet she had totally come through for him. She'd spent the entire day by his side on Sunday. The funeral mass, the cemetery internment, the reception afterward—she had been right there, with him. A silent, steady support.

He wasn't sure he could ever explain to her how much that meant to him, how much he appreciated the sacrifice of her time to attend something so uncomfortable and sad, for someone she had never met, or how grateful he was for the buffer she created between himself and his mother. Having Gwenna with him allowed him to stand straight and concentrate on giving his baby sister a final and fitting tribute to the loving and beautiful person she had been.

Now he was exhausted and mentally drained, but he'd made it through and he would be alright. The worst was done and he could regroup, grieve, heal. But first he wanted to figure out how to say thanks to Gwenna.

They were sitting in his truck at the funeral home after the reception since she'd left her car at his place. It always struck him as odd to see Gwenna driving the massive Lexus SUV, but she had told him it was her brother's car. At the moment she was obviously waiting for him to drive or say something, but his tongue felt glued to the roof of his mouth.

Gripping the steering wheel, he tried to figure out how to explain to her what he was feeling. That he was grateful, appreciated her presence, her comfort. And that he dug her. That he was completely, totally falling for her. But he was afraid it was one-sided or that she'd tell him it was just some kind of stress-induced attraction. That under normal circumstances neither one of them would have ever glanced at the other.

Maybe that was true, but hell, did it matter?

He turned to her. She smiled at him and touched his knee.

Instead of saying what he really wanted to, he said, "You didn't eat anything at the reception, did you?"

She frowned a little. "I had a sandwich."

"I didn't see you." It was nearly four in the afternoon and he would swear he hadn't seen her eat one bite. Her poor eating habits might explain why she always looked so pale, so thin. Not that he thought she looked unhealthy, because she didn't. Her skin was smooth and shiny, cheeks pink, body curved in all the right places. But he never saw her eat and it was starting to bother the detective in him. "Let's go back in and get you something. Or we could stop and pick something up on the way back to my place if there wasn't anything you wanted at the lunch."

"Nate, I ate. I did. Trust me, I'm fine."

Her eyes didn't meet his. A bad, bad sign. He wondered if she could have an eating disorder or something. He was no shrink, but it seemed like Gwenna would be the kind to stuff her feelings down deep and deal with them in a way that would make no sense to him. The daughter, the ex-husband, the lack of a career to distract her—she had plenty of reasons to be stressed and out of whack.

"What happened to your daughter?" he asked, with about zip for tact. But he was tired and he was suddenly really friggin' worried about her.

Her eyes went wide. "Isabel? She died." Then she looked out the passenger window and bit her lip.

"I'm sorry, I shouldn't have brought it up . . . I was just wondering how. I know today must have brought up bad memories for you, with a funeral and all."

"It's been a long time since my daughter died," she said, her voice low, sad, her shoulders tense.

Considering she looked about a minute out of high school, Nate couldn't believe it was that long ago, but it was clear she didn't really want to talk about it. "I don't guess you ever recover from a loss like that."

"No." Her head swung around and she looked at him. "You don't."

"Was she sick?" Nate figured he should shut the hell up, but his mouth seemed determined to do its own thing.

"No. She was very healthy actually. It was just an accident. A horrible, unexpected accident. It was at our castle in England . . . she fell on a sword."

"A *sword*? Jesus." Nate covered her hand on his knee with his and gripped her tightly. "Shit, I'm sorry. I shouldn't have brought it up." And he felt guilty as hell that he had. A sword. God, he wanted to throw up at that image.

But she gave him a brief smile. "It's alright, Nate. I'm actually okay, for the most part. I did have what amounted to a breakdown after, and that pain, that grief has changed me permanently, but the thing is, I'm still here, sane. Functional. I've been through the worst that could ever happen, and finally, I feel like I've regained myself as a woman. I can actually look to the future with something like pleasure for the first time in what feels like literally forever."

"Good." He squeezed her hand harder. "I'm glad to hear it." Which wasn't exactly profound or poetic, but hell. It was what he felt.

"So are we going to call it a day and meet back up tonight? Or would you like to go with me to pop by my friend Brittany's house? She and the baby are home from the hospital and I wanted to pay her a visit and see if she needs anything."

Go back to his place alone or hang out with Gwenna? No contest. "Sure. I'd love to go with you. Just tell me where to drive."

Gwenna really needed some kind of pill to cure her of poor decision-making skills. Or maybe it was more that she suffered from appallingly bad luck.

Either way, it was horribly ironic that she would show up at Brittany and Corbin's to see baby Ava at the same time Roberto was comfortably ensconced in their sitting room and having a chat.

Brittany had warned her at the door, with a whispered "Donatelli's here," and a curious glance in Nate's direction.

But when Gwenna had suggested they come back later, Brittany had waved her hand in dismissal of the idea, and Nate had said, "Your ex-husband's here? I would *love* to meet him." He stuck his hand out and shook Brittany's with a firm "I'm Nate Thomas. It's a pleasure to meet you. Congratulations on your baby. Gwenna says she's beautiful."

"Oh, thanks so much. I'm Brittany Atelier. Come on in." She smiled at Nate and gestured for them to come in. "Where have you two been? You're all dressed up."

"A funeral," Nate said quickly.

"Oh, I'm so sorry." Brittany glanced between them. "Well, we're glad you could stop by. Sorry it's not the greatest timing. I didn't know . . ." She jerked her head toward the interior of the house. "You know how he is. Like a freight train rolling through."

"Trust me, I know," Gwenna said wryly, hoping like hell that Brittany would catch on that Nate was mortal. But given that Brittany was the child of Roberto and a mortal mother, she had particularly good instincts when it came to telling mortals from vamps.

Gwenna just didn't want her to say anything she shouldn't in front of Nate. It occurred to her as she anxiously followed Brittany into the house that she really should have called ahead. This was a lousy spontaneous plan. But she had been avoiding letting Nate go home by himself, and the other reasonable option—grabbing a bite to eat—was out of the question given that she wouldn't eat and he already appeared to suspect her of anorexia.

But now she was walking into God only knew what sort of confrontation.

"Maybe we really should stop by another time."

"We're already here," Nate said, looking down at her, his eyes flashing. He was ready for a fight with Roberto, she could see it.

In theory, the idea of two men squabbling over her was sexy. In reality, it was a bit embarrassing.

Especially when Roberto wasted no time in being rude. As the round of introductions were made, he casually looked Nate over and said, "So you're Gwenna's latest boy toy. What are you . . . cop, fireman, construction worker? She's been in a workingman phase recently."

He couldn't have shocked her more if he'd stood up, dropped his drawers, and did a naked tap dance. "Roberto!" What was almost as amazing as his words was that she could still be surprised by anything he did. If he wanted to embarrass her, or destroy any relationship she might have with Nate, he was determined to do it. And Roberto was an intelligent strategist. Instead of playing the irrational jealous ex-husband—which he was—he had simply painted her a tart. The complete and total bastard.

But Nate didn't look particularly shocked or disgusted. He wasn't recoiling from her or demanding she find her own ride back to his house. He just met Roberto's look dead on and said, "I'm a cop, and yes, I'm her latest boy toy. You must be the asshole ex-husband she complains about. The one who has nothing better to do than be pathetic and call his ex-wife seventeen times a day."

Yikes. Roberto's face turned the color of an eggplant. And he had a tick in his left eye that spelled serious trouble. Gwenna reached out for Nate's arm. They needed to leave.

"Well, now that we're all clear on who's who . . ." Brittany smiled cheerfully at each of them, obviously determined to brazen through the awkwardness. "Who wants to hold the baby?"

Corbin, Brittany's husband, looked irritated with all of them, and unwilling to part with his daughter. But he didn't protest when Nate said, "I would love to hold the baby."

Passing Ava over with multiple warnings about her floppy head, soft spot, and umbilical cord stump, Corbin watched Nate suspiciously as he adjusted Ava into a cradle position. But Nate looked like he knew what he was doing, and he was comfortable holding her. He ran his finger over her lip and smiled down at her.

Gwenna was unprepared for the kick in the heart that gave her. Not to mention the unexpected rush of heat in her inner thighs, which was just wrong. She should not be feeling any sort of desire for Nate Thomas with her ex-husband and an innocent baby present. Nate made a funny face at Ava and said, "You're so pretty, yes, you are. You're just gorgeous," in a singsong voice.

And there it was again. Lust. The man solved murders, cared about women and children, wanted to beat up her ex, and was good in the sack. Damn it, she was in trouble.

Brittany was watching Nate in pleased amusement, Corbin was relaxing, and Roberto looked like he'd swallowed a hard-boiled egg. Nate seemed intentionally oblivious to Roberto, and quite enamored of little Ava. Gwenna found herself quite enamored of Nate, and wishing a meteor would hit Roberto. The latter wasn't a new feeling. The other thing, about Nate, was so fresh, so unexpected, so outside of her normal dull existence, she wasn't at all sure how to deal with it.

Because the absolute only thing wrong with Nate, that she could see, was that he was mortal. Which was more than a bit of a problem, it was a catastrophe, and one she needed to remind herself of repeatedly, particularly after sex when she was inclined to think that it wouldn't be a bad idea to spend a decade or two naked with Nate.

Roberto stood up. "A word in private, Gwenna."

That ought to be a good time. "Sure." Normally, she would put him off, but she didn't want any confrontations with her ex and Nate, nor did she want Roberto doing something like wiping Nate's memories out, which he was perfectly capable of doing. And think what a bloody shame it would be if Nate didn't remember their massage table encounter. Besides, if she tried, she could usually hear Roberto's thoughts, and at the moment he was actually more hurt than angry that she was with another man. It had nicked his heart, given the morose thoughts he was having, which almost made her feel indulgent toward him.

She didn't suppose she would have appreciated seeing Roberto with another woman, either. Oh, wait. She had. A dozen times or more while they were still married.

Sympathy disappeared. As did her patience and her politeness. "You know what, actually, I've changed my mind, Roberto. I'm not in the mood to talk to you. And Nate and I have plans and we really need to get going. So unless you have something earth-shattering and vital to either of our existences, you can wait. In fact, why don't you send me an e-mail? That would be best all round for everyone."

She turned and gave Brittany a kiss on the cheek. "I'll stop by at a better time."

"Okay. Good to see you." Brittany reached to take Ava from Nate.

Corbin touched Gwenna's sleeve. "Your brother stopped by last night after the . . . event. Perhaps you should speak to him about ze future."

Gwenna stared at Corbin. What the hell did that mean? "Alright, then. If you think there's something to be discussed."

"Yes, I do." He was giving her all kinds of meaningful looks, so she tuned in to his internal thoughts, knowing he was giving her permission.

Chechikov is mortal now, and in hiding, you know zis, yes? Well, beware of his wife. There is something I do not like about her, and Ethan said she was at the ball last night with Ringo. That makes me suspicious of her.

"Okay." It occurred to Gwenna that maybe Corbin would be a good person to discuss the slayers' loop murders with. He knew all the parties involved, and he would focus in on the important facts, not harass her with safety tips. "Let's talk later." She was forced to say it out loud since Corbin was no longer vampire and couldn't hear her thoughts in return. He had used a vaccine he had created on himself, returning to a mortal state, and he had done the same to Chechikov as punishment for kidnapping Brittany.

Corbin nodded. "I'm looking forward to it."

"I heard that, by the way," Roberto said. "If you let in one, you let in all of us. But in this case, I agree with Atelier. I'm suspicious, too. Though I don't think it's any concern of Gwenna's."

Wonderful. Leave it to Roberto to get the last word in.

"Heard what?" Nate asked. "What are you talking about?"

Roberto raised an eyebrow. "Mind your own fucking business."

"Hey!" Brittany shot him a dirty look, and turned her daughter away from Donatelli. "Watch your mouth in front of the baby."

"She's an infant," Roberto protested.

"Precisely," Brittany snapped at him. "We had a deal. I said you could visit Ava if you were on your best behavior and didn't do anything to corrupt her."

Roberto looked so confused Gwenna felt the urge to laugh. In his world of wheeling, dealing, drugs, and stealing, using off-color language was hardly the worst offense he could make.

"Using a swear word in front of a three-day-old baby is going to corrupt her? I find it hard to believe your mother didn't swear in front of you and you turned out just fine."

"Leave my mother out of this." Brittany's cheeks turned pink.

"Donatelli, watch what you say to my wife." Corbin was off the couch and over to Brittany.

"What? I just said—"

Gwenna interrupted him, enjoying that particular novelty. "Roberto, why don't you head out with Nate and I? I think we're all finished being a dysfunctional family for the moment, and I suspect Brittany could use a rest."

"You go ahead," Roberto said. "I want to speak to my daughter."

Brittany rolled her eyes.

Gwenna sighed. He just couldn't keep quiet. Now she was going to have to lie to Nate yet again. Better to do it in private, though. So she just waved to Brittany and Corbin and took

Nate's hand—sure to inspire murderous thoughts in Roberto's mind—and went out the front door.

"Daughter? Who the hell is his daughter?" Nate glanced back at the house as he pulled his keys out of his pocket.

Gwenna jumped in the passenger side as soon as he clicked the door unlocked. She decided to go with the truth, as close there to it as she could. "Brittany's his daughter. Ava is his granddaughter."

"What? How is *that* possible? He can't be any more than forty. Which makes him too young to be Brittany's father, and too old to be your ex-husband."

There was possibly truth to that. Roberto was fourteen years older than her, and he hadn't aged well. He looked a decade older than his mortal age at death. He had been the adult when she had met him, in his thirties, and he had taken advantage of her naïvety. No question about it.

"He's a bit older than forty." A lot older. "And he had a misguided youth. Brittany's mother was an exotic dancer he had no business having an affair with at his age." Let Nate interpret that however he chose. "But he did, and there you have it. Brittany is the result. It's only been a few months since DNA testing proved his paternity. Neither of them knew he was her father."

"Wow. That's a little awkward, huh?"

"Very awkward. But Brittany is a generous person and she's willing to give him a chance to be in her life. Hopefully for both their sakes, he won't screw it up." She clicked her seat belt. "I'm sorry about that. I had no idea he would be there."

"Not your fault. And hell, he doesn't bother me. Just another prick who thinks he's right—I deal with them every day." Nate put his hands on the steering wheel, the car already running. "So where are we going now?"

Gwenna ran her hand through her hair, flipping it back over her shoulder. She was anxious, restless, irritated, and not sure why. Maybe it was the obvious—that she needed to let go of Nate. It was very selfish on her part to drag him into vampire politics and the personal squabblings of their inner circle. She felt guilty that she was lying to him repeatedly, giving him only bits and pieces of information. Granted, it wasn't like it was possible to be totally honest with him, but it was still troublesome.

A small part of her also realized that Nate was still a man. And she was supposed to be entering a new, totally independent phase of her life, and how much could she really do that if she was involved with a man like Nate, who was confident and protective, saw the world entirely in black and white, and was maybe even just a bit controlling?

Those things were all true, and Gwenna knew that she couldn't continue to see Nate. It wasn't practical. Smart. Or good for her mental health.

Yet they still had now. Today. She wanted that. Wanted him.

"Let's go to the casino," she said. "I feel like gambling."

Nate gave her a funny look. "You don't have plans to meet Slash, do you? You know how I feel about that."

That had never occurred to her. She had just been envisioning metaphorically tossing her inhibitions down the craps table along with the dice. "No. If I did, I would tell you." Probably. "Though I still think it's a good idea. Otherwise, we might have to wait weeks while you try to figure out who he is. I've been searching for any sort of link to his real identity, and it just isn't there. He's totally covered his tracks."

"I appreciate you wanting to help, but let me and the department handle this, Gwenna."

That attitude struck her as patronizing, even as she realized that Nate had no way of knowing she was a vampire, and not in the danger a regular mortal woman would be. But she just didn't understand his unwillingness to accept help. "But what if someone else is killed in the meantime?"

He didn't have an answer for that obviously. Nate made a sound of exasperation. "What do you want me to do? Send you out there to get killed? I don't think so." He reached out and touched her cheek, softly sliding his finger across her skin. "Is it crazy to say that I care about you? That I want to keep seeing you."

Gwenna closed her eyes for a brief second to gather her emotions. She wasn't prepared for Nate's lips to brush over hers while she did.

"I really like you," he said in a low voice that did all manner of shivery things to her insides.

She opened her eyes in time to see his expression, dark and sensual and entrancing, as he bent over her, kissing both corners of her mouth.

"I want to be with you."

Now was the time to tell him they had no future, that it was fun while it lasted, but the reality was such that they could never be together. It was the absolute perfect opportunity to settle the issue, to put the brakes on any sort of relationship. Easy enough. She just had to say it.

"I want to be with you, too." That wasn't saying it. Damn it. Why the hell had the truth come out of her mouth? Here she was lying right, left, and sideways, and when she actually needed to lie, she blurted out the bloody truth?

And now Nate's tongue was in her mouth, so there was no way to correct or retract her statement. She was too busy snogging.

He broke away, breathing hard, hand buried in her hair. "The casino to gamble or straight up to your place so I can fuck you?"

Oh, my. Gwenna wished a gearshift wasn't between them and that they weren't still sitting in Brittany and Corbin's suburban driveway. Why wait, really? But there was something to be said for anticipation. "How about we get drunk, lose a pile of money, then go up to my place so you can fuck me?"

Gwenna was so proud of herself. She'd said the *f* word again, and this time in a sexual context. It felt sassy and raunchy, and she was rather fond of it.

Nate clearly was, too. His eyes went dark and he groaned, glancing down at her chest, his finger wandering between her thighs. "Jesus, you're killing me."

Gwenna was spreading her legs a little so he could slip under her skirt, when a knock on the window sent her jumping three feet in the air.

"Christ." Nate pulled back and made a sour face at whoever was behind her shoulder. "What the hell does he want?"

Oh, no. Gwenna turned and saw Roberto a mere twelve inches away from her on the other side of the window. Not good.

He looked like he could eat glass and like it.

And somehow she couldn't force herself to speak.

But Roberto wasn't at a loss for words. "Can you move your slutty little make-out session elsewhere? My car is in front of you in the driveway and you're blocking me."

"Oh. Sorry." Her cheeks were burning. She had no reason to be embarrassed or ashamed, but she felt very exposed.

Nate didn't bother to say anything. He just put the truck into reverse and pulled back, leaving Roberto standing in the driveway glaring at them.

"What does your ex-husband do for a living?"

"Real estate development is what he officially calls it. You would call it the Mafia, I imagine."

Nate stomped on the brake harder than was necessary at a stop sign. "Your ex is *mob*?"

"Of course he is." Gwenna was irritated that yet again, in the middle of a moment she was quite enjoying, Roberto had inserted himself. And now they were still talking about him. "Didn't I tell you that?"

"No, I don't think you mentioned that little fact."

"Does it matter?"

"Maybe. I don't know. And you married him? How old were you?"

"I was eighteen when I met him. He was very charming." Lots of sweet words and grandiose promises. And to be fair, he'd kept most of those promises. He just could never separate right from wrong with any sort of finality. Roberto had very wide moral boundaries.

"He looks like a snake oil salesman."

"Yes, well, I was an idiot. What can I say?"

"I didn't say you were an idiot. You were young, he was charming. We all make mistakes."

"Can we not talk about him anymore, please? I am so utterly sick of everything I do being affected by Roberto. He has no business being here in this truck between us right now." She wasn't sure why she was so thoroughly hot under the collar, but she was. Why couldn't she even have an affair unencumbered? Everyone else did. Every mortal and vampire on the entire goddamn planet was entitled to a little fun, a frivolous sexual fling just because it felt good. Not her. She had to have her ex-husband sitting on her lap while she tried to get naughty.

Nate glanced over at her. "You're right. Sorry." He gave a laugh. "Do you know when I first met you I thought you were a ditzy blonde?"

Gwenna felt her eyebrow shoot straight up to her hairline. What exactly about that statement was causing him amusement? "Is that to say you no longer think I'm a ditzy blonde? Thank you, I think." She didn't feel warm and fuzzy at the backhanded compliment.

"But now I think you're one of the most amazing, intelligent, compassionate, beautiful women I've ever met."

Much better.

"And I feel like you walked into my life at the right time, for a reason."

He was facing the road, so she couldn't see his eyes, but his voice was firm, confident. "And I'm not such a pussy that your obnoxious ex-husband with mob connections is going to scare me away."

"No?"

"No. So we're going to see where this thing between us goes."

Well, since he had decided . . . It would be rude to tell him no. But there was that niggling little part of her that kept insisting there had to be a way to tell Nate the truth. That maybe he was open-minded enough to accept her vampirism. Because she really and truly wanted to see where a relationship between them could go as well.

"That sounds like a plan, Nate."

She had one, too. When they got to the Ava, she was going to take him upstairs and show him that she was a girl with bite. Literally.

Thirteen

Ringo stared at Sasha in disbelief. "What do you mean, no?" She couldn't just rub all over him and get him hard and then bail on him. It did not work like that.

"Nyet." She shook her head, zipping the pants he'd just undone back up. Yet at the same time she leaned forward and kissed him again vigorously, her breasts pressing against his chest.

No, no, no. That wasn't going to work. "Hey, back off, Bond Girl. You can't be doing that. We either have sex, or you've got to stay the hell off of me."

She looked at him blankly, just shrugging her shoulders, fingers playing with the back of his neck as she grinded her body against his. What was the Russian word for *dick tease*? Jesus. Sasha was gorgeous, tall and thin and exotic, with piercing eyes and legs meant to wrap around a man. Except there was no wrapping going on and he was losing patience. The chick wanted to make out and leave it at that, and he wasn't in fucking high school. That pet-and-cuddle shit didn't cut it for him. He wanted something real. Something to take the edge off his frustrations and anger, and to help him forget that he missed his dipshit of a wife.

Kelsey would never tease. She took it as hard as she gave it, and he respected that.

"Look, I know you don't speak English, but I'm telling you that this isn't going to work. The clothes have got to come off." Ringo went for the zipper on her jeans again.

She slapped his hand. Hard.

"Oww, Christ!"

Lifting her hand, she pointed to the big-ass rock of a diamond on her ring finger. "*Nyet.* Gregor."

So she suddenly had a conscience about the fact that she was married? Ringo stared at her in disbelief. They were kissing and pawing each other in Gregor's freaking hotel suite at the Bellagio, and that was okay, but she drew the line at penetration? That was the good part. Man, he didn't understand women.

Of course, he was only with her because she was slipping him a little cash to get her into vampire-restricted events, like that Inaugural Ball the night before. He wasn't sure why she had wanted to go—she had just looked around and left without a protest when security had ousted them since he wasn't exactly welcome and neither was she since she was married to Chechikov, Carrick and Donatelli's political enemy. But he'd been willing to do it for the money, because he owed Donatelli for stealing his heroin and prospects for employment weren't looking too good. Nobody was in the market for an assassin at the moment.

Ringo figured it hadn't hurt to be seen with Sasha, either, since she was a very attractive woman, and he wanted to make his wife jealous. He missed Kelsey and was pissed at her for abandoning him. She had always stood by him before, and the fact that she'd just walked out, for such a lame reason, had hurt. Down deep, where it sliced and burned.

"Who gives a shit?" Ringo slid the ring off her finger and plunked it down on the coffee table. "There. You're not married."

He expected her to get ticked, and that was fine with him, because he was about sick of this broad, but she just lifted her eyebrow and gave him a smirk. She said something in Russian and reached into her pocket. That better friggin' be a condom she was pulling out, or he was walking.

Even better. It was a bag of heroin in powder form. Ringo was a solid twenty-four hours out from his last hit, and he was feeling it. It made him anxious and impatient and irritable. The sight of the bag in her hand made his leg twitch, his body burn, his mouth dry and thick.

He reached for it. She turned and dumped the powder into a glass sitting on the coffee table. A used glass, blood dried on the rim and pooling in a sticky circle on the bottom. Ringo moved forward to take it from her, not worried about cleanliness or clumping. He would just add a fresh shot of blood before he drank it. Hell, maybe he'd add hers. She was mortal, after all.

Giving him a smile, she darted away from him, went to the wet bar behind the sofa, and reached into the little fridge. She added a splash of blood to the glass and swirled it around. That was more like it. Nice, chilled drug blood and a hot chick waiting on him. That's how he wanted it. Then as he was reaching for the glass, she suddenly and inexplicably dumped the whole thing down the sink with a flick of her wrist.

Ringo watched her in disbelief, before knocking her aside and swiping his hand across the disappearing fluid, mopping up what was still clinging there. He licked his blood-smeared skin, intense painful disappointment coursing through him, pitting his stomach, and tensing all his muscles. There was hardly any left, but he sucked every last speck off his hand, going back with his finger in the sink basin over and over again until there was nothing left.

Then he lifted his head and glared at her. "Why the fuck did you do that?"

It took him a second to realize that she had just shoved a knife into his heart.

The pain exploded, mingling with the beginning high of the heroin, and he stared at her in shock, unable to react.

"Because I want you awake when I kill you," she whispered, hand still firmly on the knife handle.

No way. The conniving little bitch spoke English.

Ringo fell onto his knees.

"Let's just go straight upstairs," Gwenna said as they parked in the garage at the Ava. She felt anxious to get Nate alone, like it was really important that she tell him the truth now.

He glanced over and grinned at her. "I thought you wanted to get me drunk before you take advantage of me."

"I've suddenly got nervous that you might pass out on me before we can get to the good part."

Laughing, he hopped out of the truck and came around and opened her door. "Whatever you want. I'm game."

Damn it, he was so adorable. Gwenna leaned forward and kissed him. "Thank you for being so accommodating."

"You have no idea how accommodating I can be."

That sounded promising.

Gwenna slid a leg over to climb out of the truck and smiled, taking the hand Nate offered. He was smiling, too, still wearing his suit from the funeral, and looking a bit rumpled in it. He wasn't really a suit kind of guy. He was jeans and boots, sweatshirts and T-shirts. She was about to respond, to toss off some witty reference to his sexual prowess, when she smelled the scent of vampire in the air.

Her face must have revealed her curiosity, because he said, "What?"

Then they both heard the popping sound. Nate reacted before she did, shoving at her, pushing her back in the car, his hand on her shoulder gripping her jacket as he tried to haul himself back into the car.

"Get down," he rasped, hands trying to push her head against his stomach and out of range from the shooter, as he stopped trying to get into the car and stood straight up.

He was trying to shield her, but she couldn't help him that way, and she knew without a doubt a bullet wasn't going to hurt her, so she fought him to stay upright.

But it was too late. There was another popping sound and Gwenna watched in horror as Nate's expression froze, as he started to tip forward, blood spreading across the pristine white front of his dress shirt. "Nate!"

His eyes were rolling back into his head, and he swayed on his feet. Gwenna grabbed the lapels of his jacket and dragged him into the truck, going for speed instead of caution. He was on his side, legs crushed awkwardly, but she just leaned over him and yanked the door shut with trembling fingers.

It was then she saw who had shot Nate. It was Smith, Roberto's bodyguard. He was standing in the middle of the row they had parked in, a gun in his hand and a smug smile of satisfaction on his fat lips.

Oh, God. Gwenna thought she was going to throw up as she realized that Roberto had ordered him to do this. To kill Nate, because of his involvement with her. For a second, the world actually tilted as she went dizzy with shock. Swallowing hard, she fought to keep the bile down, and shimmied into the driver's seat. The hospital was just up the road. They would save Nate. Mortals survived gunshot wounds all the time. Modern medicine was astonishing. She would not let him die because of her.

But when she slowed down to let the gate open so she could exit the parking garage, she glanced at Nate. And realized that no one was going to save him. It was too late. He was already dead, eyes wide open and vacant.

"No!" Tears blurred her eyes, and she slammed on the gas, hurtling out into the street, not even sure where she was going, the jerk of the vehicle jarring and intense. Mind numb, she sideswiped a parked car, before having the wherewithal to pull over and park on the side of the road, shaking and crying. "Oh, shit, oh, shit, this isn't fair." She reached for Nate. He slumped against her, slack and completely unresponsive. "Damn it." With trembling fingers, she checked for a pulse in his neck, knowing she wasn't going to find it.

The look of death was unmistakable, and Nate had it. A quick pull back of his jacket showed one of the bullets had gone right through the heart. Gwenna held him in her arms and fought the total overwhelming and paralyzing feeling of panic. She didn't know what to do. She had absolutely no idea what to do. But there was nothing *to* do. He was dead. Nate was dead because of her.

He was dead, and she would live forever, and Roberto still had his iron fist of control wrapped firmly around her . . .

Gwenna sat up straight. Unless she used her blood. Gave it to Nate. Turned him to vampire.

She had never done that, never used the power of her blood, never needed to, and had never wanted the responsibility. The one person she would have turned was her daughter, and Isabel had rejected the gift, had ensured her mother or uncle could never turn her by committing suicide. Isabel had pinned herself with a sword to the boards so she wouldn't inadvertently jerk about, then had decapitated herself.

That her daughter had wanted to die that badly had nearly destroyed Gwenna.

Knowing she was responsible for Nate's death very well could destroy her.

Gwenna shifted back over behind the wheel, letting Nate's head fall into her lap. Smoothing his hair back, she shifted gears, hit the gas, and pulled out onto the street. There was no way she was going to just let Nate go. His house was only a few minutes away and she would have privacy to drain him and then feed him her blood.

If Roberto thought she was going to crumple into a puddle and let Nate die, he had another thing to learn about Gwenna Carrick. She may be quiet and unassuming, but she was also stubborn and logical.

And logic was telling her the vast majority of people would choose life as a vampire over death.

So that's what she was going to give Nate.

"He's dead. Are you sure?" Donatelli stared hard at Smith. His men weren't exactly Mensa material and it was vital to verify important little details with them.

"I guess so. I mean, I shot him through the heart." Smith's look of satisfaction and pride turned to puzzlement. Worry. "He should be dead."

"Didn't you check his pulse?" That's all he needed was the damn cop only wounded. Gwenna would get off on nursing him back to health, which would totally defeat the purpose of shooting the bastard in the first place. He wanted Nate Thomas out of Gwenna's life. Permanently.

"No, I couldn't check his pulse. She pulled him into the car and drove away. But he really did look dead."

Roberto stopped pacing and closed his eyes as the whole room went red with his rage. "Excuse me? *Who* drove him away?"

"Ms. Carrick." Smith bit his lip, like he couldn't quite figure out why that might be a bad thing.

"You are a complete moron." Donatelli struggled to breathe. "You were supposed to shoot Thomas when he was by himself, not with Gwenna."

"Why?"

"Because . . ." He clenched his fists over and over, mind trying to devise a punishment heinous enough for Smith and his stupidity. "Because Gwenna likes the man, you fool. And she's a sucker for a sad story. If she thinks he is dying, she'll turn him into a vampire. Then I'll have the guy drooling over her for who the hell knows how long instead of just a year or two! God!" He picked up what was closest to his hand—a table lamp—and hurled it across the room.

It exploded against the wall with a horrific crash and dropped to the floor in a hundred pieces of ceramic and glass.

"Sorry," Smith said. "I didn't even think of that."

Well, obviously.

Though Gwenna didn't really give a damn what the neighbors might think, she didn't want to deal with any suspicious inquiries, so she kicked open the fence gate, breaking the lock, and dragged Nate into the backyard. Punching her hand through the glass of the slider, she undid the lock and opened the door. Nate was heavy, even for her, and she barely made it to the sofa in his den before she lost her grip on his arms.

Her balance compromised by gravity as he dropped down onto the sofa, she stumbled and fell on top of him, breathing hard, her stomach churning, eyes burning. It had been at least five minutes since his heart had stopped beating and she couldn't wait another minute. Peeling down his T-shirt to give her clearance to his neck, Gwenna closed her eyes and punctured his flesh with her fangs.

This was the first time she had drunk his blood, other than that one quick taste during sex, and she felt the hot swell of regret. It shouldn't have been like this. She should have told him the truth and let him decide whether to stay or walk away. She shouldn't have waited.

It took several minutes to drain him completely and Gwenna was nauseous and panicking by the time she was finished. She almost never bit mortals anymore, not since blood bags, but when she had, there was always a flow of thoughts and emotions, human life, along with their blood when she fed.

With Nate there was nothing. It was absolute silence and that terrified her.

"We're going to fix this, Nate, I promise." Gwenna had no real idea what she was doing, but she didn't see any other way to go about it, so she sliced open her wrist with her teeth and dripped the blood from the wound into Nate's open mouth. The hot liquid sort of pooled on the top of his teeth and tongue and dribbled out the corners of his mouth and down his neck.

"Shit." Gwenna pushed up on his chin and forced what would be a swallowing action if he were still alive. Maybe it was too late. Maybe a mortal had to be alive still, if only by a thread, to make the change. Without functioning organs, maybe this wouldn't work.

Yet when she opened his jaw again, she saw the blood seemed to have dissipated, so she squeezed her wrist hard and pumped more into his mouth, filling it to his teeth. Then she shoved his mouth together, held it there for a moment, opened, and started the process all over again.

After the fourth time of filling his mouth with blood and forcing it down his throat, he bit her. Weakly, but he caught the tip of her finger with his teeth when she was prying his lips open.

Gwenna jumped in shock, than gave a sigh of relief. "Oh, Nate, God, please be okay." She forced her wrist over his mouth again, and this time he clamped on and sucked of his own volition. Sliding alongside of him to get a more comfortable position, Gwenna held her wrist up to him, but let her head drop into the crook of his arm. She needed a minute to regroup, to think, to figure out how to explain this to him, and to let go of the fear and panic that had engulfed her. She took a few shuddering breaths and relaxed her body, taking comfort in the hard pull of Nate's mouth on her wrist. He was getting stronger, she could feel it, taking more of her blood with each subsequent suck and swallow.

It was working. His body was starting to twitch and move next to her, little jerks and spasms. She was starting to feel weak from the loss of her blood, so she detached herself, figuring she could feed him from a bag if he still needed more. Yet she couldn't bring herself to move away from him. Hand on his chest, she felt the reassuring rise and fall of his breathing and let the tears run down her cheeks.

Four days wasn't a long time to know a man. Not when superimposed over the length of her life. But at the same token, those nine centuries of living had taught her to measure a person's integrity quickly, and she knew that Nate was a solid human being. His caring and concern for his sister were evidence of the quality man he was.

Her entire life, she had been refusing to be honest with herself about Roberto. Despite his positive attributes, he was, in essence, rotten to the core. She had never wanted to admit that, had told herself that everyone was complex and multilayered and no one was perfect. She had still cared about Roberto because she had loved him once fully and completely and they had shared a life, a marriage, no matter how rocky those years had been. And she glossed over Roberto's flaws because of her own guilt. They had created a daughter, the most obvious and enduring connection between a man and woman, and she had never told him. It didn't seem right to cast stones at him for his behavior when she wasn't exactly beyond reproach.

Yet the time had come to tell Roberto the truth about Isabel. And to admit to herself that a man who would order Nate shot, order Kelsey drained of blood, and earn his money via illicit drug dealings was not worth even her sentimental holding on to the past.

Because she had done just that for so long, though, Nate Thomas had taken a bullet and died. It made her feel sick, and she wouldn't blame him if he despised her after he woke up and found himself a vampire. She would be profoundly disappointed, and yes, heartbroken, because she truly cared about Nate, but she would understand his feelings.

"Gwenna?"

She sat straight up and looked at Nate. His eyes weren't open yet she had definitely heard him, shaky and steady, but sounding very much alive. "Yes, it's okay, you're fine."

"I feel like shit," he said, dragging in a ragged breath. His eyes opened briefly before fluttering shut again. "I dreamed I got shot."

"Just go back to sleep, Nate. You'll feel better after you've had a few more hours of sleep, I promise."

From the looks of it, he already was. Gwenna touched his clammy and sweaty forehead. He was burning up. Undoing his shirt, she ran her finger over the puckered exit hole from the bullet. Right through the heart. It occurred to her if the bullet had gone in his back, and exited out his chest, it must have lodged somewhere in his truck. It hadn't hit her, she was sure of it.

Standing up, she bent over and stripped him of his jacket and dress shirt. He slept straight through it. Balling the clothes up, she tossed them in his laundry room on top of the washing machine, and pulled a thin sheet out of his linen closet. She had no idea how long he would sleep, but she was guessing for a few hours. As she laid the sheet over him on the sofa, she glanced at the clock on his microwave in the kitchen. It was only five o'clock. She guessed he'd sleep until midnight or later. Then he would need to feed again. She would have to dash back to her place for some blood bags for the both of them, but she was concerned about leaving him just yet.

Wandering around his living room, she took in the vintage rock posters framed and hanging, the midcentury modern furniture and streamlined decor. It suited him and the low-ceiling ranch house. Everything was straightforward and uncomplicated, not the least bit fussy. A glance in his kitchen proved that he wasn't much of a cook, though he did appear to be addicted to coffee. He had three different coffeepots, a French press, a grinder, and six pounds of beans in various roasts and varieties.

He was tidy. Clean. She had been in his house before and had got the same quick impression, but moving around, really looking at everything, it was obvious to her that Nate liked order in his life. She popped her head into his bedroom and saw that he had made the bed, the rust-colored duvet pulled crisply, white and beige pillows stacked in front of the dark wood headboard. The closet was open and two ties were discarded on a chair next to the dresser. She could picture him getting ready that morning, methodical, determined, even as he was torn apart with grief for his sister.

The second bedroom shocked her. She hadn't understood that Kyra had lived with him. Yet there was the evidence in front of her in the form of a hospital bed, personal effects like books and magazines, a bulletin board with a collage of photos. Women's clothes hanging in the half-open closet.

Gwenna felt her heart swell as she moved into the room, running her hand over the glossy issue of *Cosmopolitan*, pristine and unread on the nightstand. Studied the pictures of a pretty young woman with the same caramel-colored hair as Nate and chocolate brown eyes, posing for pictures with her girlfriends, tanned and healthy, and vital. Pictures of her with Nate, laughing and making faces in front of the Hoover Dam. Later pictures, obviously, in front of a Christmas tree, where her hair was falling out and her eyes had dark circles under them, her cheeks sinking in. But her smile still firmly in place, her eyes knowing and at peace with her fate.

Nate stood next to her, his arm protectively around Kyra as she leaned against him. He was holding her up, his strength enough for both of them, and Gwenna knew right then, beyond a shadow of a doubt, that she had fallen in love with Nate Thomas. He wasn't a man who would ever doubt himself. He wasn't a man who would crumple and not be able to walk forward. He knew who he was, held firm to his convictions, his truths, his love. There was a strength in him, one that she appreciated and envied, and she was in love with him.

Now she could only hope that when he woke up and she told him the truth, in its unfathomable entirety, he wouldn't turn that decisiveness against her and walk out of her life.

Fourteen

"Where's my husband?" Sasha asked.

Ringo took a step back, hand holding on to the knife she'd driven into his chest. It wouldn't kill him, but it hurt like a mother and he wanted it out. And then he was going to stab the crazy bitch in front of him with it.

"I don't know where your husband is and it's not my problem if you've lost him." The knife handle was slick with his blood and he couldn't get a good grip on it to tug it out.

This was so typical of women. Constantly playing head games. And if the dumb broad thought he was going to die from a knife to the heart, she was about to get a little reality check. He didn't appreciate the blood loss, but he could take her down in about half a second, given she was mortal and he was a vampire.

"He has been missing since yesterday and you know where he is. You are on the loop, yes?" she asked.

Man, it was crazy how excellent her English was given that for months she'd been claiming not to understand a word of it. Ringo shook his head, getting a little annoyed that he couldn't get the knife out. "I don't know what you're talking about."

"I promise, we can work an arrangement, you and I. But you have to tell me where he is. And help me get to Carrick's sister."

"Carrick's sister?" What the fuck was she talking about? "What does Gwenna have to do with anything? I'm sorry, you've totally lost me and I've decided I don't give a shit about any of this." He was quitting. A little cash and a piece of ass were not worth this aggravation. He wasn't feeling all that great anyway. He wanted to get back to his apartment and drink some blood, take the last of the heroin he had. That would even him out, because he was really starting to feel like crap. His chest pain was agonizing, his stomach was revolting, and the room was spinning a little.

Ringo shoved past her, heading for the front door.

She ran and threw herself in front of it, blocking his exit, her chest heaving, expression crazed. "No! You cannot leave."

"Who's going to stop me?" She was married to a vampire. She had to know he could snap her like a pencil. Though now the room was really dancing in front of his eyes, spotted and dark. Ringo shook his head hard to clear it.

"You're dying, you know," she said.

"I don't think so." But he felt something like panic, and he renewed his efforts to pry the hot, wet knife handle out.

"Yes, you are." Her face wavered in front of him, but he could see her conviction, her revulsion. "That knife has a wooden tip to its blade. You cannot retract it yourself. It requires someone else to pull wood out of a vampire, and I am not going to do it."

Well, that threw a fucking monkey wrench in his day.

There was a knock on the door right behind Sasha's back, and Ringo was instantly aware that it was his wife standing there. He could smell her vanilla lotion scent and feel her anxiety. Sasha didn't open the door, but charged at him full force, knocking him to the ground, her hand shoving and pushing at the knife, driving it deeper.

Ringo's chest exploded in pain and he let out a yell, trying to toss Sasha off, but discovering that his arms didn't seem to work anymore. He was pinned, everything dark and hazy, his body wracked with pain, his brain scattering around, trying to find a solution, but not coming up with any sort of plan.

Then the door crashed open and he heard Kelsey's voice. "Get your slutty Russian hands off my man."

Sasha went backward, completely disappearing, and Kelsey's head bent over him.

"Hey, babe," he said, trying to smile, relief coursing through him. "I am really friggin' glad to see you."

With one swift motion she yanked the knife out of his chest and pressed the open wound with the material of his T-shirt. She bit her lip, tears in her eyes. "Damn it, Ringo, why did you do this?"

Like he stabbed himself? Having the knife gone gave him instant relief from the excruciating pain, though he still felt numb and disoriented. He swallowed hard, reaching out to flick his finger on her bottom lip. "Shit, Kels, I didn't do this on purpose. I had no idea the bitch was crazy."

She sighed and caressed his cheek. He liked her soft touch on his skin. "I miss you," he told her. "Come home."

"We have serious issues we need to work out," she said sternly, right before she kissed him.

"What issues? The only issue is that you left me." He was still ticked about that.

But Kelsey pulled back. And when she did, Ringo saw his brother Kyle standing behind her.

Jesus Christ. Ringo lifted his hand, wanting to touch Kyle, whose mouth was moving as if he were speaking, but there was no sound. Kyle's hands were on Kelsey's shoulders.

When Ringo sat up and tentatively swiped at the spot where Kyle's hand was, he felt nothing but air. His brother was gone.

Kelsey didn't seem to notice. She just took his raised hand and squeezed it. "You have to get clean and stay clean."

The heroin felt like the last of Ringo's worries at the moment. He craned his neck to see around her. "Where's Sasha?"

"On the floor. I accidentally knocked her unconscious."

He suspected there was nothing accidental about it. But he was damn glad for his wife's timing. "How did you know I was here?"

"Kyle told me."

Gwenna booted up the computer in the corner of Nate's living room. He was still sleeping soundly, and she could get online and check her e-mail while keeping an eye on him. She wasn't surprised to immediately see an e-mail from Slash.

I didn't see you at the concert. Were you there?

Feeling impatient as hell with Slash, Gwenna replied:

Yes, but I left early. Though how were you going to find me anyway? You don't know what I look like. Are you sure you're really even in Vegas?

Testy, but oh, well. She was over Slash and his vague e-mails. She could really care less if he was a lunatic killer. Let him show his true colors if he was, damn it. Clicking on to the next e-mail, she saw FoxyKyle had posted to the loop.

That name was just so irritating. Foxy didn't have anything of import to say, just a mention that she would be off-line for a few days. Though when Gwenna thought about it, that could potentially be considered odd. Foxy was always online, for the most part. Usually a day didn't go by without at least one post from her.

Gwenna was suddenly determined to figure out who FoxyKyle was. She started by googling Foxy's user name and working backward through the pages. Then just the e-mail address. A half an hour and dozens of pages later, Gwenna found a student roster for UNLV from 2005 with Foxy's e-mail address listed next to the student Kyle Martin. So she researched Kyle Martin and found that he had been shot and killed by a burglar in California while visiting his brother. The brother's name was Ringo Columbia.

Bloody hell. Gwenna pushed her chair back and stood up, still reading the screen. The brother was mentioned as being a former Marine. But that was it. Nothing to indicate it was anything other than a terrible accident, despite the fact that the burglar was never apprehended. And why was she just now remembering that Kelsey occasionally called Ringo Kyle? It was some kind of pet name she had for him, which was in fact his dead brother's name. That struck Gwenna as rather appalling now that she understood the significance.

Leaning on the desk, she closed her eyes and took a deep breath. If Kyle was dead, it only stood to reason that the person with access to his e-mail account would be his brother. Andrew and Johnny had been drained of their blood and stuffed in out-of-the-way corners. Ringo Columbia was a vampire and an assassin. He knew how to kill and did it easily, without remorse.

But would he do it alone?

Or on someone's orders?

Gwenna turned the computer off without properly shutting it down. She just flicked the switch, checked on Nate to make sure he was resting comfortably, and headed out the back door, stepping carefully over the broken glass.

There were a few people she needed to talk to and it couldn't wait.

Nate woke up when his cell phone rang. He rolled on his side, determined to ignore it. He felt sluggish and hot, mouth dry and muscles stiff, and he wasn't exactly sure why he was on the couch instead of in bed. His house phone starting ringing as he dozed off. Then his cell phone again.

He sat up with a huge effort and decided if that was his mother, he was going to divorce his parents. Though you probably couldn't do that at thirty-three years old.

Looking around for his cell phone, he spotted it on the coffee table, and leaned over with a groan to grab it. Every inch of him hurt like hell. "Yeah?"

"Hey, it's Jim. You need to get down here. We've got ourselves another body."

Nate rubbed his head, hard, in an attempt to jump-start his brain. He still felt foggy and vague. Must be the result of the funeral and lack of sleep. "Shit. You're kidding me. Where?"

Speaking of where, where was Gwenna? Nate looked around his living room. He didn't see any sign of her. Nor did he remember taking her home. The last thing he could actually remember with any certainty was heading to the casino. Then he'd been asleep, dreaming he'd been shot.

Jesus. He must have really lit into the booze at the casino. Not cool.

Now he had a hangover and another dead body.

"Our boy's getting bold. This one was right out in the open, tossed into a lounge chair by the pool at the Ava hotel."

Nate snapped wide awake, fear gripping his gut. "Was the victim male or female?"

"Male. But this dude's older. Forties. And a big guy. It couldn't have been an easy thing catching him off guard, whacking him, and plopping him by the pool."

It wasn't Gwenna. That's all Nate really heard. Taking a deep breath, he stood, his stomach burning. He really felt like shit.

"Give me twenty minutes to get there." He needed to drink about a gallon of coffee first. "And what time is it anyway?"

"Aahh . . . eleven p.m."

"Are you serious?" How could he have had time to get shit-faced at the casino and pass out and still be home by eleven? That was freaking pathetic. "And just so you know, Gwenna Carrick and I were at the Ava around five o'clock today. She lives there. Her brother owns it."

"Now why does that not surprise me?" Jim said wryly. "Your chickie pops up everywhere there's a body, Thomas. Might be a really good idea for you to stay away from her while we're piecing this thing together."

That would be the logical thing to do. Nate scratched his chest. He had a nagging itch right around his pectoral, left side, and for whatever reason he wasn't wearing a shirt. It was really irritating to him that he couldn't remember anything. Especially now that the cop in him was silently considering that maybe he'd been drugged.

But love wasn't logical. And he was pretty damn sure he was in love with Gwenna Carrick. "Yeah, I hear ya." That was nice and noncommittal. Because while he knew he shouldn't see Gwenna, he wasn't at all sure he could go cold turkey and cut her off.

"Another thing. Latest victim still had his wallet in his pocket. If we can believe the ID he was carrying, his name's Gregor Chechikov. Just from doing a little preliminary research in the last thirty minutes, we've already turned up a conviction in Chechikov's history. Seems he had some Russian Mafia connections and got caught in a sweep in New York ten years ago, though he never did any time. He plea-bargained and went home to the Motherland."

"This guy's mob? Fuck." Nate stood up, shook out his sore legs, and walked slowly to the kitchen to start his coffee. "Do me a favor and start a search on a guy named Roberto Donatelli. See what you turn up."

"Sure. Who is he?"

"He's Gwenna Carrick's ex-husband."

"Mr. Carrick, we have a bit of a problem."

Ethan turned away from his computer screen in his office and gave Sam, his head of hotel security, his full attention. "What now?" He already had his casino crawling with cops after a sanitation worker had gone to strain the pool at its 9 p.m. closing and found a dead body sitting in a goddamn lounge chair.

A body that Ethan knew immediately on sight was Gregor Chechikov, though he had played dumb. There was nothing to connect him to Chechikov in the mortal world, and if he admitted to knowing the victim, it would only complicate their investigation. Though it was unlikely they would ever solve the crime.

This was an internal vampire affair. And a huge problem. Someone had known Chechikov was no longer vampire, but returned mortal by Atelier's vampire vaccine. They had known that and killed him. Or maybe they hadn't known why, they had just ascertained he was mortal and took advantage of the fact. Either way, someone had wanted to kill a man who was something of a cult classic in vampire culture.

His death was going to infuriate a large number of vamps. Not a great way to start a new term as president. Not to mention he was mad as hell that, despite recent security increases, someone had managed to plant a body on his property. "When do the police expect to be done by the pool?"

"They'll probably be here all night. And we'll have to keep the pool closed tomorrow."

"Wonderful." He'd already called his secretary in to have her schedule an emergency meeting with his cabinet members to discuss the situation. "So I'm sorry, what's the new problem?"

Sam handed him a DVD. "Why don't you pop that into your computer and take a look. It's the security tape from this afternoon of the parking garage."

Ethan did as suggested and a minute later he was staring at the empty parking garage, a red Toyota cruising down the row of cars. "What am I looking for?"

"May I?" Sam leaned over and moved the cursor to speed the video up. He stopped it. "Watch the Ford Explorer."

Studying the black-and-white images, Ethan watched a man get out of the Explorer, come around to the passenger side, and open the door. Presumably it was either to let a woman out, or to get something from his truck, but they could see clearly into the vehicle and there was nothing there. There was also something familiar about the guy.

"Do I know this guy? I think I've seen him before."

"He's, uh, a friend of Ms. Carrick's."

That's who he was. Gwenna's mortal boyfriend. "So are you assuming he's driving Gwenna home here?" That wasn't all that newsworthy, in Ethan's opinion.

"Yes. But watch."

And Ethan saw Gwenna's friend take a bullet in his back, pitch forward, and get hauled into the truck from invisible hands. "Bloody hell. That's Gwenna driving him away, isn't it? And who shot him?"

"Vampire. He's not on the tape. Though the guy in the booth down there remembers Gwenna leaving, driving erratically. Then right after her was a big guy he described in good detail, because he and the guy had a conversation about female drivers as they watched Gwenna jump the curb."

"Does the guy sound like anyone we know?"

"It sounds a hell of a lot like one of Donatelli's employees to me. Though that's just speculation on my part. I didn't see him."

Ethan stopped the tape. "Damn it. That would be right up Donatelli's alley, wouldn't it? To kill Gwenna's boyfriend." Which wouldn't make Gwenna happy, which pissed Ethan off. Donatelli needed to leave her alone, once and for all.

Sam nodded. "Donatelli's never been right in the head when it came to Ms. Carrick."

"Where do you think Gwenna went?"

"No idea."

Ethan picked up the phone and dialed his wife. "Hey, it's me. Have you talked to Gwenna tonight?"

"No, but I know she was going to a funeral today with Nate Thomas, her hottie mortal boyfriend."

"Is that his name?"

"Yep. Why? Do you need to talk to Gwenna? I'll tell her to call you if I see her."

"Thanks, babe, I'll see you later. I love you."

Ethan hung up, not even waiting for Alexis's return endearment, which would get him in trouble, he was certain, but he was suddenly worried about Gwenna. Terrified she might have done something stupid. He stood up.

"Find Donatelli. I need to talk to him."

"Sure."

"And didn't you tell me the detectives on the scene downstairs were named Connors and Thomas?"

Sam pulled out his Palm and clicked on a few things. "Yeah. Detectives James Connors and Nathaniel Thomas. I met Connors. Big guy. Said his partner was on the way."

Shit. Fuck. Damn. Ethan rubbed his temples. "Well, guess what Gwenna's little mortal friend's name is? You know, the one we just watched on tape bite it by a bullet?"

Sam's eyes went wide. "You can't be serious."

"Oh, I am. Alexis just said his name is Nate Thomas. Which means Gwenna turned him vampire. And we have a fledgling vampire downstairs picking over Chechikov's body."

Gwenna held her breath until Alexis hung up the phone.

"That was Ethan, as I'm sure you guessed. He's looking for you."

"Thanks for not telling him I'm here."

"Yeah, well, you owe me big time. He's going to want to beat me when he figures out I lied to him."

Pacing back and forth in Alexis's apartment, Gwenna realized her feet hurt. She'd been wearing her heels from the funeral since early that morning. Her toes were pinched and she'd been up for twenty-four hours so she could attend Kyra's funeral with Nate. She was anxious, exhausted, strung out, mind racing in seventeen different directions. "I know. And I appreciate you putting yourself on the line for me. But the thing is, I have to keep Ethan out of this. First of all, it would be political suicide. But more important, this is between Roberto and myself. We have unfinished business that I need to take care of."

"I think you're making a mistake." Alexis sat at her dining room table and watched Gwenna, hand propping up her chin. "If this involves the slayers' loop in any way, Ethan needs to know. It will make him look like an ineffectual president. And you know what Donatelli is like. Confronting him alone is not a good idea."

Gwenna had told Alexis everything because she had needed a sounding board, someone to help her sort out the situation. But Alexis clearly wasn't seeing eye to eye with her. "Roberto would never hurt me."

"What if it's Donatelli who gave Ringo the orders to kill those guys?"

"I just don't see to what purpose that would serve Roberto. It's too risky and he's not stupid. He's in the perfect power position as vice president. Why would he jeopardize that?" It wasn't the way Roberto operated. He went for power, always power.

"Yeah, well, I can't even begin to guess what's going through Donatelli's head. But there was a little development in this whole thing tonight. Another body was found, and I can guarantee you this will send these murders straight to the front page of the *Review-Journal*."

A chill went down Gwenna's spine. "Why?"

"Because the body was found right here at the pool at the Ava. And the victim is none other than Gregor Chechikov."

"What?" Gwenna stopped pacing and stared at Alexis. "Gregor? Oh, shit." That did point the finger rather blatantly at Roberto. Why she wanted it not to be him, she couldn't explain. But she had another more pressing thought anyway. "Are the police here?"

"Oh, yeah. All around the back. It's a mob scene, and I expect the media to show up at any given minute. A murder at a casino is news."

"I've got to go." Gwenna kicked off her heels. "Do you have sandals I can borrow?"

"Sure. In the front closet. Take your pick." Alexis narrowed her eyes. "But where are you going? You shouldn't see Donatelli alone. Take someone with you."

"I'm not going to see Roberto." Not yet, anyway. "I have to check on a friend."

"Didn't you just come from Nate's house?"

"Actually, that was earlier." And she had the horrible sinking feeling that he was no longer tucked up under a sheet on the sofa, but was downstairs rummaging through poolside evidence. "I went and saw Brittany and Corbin."

"Why? Did something happen to Ava?"

"No, of course not. I just had to ask Corbin something." Or more accurately, beg him. But it had worked. Corbin had given her one dose of his vampire vaccine.

She had the power to return Nate to his mortality.

But first she had to find him and make sure he wasn't wandering around as a fledgling vampire, utterly clueless as to what she'd made him.

Nate peeled off the latex gloves he'd been wearing and rubbed his forehead. God, his stomach hurt. It burned intensely, like he was hungry. Yet when he'd had some coffee and a bagel on the way over, he'd spent the next twenty minutes puking it all back up in the casino parking lot.

"You okay?" Connors asked him, moving past with a uniformed officer. "I saw you tossing your guts out back there."

"I think I have the stomach flu or something." He hoped. Because he didn't like the alternative—that Gwenna had drugged him. Which probably proved he'd been in police work too long if he could even consider that a possibility. But either way, he was finding it difficult to concentrate.

"Yeah, well, don't breathe on me. I don't want your fucking flu cooties."

"Thanks for the sympathy." Nate gripped the back of a pool chair when a hot wave of dizziness rolled over him. "Shit the bed, this sucks." He closed his eyes and took a deep breath in and out, his stomach churning painfully.

"Give us another thirty minutes and you can head on home. We'll have ourselves a big old sit-down tomorrow with all the medical evidence from our rapidly growing body count. We'll plan a strategy, which will include begging the department for some manpower to assist us. We can't follow up on all three of these by ourselves."

At the moment, just standing felt like a challenge to Nate. And Jim smelled funny to him, sort of sour and sweaty, nauseating. Nate leaned over and threw up again, aiming for the potted plant on the concrete sidewalk.

"Thomas! You're contaminating a crime scene. God, go home." Jim grabbed his arm and pulled him along the pavement. Then jerked him to a halt again.

Nate was stumbling to keep up, concentrating on keeping one foot in front of the other, his eyes on the ground.

"Uh-oh. Here's trouble," Jim muttered. Then louder, "You're not allowed in here. You have to stay behind the tape, miss."

Nate forced his head up. He knew it was Gwenna. He could smell her skin, the strawberry lotion she used on her hands, and he could hear her heart pounding anxiously.

Her heartbeat? Nate shook his head to clear all the sounds, the crazy thoughts. What the fuck was the matter with him? His teeth hurt, right in front. "Gwenna, go back upstairs. I'll call you later."

She reached across the crime-scene tape and ran a cool hand over his forehead. "I'm heading out to run an errand, but I need to talk to you."

Nate pulled away. "Don't touch me, babe, I have the flu. I don't want you to catch it."

"Have a sip of this." Gwenna put a takeout cup with a straw in his hand. "It will make you feel better. Then when you're done here with Gregor, call me so we can chat."

"I don't think I should drink anything. My stomach will just toss it back up." But it did feel cool in his hand, and it smelled sweet. "What is it?"

"It's a British cure-all. Just drink it."

She looked so worried about him that Nate sipped from the cup, sucking hard on the straw. The drink moved over his tongue, immediately soothing his dry mouth. It hit his gut like water on a smoldering fire. "Hey, that's pretty good." He took another sip and realized that he had drained the whole cup in about two seconds.

The burning in his gut abated and his teeth stopped throbbing. "Thanks. That helped."

Taking the empty cup back, Gwenna looked him straight in the eye, leaning over the crime-scene tape, and whispered, "Would it be insane and completely inappropriate to say that I'm falling in love with you?"

Those words were as soothing as her cure-all drink. "No." He squeezed her hand. "It wouldn't be crazy. Because I'm falling in love with you, too."

She kissed him before he could protest she'd catch his germs. "Be safe. I'll see you later."

In his foggy state, Nate realized something as he watched her beautiful figure turn and walk away. She had said she was running an errand. Where the hell was Gwenna going at midnight?

And had she mentioned the victim by name?

Clenching his fists, Nate wiped his sweaty forehead and went to find Jim. They had a big problem.

The woman he was most likely in love with was knee-deep in what were potentially mob murders.

That ought to do wonders for his career.

Fifteen

Roberto's bodyguard, the one who had shot Nate, opened the door for her at Roberto's suite.

Gwenna was so furious she reached up and slapped him straight across the face. She had never hit another human being in her life, but it felt pretty damn satisfying.

"Ow." His head snapped back and he glared at her. "What was that for?"

"For strolling up and shooting my boyfriend in cold blood."

"I was just doing what I was told," Smith said sullenly.

"Well, maybe you should try thinking for yourself once in a while."

Smith looked confused as to how to even respond to that, let alone do it. He just stared at her.

But Gwenna shifted her attention to Roberto, who was entering the room with a buxom blonde wearing tight jeans and a tank top, clinging to his arm. "Are you harassing my help?"

It was a mere shadow of what she felt like doing to Roberto. "I'm just offering Smith my opinion. Who's your little friend, Roberto?"

"Oh." Roberto glanced at the woman like he'd just realized she existed. "This is Katie. Katie, this is my ex-wife, Gwenna."

But the blonde frowned. "My name's not Katie. It's Sarah."

Gwenna rolled her eyes in disgust.

"Are you sure?" Roberto asked, studying Sarah's face. He even glanced at her backside. "I could have sworn you were . . . well, never mind. Sarah or Katie, whatever."

"So you get to do this," Gwenna said, waving her hand at Katie-Sarah. "But you couldn't let me date? Not even after all this time, not after the way I was completely and totally faithful to you. You can screw everything that walks but I'm not entitled to one speck of happiness with another man? You are a selfish, cruel bastard."

"I'm selfish because I want to love you? You know I'd ditch Katie in a second if I thought you'd come back to me. I only want you, and we belong together."

Sarah's mouth dropped open. "What's going on here? Maybe I should leave. You promised me we'd have fun and I'm not having fun."

Did Gwenna care? "There's the door."

With a sniff, Sarah grabbed her purse off the console table and started for the door. But on the way, she intentionally slammed into Gwenna with her shoulder, knocking her off balance.

Gwenna stumbled but recovered and glared at the mortal girl. "Watch it."

"Make me."

Someone obviously had a lot of bar brawling experience. Sarah looked eager to go a round. But little did she know Gwenna was one seriously steamed vampire. She felt capable of outbitching the best of them. "Do not mess with me. I am absolutely not in the mood."

But Sarah couldn't take a hint. She reached out and shoved Gwenna.

You know, there was really only just so much she could tolerate. Before Sarah could even blink, Gwenna twisted her arm behind her back and marched her to the front door. She opened it with her right hand and shoved Sarah out into the hall with her left. Then slammed the door shut.

Roberto was fighting a grin when she turned back to him. "Don't smirk at me!" she snapped. "I am only going to ask you once. What was your purpose in having those boys on the loop killed?"

His smiled disappeared. "What loop? I don't know what you're talking about."

Knowing Roberto was generally too smug to bother hiding his misdeeds, she wondered why he was denying it. Unless he hadn't actually ordered Ringo to kill Andrew, Johnny, and Gregor. Roberto did look legitimately confused.

"The boys from the slayers' loop. And Gregor Chechikov."

"Chechikov is *dead*? Who told you that?"

"Alexis. Gregor's body was found by the pool at the Ava. Are you honestly telling me you didn't know that?"

"No." Roberto's face had got pale and still. "That must be why Carrick's called me three times. I was ignoring his calls because I was, uh, busy."

"Yes, I imagine you were." Gwenna crossed her arms over her chest. "Katie-Sarah looks like a handful."

"Jealous?"

He wished. "Hardly. Now be honest with me, Roberto. Did you have anything to do with Gregor's death?"

"No, damn it. I had no idea the bastard was dead until you just told me."

She couldn't fathom why she would ever believe a word that came from his mouth, but after nine hundred years of knowledge of his character, expressions, and body language, she was certain he was telling the truth. "Did you tell Smith to shoot Nate?"

Roberto rammed his hands in his pants pockets and looked at the floor. "Yes."

At least he didn't look proud of the fact. Though she still felt repelled by his behavior. And so, so sorry that Nate had paid the price for her relationship with Roberto. "Did you introduce Ringo Columbia to drug blood?"

"I offered him a choice. He took the heroin with no encouragement from me."

"Did you have Kelsey shot last year?"

"Not intentionally. She was collateral damage."

Gwenna was disgusted. "You do realize that I disapprove of all those actions."

His chin lifted up. "Yes."

"Which means that inherently we have an entirely different set of beliefs by which we live our lives."

"Possibly."

"And therefore it is impossible for us to coexist in a mutually satisfying and healthy adult relationship."

His arm dropped. "If you would just—"

She cut him off. "Shh. Come now, be honest. You've been doing an excellent job of it so far in this conversation."

"Gwenna." Argumentative tone shifted to discouragement as Roberto's shoulders drooped. "Don't do this. Come home to me. Let me love you."

Taking a deep breath, she shook her head. "You're not going to love me when you hear what I've kept from you."

"Kept from me?" His disdain was back. "What? A boyfriend before this one? That doesn't bother me."

"No." Gwenna ran her hands down the front of her dress and forced herself to maintain eye contact with him. This needed to be said and she would not cower. He was entitled to the truth as much as she was. "Do you remember when we met? The first time?"

"Of course. You were playing the harp when I came into the hall." He smiled. "That day changed my life."

"Mine, too. And after that . . . after we had made love that first time, when you left me . . ."

"I was coming back," he said, his voice soft. "I was always coming back. I had to go to Italy to claim some property. If Ethan had been home, I would have married you before I left, but I wanted to do the proper thing. I wanted your brother's permission. Then I came back and was told you had died. No one told me Ethan had turned you until three centuries later when we met again in Italy."

"There was something else you weren't told. I didn't die of a fever. I died immediately after childbirth." She waited for that to sink in.

His jaw dropped. "Are you saying you were pregnant when I left? That you died giving birth to our child?"

"Yes. I bled out after our daughter was born and Ethan turned me into a vampire."

"I'm sorry. I had no idea. None."

"I know."

"It was a daughter? She was stillborn?"

Roberto was moving to reach for her, but Gwenna evaded his touch. She wasn't done. "Yes, a girl. Isabel. And she was not stillborn. In fact, she lived to the age of twenty-five."

That was a rather priceless look on Roberto's face. "What? Explain yourself, Gwenna."

So Gwenna did. She told Roberto about Isabel. About her life. Her death. What she had sounded like, looked like, acted like.

"I wish we'd had photography in those days. I would give anything to have a picture of her," she said, after she'd covered the basics, and was waiting for Roberto to say something. Yell at her. Condemn her. Make her cry.

His face was stricken. And he did something she could never have expected. His voice wobbled and said, "At least you know what she looked like at all. You took even that from me."

"I didn't know where to find you."

"But you could have told me later."

"Yes, I could have." Gwenna hugged her arms to herself. "So we're both flawed."

"And this is good-bye."

"What?" She looked at him in confusion.

"Good-bye, Gwenna. I need you to leave."

Roberto wasn't looking at her. And she realized that this was it. He had made the decision to stop pursuing her.

Immense relief washed over her. There was a sadness, too, for all they had shared, and all the mistakes they had made. But mostly, she felt empowered with knowing that she had told the truth, stood up to Roberto in essence by not fearing his reaction, and had ultimately won her freedom.

"Good-bye," she said, reaching out and touching his arm.

Then she left the Venetian and went to find Kelsey Columbia.

Gwenna rang Kelsey on her cell phone as she went down to the parking garage to collect the car she'd borrowed from Ethan. She needed to warn Kelsey to stay away from Ringo. If Roberto hadn't ordered hits on the slayer members, then someone did. Or Ringo had acted alone.

But somehow Gwenna thought Ringo didn't have convictions or passions or a plan. He merely acted in the interest of making money, to buy his drugs. Either way, Gwenna wanted to make sure Kelsey didn't renew any contact with him. He was potentially a very dangerous man.

"Hello?" Kelsey answered on the fourth ring.

"Kelsey, it's Gwenna."

"Hey, Gwen, what's up?"

"Listen, are you alone? Or are you with that David Foster guy still?" Alexis had told her Kelsey had gone home with the bass player from The Impalers. Gwenna had a vague memory of a charming smile when he'd seen them leap up onstage, but they hadn't been formally introduced.

"Why would I be with Davey?" Kelsey sounded genuinely puzzled. "I'm at home with Ringo."

"What?" Gwenna dropped the car keys as she tried to unlock the doors. "Why? You left him."

"We're back together."

"But . . . he tried to prostitute you for drugs. You left and you were going to play tambourine for The Impalers." Shit. Ringo was probably sitting in the room right behind Kelsey. How on earth could she warn her the man was a murderer with him listening to every word Kelsey spoke?

"Oh, that wasn't going to pan out. Davey only said yes to get in my pants."

It continued to amaze Gwenna that Kelsey was almost always actually paying attention. She looked and sounded ditzy, but she was usually spot on about people. "Can I meet you somewhere? I need to chat with you."

"Right now?" Kelsey sounded doubtful. "We're kind of making up here, Gwen. I'd like to hang out with Ringo if you don't mind."

"It's really, really, really important. It will only take ten minutes, I promise. Meet me at the fountain in the lobby of the Ava in fifteen minutes, okay?"

"Alright." Kelsey still sounded skeptical.

"I need sexual advice," Gwenna lied, feeling a little desperate. "I don't think I'm making Nate happy."

"Oooohhh. Okay, sweetie, I'll be there. I have a book and a DVD I'll bring for you."

"Brilliant." Gwenna only hoped it wasn't a home recording.

Nate was debating going back to his place and passing out when he recognized a familiar face behind the yellow tape. Wonderful. Just what he needed to complete his day from hell—Gwenna's ex-husband arguing with the officer guarding the area. Yeah, he needed this guy around like a fucking hole in his head.

Still feeling less than one hundred percent, Nate went over and eyed Donatelli. "What do you need, Donatelli?"

The man's eyes widened and he let out a snort. "I should have known. Of course Gwenna wouldn't let it alone. She saved your sorry ass, didn't she?"

"Saved me from what?" Nate waved the officer off.

"Death. Or did the bullet miss?"

"What are you talking about?" Not in the mood to play head games, Nate started to move away, though he did think it was odd that Donatelli would mention getting shot after Nate's strange dream. "You need to stay away from this crime scene or I'll get a lot of enjoyment from throwing you out of this hotel."

"I heard you need an ID on the victim. I believe I can be of assistance."

"Oh, yeah?" Nate eyeballed him. "Who told you that?"

"Ethan Carrick. One of his security men overheard your team mention Gregor Chechikov . . . I have known Gregor for a number of years. I'm sure I could tell you conclusively if the victim is Gregor or not."

Interesting that Ethan Carrick had communicated that information to Donatelli after he had sworn he did not know the victim by sight or by name. It made Nate question the integrity of Gwenna's brother, too, and wonder just how he had earned all his giant piles of money. He had no doubt that Donatelli knew Chechikov. Nate was guessing they both had a lot of mutual acquaintances in the Mafia. What was interesting was that Donatelli would seek him out and confirm the relationship when it wasn't necessary.

"Fine. Come on over and take a quick look." He was curious what kind of reaction Donatelli would have, because he was fairly certain the victim was Gregor Chechikov based on his passport picture tucked into his jacket.

"How did he die, by the way?"

"I'm not at liberty to say."

Donatelli followed him. "Has anyone contacted his wife?"

"No. Any idea who his wife might be? We haven't found a next of kin yet."

"Her name is Sasha Chechikov. She's very young, early twenties. Very beautiful. I'm sure she'll be quite devastated to learn she's a widow." This was clearly sarcasm given the smirk on Donatelli's face.

"Does she live in Vegas?"

"She and Gregor have been here for the last six months, though I don't believe Gregor intended the move to be permanent. It was just a temporary move for business reasons. They've been living at the Bellagio."

"Thanks." Nate led Donatelli to the brawny Russian still lying on a chaise where the killer had left him. It was starting to really infuriate Nate that the deaths were piling up so quickly, and there was no time even to get physical evidence analyzed before the next victim turned up. The killer was arrogant and clearly very driven to commit his crimes.

If Gwenna was right, and his intent was to rile up the faux slayers, then three deaths immediately ought to do it. Which might lead to more murders. Though Nate found it hard to believe a Russian mobster was on a vampire slayers' loop. They hadn't uncovered his name at present, and they had two-thirds of the members identified.

"Here he is." Nate took a deep breath. He still wasn't feeling all that great, and the overwhelming stench of death that wafted up from the victim was making his stomach churn again. While Nate wouldn't say he was used to the odor of death, he'd been exposed to his fair share of it, many victims in far worse shape than the guy in front of him. Yet for some reason tonight it seemed thick and noxious, crawling up his nostrils, tightening his gut, and making his gums itch.

"That's Chechikov." Donatelli raised an eyebrow. "He's looked better, but it's definitely him. Wonder who he pissed off this time."

Clearly Donatelli and Chechikov hadn't been great pals. The guy didn't look broken up in the least. "So you're saying he had a lot of enemies?"

"Oh, yeah. A lot that go back centuries."

"Centuries? Like a family feud?" Nate grabbed the back of a pool chair, struggling to keep from getting sick or going down and kissing the concrete.

"If you need to feed, why don't you go inside and ask Carrick for some blood?"

Nate felt saliva puddle in his mouth and his stomach burned, as he watched Donatelli in confusion. "What?"

They stared at each other, Donatelli's brow furrowed, Nate getting dizzy.

"She didn't tell you, did she?" Donatelli asked.

"Who tell me what?"

"Gwenna. That she turned you into a vampire."

The words took a second to process their way through Nate's foggy brain. "A vampire . . . you're insane."

"No. But I am a vampire. As is Gwenna. And now are you. I ordered you killed, and you took a bullet in the garage at the Ava from one of my men. You died. Gwenna turned you, something I hadn't intended to happen. And now it seems she's lied to you."

Nate just stood there, feeling a full sentence behind Donatelli's convoluted explanation. Vampires were not real. Yet there seemed to be a whole lot of people who thought they were. "You know what, it's time for you to leave." He didn't have time to listen to that crap. Even if Donatelli had somehow managed to describe Nate's dream. That was just a freaky coincidence.

And he needed to get home and to bed before he passed out on the pavement.

"I'm leaving. But before I go, turn around with me and look in the pool. Neither one of us has a reflection."

If he had been himself, Nate would have reached the point where he just grabbed Donatelli by the collar and bodily removed him. But he was sick as a dog and brain dead, so he turned automatically, his skin clammy and everything sharp and focused, a slight buzzing in his ears.

Huh. He didn't have a reflection. That was fucking weird. Especially considering the evidence bag in his hand did. As did the chair behind him.

"This is vampire business," Donatelli said, gesturing to Chechikov. "The police will never solve the crime." He then held the cup he'd been carrying around toward Nate. "Have a drink before you drop, then I suggest you go find Gwenna and ask her why she would turn you and yet leave you without the knowledge to survive."

The cup Donatelli had handed him smelled fantastic. Sweet. Necessary. He shouldn't touch it since it had been handed to him by a crazy man, but he was beyond thirsty and he couldn't control himself. Nate tipped it back and drank it all in one swallow. It was the same taste and consistency of what Gwenna had given him, and it had the same effect. He felt immediately better.

"What is this?" Prying the lid off, he glanced inside. It was red, staining the sides, and it smelled like . . .

"Blood."

It was. And Nate felt panic rise in his throat.

He needed to find Gwenna.

Sixteen

Gwenna had ringing ears and a DVD on sexual positions in her possession when she went back to the casino, hoping Nate hadn't left yet. The only thing she had concluded from her meeting with Kelsey was that Ringo wasn't lacking for sexual satisfaction or creativity, both of which she could have done without knowing. For eternity, really. Kelsey was in no way afraid of her husband, despite Gwenna's attempts at hinting he was a loaded cannon. Nor did she seem to have any interest in leaving him. The only thing Gwenna could feel the least bit reassured about was that Ringo killed for money, not malice. If he was responsible for murdering the men on the slayers' loop, there was someone who had paid him to do it. That's who Gwenna wanted to uncover.

She was walking through the lobby, pulling her phone out so she could call Nate, when someone touched her arm.

"Excuse me."

"Yes?" Turning, she recognized the guy behind her. It was one of The Impalers. David Foster. The one she had sort of done a body grind behind when she'd been plastered on martinis before she'd been hauled offstage by a bouncer. An incident she'd just love to forget actually, though the follow-up sex with Nate had been lovely.

"Don't I know you from somewhere?" He had a friendly face, with a nice straight smile.

Gwenna gave a noncommittal shrug, embarrassed as hell. "I don't think so."

"Are you sure? I could have sworn . . ." Then he stuck out his hand. "Anyway, I'm David Foster."

"Gwenna Carrick. It's a pleasure."

His face lit up and he snapped his fingers. "That's where I know you from. You're Carrick's sister. Not that I've met him or anything, but he seems cool."

"Thanks, I like him well enough." Worried about Nate, Gwenna removed her hand from his and gave him a smile. "Well, I hate to dash off, but my boyfriend's not feeling well and I want to check on him."

"Sure, that's cool. I hope he feels better. Nice meeting you." David gave her a wave and took a step back. "And do yourself a favor, Gwenna, and stay away from Slash."

Gwenna stared at his back, heart pounding as she processed his words. "What?" she asked, but he was already gone, walking with vampire speed, brushing past mortals so quickly they would only notice a breeze and briefly wonder where it came from.

He knew about Slash. He knew she knew Slash. What the hell did that mean?

Rushing through the lobby at vamp speed herself, she headed for the pool, and just about collided with Nate coming into the hotel through the glass double doors.

The color was back in his face, but he didn't look good. He still had the look of a man about to lose his lunch at any given minute. There was a glaze of pain over his eyes that worried Gwenna. She wondered if his actually dying and returning to immortal life was somehow a bigger problem than she could have guessed. It had been her impression most mortals took to the change easily, but it was clear Nate wasn't.

"I need to talk to you," he said.

"Okay, let's go to my room." She tried to take his hand, but he pulled away. Hoping it was from his nausea and nothing more, she gestured to the pool. "I guess you were called to the murder. I can't believe there was another one already and that it's Gregor."

Nate was quickly moving toward the elevators, but he stopped and glanced at her. "It's amazing how all of you seem to know the victim's identity when that information hasn't been released. We're going upstairs and I want some answers, Gwenna."

It was certainly time for that. She nodded. "Yes, that's a good idea."

He said nothing else the whole way up, staring at the floor, holding his hand to his chest like he had a pain there. It made Gwenna feel horrific, guilty, appalled at what she had done, at how she had destroyed his life because she had been selfish enough to want his attentions, his affection, his normalcy. She didn't know where to start, how to explain.

But she thought she'd scream if the silence continued so she opened the door to her suite and said, "I want to tell you about the link I found between one of the loop members and a well-known hired assassin. Well, well-known in my circles, unfortunately. I think someone hired him to do these murders. Was Gregor killed in the same way?"

Nate nodded, looking wary, sticking his hands in the back pockets of his jeans. "Why do you know about assassins?"

"Between Ethan and Roberto, I know just about everyone that matters in our world, straight or not."

He gave a brief nod, than held up his finger. "Let's get to that in a minute. First, I want to discuss something else with you."

"What's that?" And did she really want to know? He looked downright furious.

"Come here." Nate gestured her to him, where he was standing by her console table. She kept fresh flowers and a stack of books there under a mirror that had come with the standard decor.

Not sure what he wanted, she did it automatically, eager to make whatever was going on right. Wanting Nate to be Nate again, looking at her with tenderness and respect. This attitude she didn't understand, didn't like.

He shoved the vase of flowers in her hand and spun her around. "Explain that to me."

She could see out of her peripheral vision that he was pointing to the mirror, but of course, she couldn't see his finger reflected in the glass. She couldn't see any part of either of them, just the flowers stable and steady even as they appeared to float in the air, nothing obvious maintaining them in place.

He knew.

"You have to keep an open mind as I tell you this." Carefully, she set the flowers down and turned to him, no idea how to proceed. "You know how you asked if I believe in vampires? Well, the answer is yes because I actually *am* a vampire."

His jaw twitched and he stared over her shoulder before locking eyes with her. "I'm one, too, aren't I? You made me a fucking vampire, didn't you? Why would you do that?"

Gwenna reached for his hand, but he didn't grip her back. "Nate, you have to understand . . . you were dead. That bullet went through your heart and you were dead almost instantly. And that was my fault. I was just trying to give you another chance . . . a choice. I'm so sorry that Roberto had you shot. I never dreamt he would do something so completely vicious."

"You should have told me you were a vampire. I thought you had some kind of eating disorder." He gave a laugh of disbelief and ran his hands through his hair. "God! This is insane. Vampires. They're not real, they're fuckin' bogeymen, made-up shit. Yet I can't see myself in the mirror and I crave blood. I drank it and it tasted so good, and now I want more. And I can feel what I think are fangs . . . they pop out whenever I think about blood, which has been about every second since I realized what I was drinking."

"I'm sorry." Gwenna gestured to the sofa. "Let's sit down, let's work through this. Ask me whatever you need to, and we'll get everything squared away. You'll get used to it . . . and I think, I hope, that being a vampire is more desirable than being dead.

And there was no way I could tell you what I was initially. You would have had me committed."

Gwenna sat down but Nate made no move to. "Yeah, but why the hell did you turn me and then just leave me? I had to find out from Donatelli, your ex-husband, what exactly I am now."

Oh, no. Gwenna felt her cheeks get hot. "Roberto told you?"

"Yes. I think he totally got off on it, too. He's not happy you turned me, because you know his plan was to whack me to get me out of your life, but he did really enjoy being the one to explain to me why I was having trouble standing. Lack of blood."

"I'm sorry. I didn't mean for you to find out like that. I thought you'd sleep through the night so I wanted to come back here for some blood bags to feed you, and I needed to check on Kelsey. When I realized that her husband potentially was on the slayers' loop and could be responsible for the deaths, I wanted to see if she was okay and warn her." Gwenna paused, realizing her words were just tumbling out. She needed to get a grip on her emotions, slow down, not panic. Nate would understand. She just needed to be calm, not defensive. She was no longer timid Gwenna, and damn it, she had reasons for why she'd done what she had. There was justification there. And she had to remember and trust and believe that Roberto's actions were not her fault. He had killed Nate, not her.

"Show me your fangs," Nate demanded, still standing in front of her.

Gwenna looked up at him from the sofa. "You don't want me to do that."

"Yes, I do. I need to see."

"Nate." She tucked her hair back, miserable, wishing she had been bolder and bit him sooner, shown him her true nature during pleasure, not like this.

"Show me, Gwenna. I have to see." He looked so agitated, she realized she had to do it.

"Fine." Opening her mouth, she gave a quick flash of her fangs, not even allowing them time to fully descend.

"Have you ever bitten me?"

"No!" Gwenna was offended, until she remembered the little love bite she'd taken. "Just once. And not to feed. It was while we were . . . I just wanted to taste you, feel you completely."

"Who are you?" Nate asked, looking at her with such profound hurt that she wanted to weep. "I don't know anything about you at all."

"Yes, you do. You don't know details, but you know me, Nate. I'm the same Gwenna you understood me to be this afternoon. The woman you said you were falling in love with." Bringing up that little confession right at the moment might be horrific timing, but Gwenna didn't want to lose the opportunity to remind him of what he felt. She did not want to lose him, period.

"But you're a vampire, with a very long past. How long?"

"I was born in England in the eleventh century. Ethan is my half-brother, and he turned me to vampire when I almost bled to death in childbirth."

Nate stared at her, cop face on. It was disconcerting the way he could completely shutter his emotions. She didn't really have any true gauge of his feelings.

"So your daughter, the one who accidentally fell on a sword, was born hundreds of years ago?"

"Yes. And she didn't accidentally fall on a sword. She lived to the age of twenty-five, then she killed herself with a sword so Ethan or I wouldn't change her to vampire." Saying the words out loud was painful, but Gwenna wanted Nate to understand she had kept the truth from him because there had no way to be honest without him declaring her insane. It had never been from malice or plain old dishonesty, but out of necessity. "It was a different time period then. She thought Ethan and I were an aberration, that we were evil."

That cracked Nate's mask. "I'm sorry, Gwenna."

She gave him a brief smile. "Yeah, me, too. I've lived a lot of years wishing I could alter the past, wishing that my daughter was still with me, wishing that she hadn't shown fear of me in the end, but I've learned to deal with it. I wouldn't say I'm entirely at peace but I'm getting there. And I'm learning to be more independent, to spend less time alone."

Nate sighed. "I want to be angry with you. I want to be furious. But I look at you . . . I see that look in your eyes and I can't do it. I can't stay angry, even when you lied to me because I know that you only do what you think is right. You're a good woman, and you'd never hurt me intentionally."

Hope swelled in her. "No, I absolutely wouldn't. I . . . I love you, Nate. And I haven't told a single man those words since my divorce, which was three hundred years ago."

Nate's head was pounding, brain struggling to keep up and process all he was uncovering. While he heard Gwenna's declaration of love, it was her latter words that made him give a laugh of disbelief. "Three hundred years since your divorce? God, that's insane. And the asshole is still giving you crap. That's just not right."

It wasn't right. And Nate was a vampire. That wasn't right, either. The very thought messed with his head. Though he knew it was true. He could feel the changes in himself, see the sharpness and clarity of objects around him, hear with a focus and subtlety that were new. He could smell every nuance of people and the world around him. Feel his fangs. Crave blood.

Scary as hell, that's what it was. But at the same time, he knew he wouldn't have wanted to die. He was more selfish and controlling than Kyra. His sister had accepted her fate with grace and dignity and Nate had admired her, had been in awe of her. He knew that he could never have just accepted death without wanting to fight, that he had the sense that he hadn't finished what he needed to accomplish in his life.

So he would accept his vampire fate. Eventually he would probably have to thank Gwenna for it. But at the moment he was too busy processing information and sensory input to appreciate that he should reassure her, tell her how he felt in return. Because he still cared about Gwenna, wanted to be with her. Even more now that he understood just how long she had been battling her ex-husband and her grief for her daughter.

But Gwenna just shrugged. "Roberto is Roberto. Though tonight I think he and I finally reached an understanding. He just may be sufficiently angry to stop speaking to me indefinitely." She stood up and came over to him. Her hand slipped into his. "I'm just sorry that it took me so long to stand up to him, to be honest with him. Because if I had done so sooner, you would still be mortal."

She looked so sad, so worried, that Nate touched her cheek. He couldn't stand a woman in tears, and she looked damn close to losing it. The last thing he wanted was for Gwenna to take this on and own it. "This isn't your fault. Don't ever say that. You didn't have me shot. Donatelli did."

"I got you involved."

"No, I got involved because there was a murderer running around killing people. You're not responsible for those deaths on the slayers' loop, either. You haven't done anything wrong. You and I chose to be together, chose to hook up because we both wanted to. End of story."

Her blue eyes stared up at him, her long eyelashes wet with her unshed tears. "Is that the end of the story? We hooked up, and that's it?"

A tear squeezed out and slid down her cheek. A red tear. Blood. Nate felt his throat close. He loved her. He did. That had to be what this was, even as he doubted it, a nasty little fear that he was wrong, that he was wanting her to be something she wasn't, wanting what was between them to be real when it wasn't. He wasn't one hundred percent sure of her, him, or what the hell love really was, but there was one thing he'd never question. He wanted Gwenna safe and he would protect her from anything, anyone. Even himself. But right now, he just wanted to hold her, to feel her against him. "No, that's not it."

Gathering her in his arms, Nate pulled her close and kissed her forehead, her temple, her cheek. "Blood tears. Do we all do that?"

"No." She shook her head against his chest, her body still stiff and unsure. "Only a few of us. Kelsey and I can do it, but no one else in Vegas that I know of."

"So you're special."

"Not so much."

Nate tipped her chin up. "You're special to me. I want to be with you, Gwenna. I want to love you."

He kissed her tenderly, enjoying the way her soft lips parted for him. His tongue was more sensitive, more attune to her unique taste. She was delicious. His. Just as he felt the urge to bite her, she pulled back.

"Good. Because I was determined to convince you we need to be together, but the truth of the matter is I don't really have time to do that right now. We have a problem."

Nate almost laughed, but she looked so serious, he didn't. "This is about the murders, isn't it? Tell me everything you know. Absolutely everything this time."

An hour later, he had requested a pad of paper and pen from Gwenna and was trying to sort out everything they knew. "The vampire world is very small, isn't it? We have the same players turning up over and over again."

"That's true." Gwenna was sitting next to him on the couch, her laptop computer balancing on her knees.

"So here's what I have. Ringo—hired assassin, worked in the past for Donatelli. Drug user. Ethan—your brother, president of vampires." That sort of blew Nate's mind. He had never considered that vampires could be real, let alone organized. Though truthfully, everything was blowing his mind. He was almost grateful for the murders to concentrate on. Homicide he understood.

Going down his list, he said, "Ethan is enemies with Donatelli, who is now VP because it was the only way for Ethan to win the election against Gregor Chechikov. Gregor, who is now dead and being hauled to the morgue as we speak." Nate made a notation on his paper next to Gregor's name. Dead. "How does a vampire die?"

"Decapitation. Wood stake to the heart. Complete burning. That's it. And technically a full draining of blood without replenishing it but I'm not sure how one vampire would overpower another long enough to do that without using one of these other methods first."

"Well, someone did it to Gregor, because the dead was definitely dead. I saw him. Smelled him."

Gwenna stopped clicking her mouse—she had said she was going to check the slayers' loop—and glanced at him. "The thing is that Gregor had been a vampire for a long time, but he was turned back to mortal recently. It would have been easy enough to kill him, if you knew he was mortal, which almost no one did, because he's been in hiding. As vampires we know immediately who is mortal and who is vamp, so Gregor had been staying far away from the public eye."

"Yet you knew he was mortal?" And how the hell did a vampire just become mortal again?

"Yes, because his mortality was returned to him by Corbin Atelier, Brittany's husband, against Gregor's will. It was his punishment for kidnapping Brittany when she was pregnant and plotting to steal her child. Corbin thought giving him weakness as a punishment was fitting for a man who would do such an appalling thing to a woman."

"That is appalling. And obviously someone wanted him dead." Nate glanced at Gwenna's screen. She had a message clicked and opened to read. "But how does a vampire become mortal?"

"Corbin created a vaccine. But it's a secret not meant for the vampire population at large. It could precipitate mass panic and protests."

"And your brother doesn't want that?"

"No one wants that. We're safer when we stick together and keep our population under control."

"So is a vampire killing slayers off the loop a coincidence or not?"

"I don't know." Gwenna gestured to the screen. "But I have another e-mail from Slash. He wants to meet me tonight at the Bellagio in front of the club."

That bothered Nate. A lot. He really didn't want Gwenna involved in this any more than she already was. "I don't think so."

Gwenna frowned. "But we need to know who Slash is." Then she grabbed his arm. "Oh, shit, I just remembered. I was heading to the pool to find you when I ran into David Foster, the bass player from The Impalers. He said the most cryptic thing to me as I was leaving—that I shouldn't meet Slash in person."

"Have you ever talked to him about Slash before? Is David Foster on the loop?"

"Not that I know of. I'd never even met David Foster before the concert, and I didn't really meet him that night, either."

"What kind of motivation might he have for wanting slayers killed?"

"I have no idea. But he can't be the killer. That doesn't even make sense. I personally think it's Sasha, Gregor's wife."

"But you said she's mortal."

"But a gigantic bitch. Kelsey said she tried to kill Ringo tonight with absolutely no reason behind it. She stabbed him through the heart with a wooden stake, and the only thing that saved him was Kelsey's intervention. Don't you think it's odd that a woman who married a vampire would attempt to kill another vampire?"

"What did Kelsey do to Sasha?" Nate had no problem picturing Kelsey ripping Sasha's head off. Kelsey had acted like a dipshit the time he'd met her, but he had sensed that she was loyal to those she loved. Loyal enough to kill. In fact, almost everyone they had mentioned or put on Nate's list was probably capable of murder given the right reason.

"I don't know." Gwenna shrugged. "I didn't ask. But I think Sasha is FoxyKyle and I think she hired Ringo to kill those boys and kill her husband."

"Why?"

"I don't know. I have no facts to back me up on this, Nate. Just my gut instincts. There is a relationship between Ringo and Sasha of some sort, obviously, and he is an assassin. And if she's on the loop, she had access to everyone who volunteered a real name. I can't imagine what her motivation is, but it just seems like she is the odd piece to this puzzle. Why the hell is she hanging around vampires, anyway? It's rare for a vampire to marry a mortal and then involve her in the vampire world."

"Gut instinct is right more often than not and I don't have enough information here. I feel like my head is racing to keep up since I've jumped in mid-action. I don't know the players the way that you do." Nate found that frustrating as well. "I'm going to trust you on this one. But who is Slash then and why does he want to meet you?"

"God, I don't know. It just doesn't seem like Ringo's brand of behavior, and I've never thought he was the sort to hang out online. And in the last week or so, he's been in a constant heroin haze according to Kelsey. I can't believe he was ambitious enough to plot all those meetings with me."

"I don't know, babe, I just don't know. But I guess if we want answers, we're going to have to show up for that meeting with Slash at the Bellagio."

"You're going to go with me?" she asked.

"Hell, yes."

"You know that it's not easy to kill me. That's why I was willing to meet Slash before. I wasn't being quite the dumb blonde you thought I was being." She gave him a small smile. "I could overpower any mortal murderer."

He was really not convinced. "While I am grateful to know that you weren't continually walking into danger with mortal strength, no weapon, and zero self-defense skills, I don't think vampire speed and strength alone could keep you out of a tight spot with a mortal who's cunning. You may think you're a tough girl, and I would have to say emotionally, yes, you're tough as goddamn nails, but you've already admitted to me you spend the majority of your time online, reading, or playing the harp and piano. Not exactly skills that can help you take down a psychotic vampire slayer."

She glared at him. But hell, he was only telling it to her straight up. Gwenna was not badass. Sorry. And truthfully, he liked her damn fine the way she was, and didn't really think he would appreciate her getting hard and vicious on him.

"You do know I have control issues, don't you? I have spent my entire life having men—specifically two men—try to control everything I do. I will not tolerate that from you."

Whoa. Back up. Nate held up his hand. "Hey, hey. I am not trying to control you, Gwenna. I don't work like that. But you've already pointed out that I'm a black-and-white kind of guy. That's true and I can't change it." In fact, he liked that about himself. It made it easier to deal with all the crap he saw on the job. "And what I'm telling you is that you're not experienced in dealing with criminals."

"I lived with one for three hundred years," she said wryly.

Nate winced. God. Three hundred years with Donatelli. Living with him. Sleeping with him. That really, really bothered him. It was strange and overwhelming enough to accept that Gwenna was a vampire, nine centuries old, that it wasn't a myth or a ghost story, but true, and she lived, normal and healthy, in the flesh. Not evil, not a bloodsucking zombie, but as a compassionate and loving woman. Who had spent a hell of a lot of years with a guy Nate wanted to throw in jail and then eat the key. Yeah, that bothered him.

It also bothered him that his entire world had shifted on its freakin' axis in one week.

"So that makes you capable of taking down bad guys with your bare hands?"

"That's not the only thing bothering you, is it?" she asked, her hand moving over onto his thigh, thumb stroking the denim of his jeans at the kneecap.

Maybe it wasn't. Nate studied her, tried to pinpoint his anxiety. "I don't know. It's just that everything has changed. This is all so unbelievable." He felt like he was dreaming, or maybe more accurately like he was shit-faced drunk, where everything was sharp and buzzing, and the world moved fast and loud around him, and he was spinning, just spinning around and around and unable to make it stop.

Gwenna didn't say anything, just gave his leg a little squeeze.

She was so beautiful, so ethereal. Now he understood that better, her intriguing mix of fragility and strength. She had been born in a century with poor nutrition and inadequate medical care, and her physical features reflected that. She was slight and fair, with big luminous eyes that dominated her face. Yet despite her appearance, her quiet demeanor, she had an intangible and unshakable strength. Gwenna had been through a lot and she was still standing.

Nate wasn't sure that he could say what he needed to without hurting her. But he was confused as hell, and it wasn't fair not to be totally honest with her.

"No, that's not the only thing bothering me. Everything's bothering me. This is all so insane . . . my sister, my parents, you, vampires . . . I have all these feelings, but what if I can't trust them? What if it's just some kind of reaction to all the stress?" Okay, that sounded wimpy as hell, but it was the truth. Nate didn't trust himself, period. He was a fucking wreck and big enough to admit that.

"You're talking about your feelings for me, aren't you?" Her voice was quiet, expression hurt.

He nodded. "Among other things." But primarily his feelings for her. He thought he loved her. How could that be real? They had only known each other a week and she had lied to him. He had gone in with the assumption she was someone other than who she was. So how did he know if he loved the real Gwenna or not? "You have to admit this is complicated. We've both been through a lot and we should take the time to make sure that . . ."

Nate stopped. He didn't even know what the hell he was saying. And given the look on Gwenna's face, she didn't, either.

Seventeen

Gwenna was being dumped. She could not believe it. Well, maybe she could. She had expected anger and recriminations for turning Nate to vamp, but she had never imagined that he would simply doubt the legitimacy of his feelings for her. Like he had some sort of posttraumatic sex syndrome that had made him want her and that was it. Nothing more. And now he had a handle on it, thanks.

"I see what you're saying. It's perfectly understandable." Actually, it wasn't. It was damn offensive, insulting, ridiculous, and just like a man. Gwenna wondered precisely why she felt the need to be polite about it. Breeding. She had been raised to defer to a man, and damn it, she just didn't see the logic in that when they were being stupid. "But that doesn't mean I like it, or that I feel any sort of patience about it. I am coming from a different place than you. I knew everything about the situation, that's true. And I have a long lifetime of mistakes to compare my feelings for you up against. I know that I care deeply about you and I don't need to think about it. I want to be with you. But if you need time, I can respect that." Sort of. And what was the matter with her? She set off to tell him to get a grip and deal, and she wound up justifying his feelings. Apparently she had a bit of a way to go with the "you go, girl" attitude.

"Thank you, I appreciate that."

"So what does this mean, exactly? We're not going to see each other? Because if you don't want contact with me, I'll introduce you to Ethan so he can help you transition to vampire." Gwenna tried very hard not to sound bitter, but she didn't think she succeeded. She refused to feel bitter, just flat out refused, and neither did she want to sound like the pitiful woman who clings when it's over.

"Of course I want contact with you." Nate looked bewildered. "I told you I'm falling in love with you."

You know, for a man who claimed he saw the world in black and white, he was tossing a whole hell of a lot of gray her way.

"But you just also said you're not sure you can trust that feeling. And I'm not exactly sure what you want me to do about it."

"Nothing. I don't want you to do anything. I want to go on like we have been."

"So, we're supposed to see each other, sleep together, solve crimes together, and the whole time I'm supposed to be giving you space to determine your feelings? So I should invest time and energy and emotional attachment without really knowing how you feel? Understanding that at any given possible second you might suddenly miraculously realize that you did not have legitimate feelings for me that can survive outside of a crisis situation and leave me? Do I have that right?" Because if she did, she was not going to play. Game over.

"Uh . . ." Nate had the exact look of a butterfly pinned to a board. "I wasn't saying . . . I mean, I don't think . . ."

Gwenna sat and waited. "I'm sorry? I didn't quite catch that."

Then he did what she supposed any man would do. He said her name in a sensual voice of capitulation. "Gwenna . . ." Maybe a little exasperation. And he moved in to kiss her.

Typical male behavior. When in doubt, turn to sex. But she found she didn't really care why he was intending to kiss her. She just wanted to feel him, taste him now that he was a vampire. Let them both get a true sense of how connected they were, their blood one and the same. Have him feel her honesty, her genuine affection and love for him.

Maybe she was flirting with disaster and asking to be hurt, but as his lips covered hers, she just wanted to feel, not think. She didn't want to worry about death or murder or vicious machinations of cruel people. She wanted to just feel good, to touch and be touched. Death was all around them, with Kyra, the murders, with the reminders of the past that hovered and clung to her, tenacious and unwilling to let go, and she still had the thick fear in the back of her throat from that moment when she'd realized Nate was dead. It was going to take a bit to recover from that blow, from the decision she'd made to turn him, for both of them.

So Nate was experiencing doubts and confusion. That was to be expected, and ultimately she knew if he chose to move on from her, she would survive that, too. If she had learned anything at all, it was that she needed to embrace life, to enjoy each night as it arrived.

Opening her mouth for him, Gwenna kissed Nate back, sliding her hands up his neck. He had such a firm, strong body, and such a fierce sense of justice. It was very sexy, as was the fact that he was using his tongue to do delightful things inside her mouth.

"You taste the same, but different . . ." he murmured. "Richer, sharper somehow."

Gwenna used his short hair to tug his head back away from her face. She bared her neck for him. "Bite me. Taste me, Nate."

His breath hitched. "No."

Yet she could see the interest, see the lust in his eyes, see the way his lips kept parting, and his new fangs descended. She wanted him to experience the thrill of drinking blood for the first time with her, wanted him to see inside her thoughts and feelings.

"Yes." She kissed him passionately, nipping at his bottom lip, her thigh moving along the front of his jeans, where he had a healthy erection. "Yes." Their mouths ground together, their heart rates increasing, their breath eager and erratic.

Once again she tipped her head and offered her flesh to him.

And this time he took it. His tongue danced over her neck, then while he gripped her shoulders tightly, his teeth invaded her. Gwenna shuddered at the faint pain suffused with pleasure, at the tug and pull of his suction, at the connection that flowed between them. It was as intimate as sex, and heat rushed over her, pooling in her inner thighs, and tearing a deep moan from her.

Nate watched Gwenna's eyes roll back in ecstasy before he lost the ability to focus and closed his own eyes. It was unbelievable, the sensation of Gwenna's hot blood rushing over his teeth and tongue, bringing with it a surge of her thoughts and feelings. He could feel her body against his, feel the warmth of her leg and hands and neck, at the same time he heard the beating of her heart and an acute sense of pleasure in her own words, her random snatches of thought, feeling, language, straight from her mind to his. It was overwhelming, arousing, to know that she cared about him, to hear that loud and clear, and understand how much she desired him.

He'd never felt the kind of connection with a woman that he did with Gwenna. He thought it was love, wanted it to be love. But whatever it was called, the intensity of joining with her, invading her body with his sharp new fangs, and drinking her sweet, thick blood, was more satisfying that anything he had ever experienced in his life.

It was hard to believe that he had died that day. That he had died and Gwenna had saved him. How the hell did he express gratitude for that?

"Just go on as you did before. And we can both be grateful that you're not dead."

Nate pulled his mouth from her neck and licked the traces of blood off his lips. "You can hear my thoughts, too?"

She nodded. "We're connected during an exchange, and probably during sex. We share blood now."

He hadn't thought of it that way.

"Though it's not always cut and dry. There are a lot of mysteries and nuances to being a vampire. We are all strangely unique."

"Because vampires are still people."

She gave a soft laugh, running her finger over his lip. "That's true."

"And there are good and bad people." Nate watched the blood trickle down Gwenna's skin, sluggish and vibrant red, from the two puncture wounds on her neck. It seemed natural to lean over and lick them clean. Shocked, he pulled back and saw that his action had not only removed the blood, but healed the wounds.

She smiled. "Thanks. And yes, there are good and bad people and I would love to catch ourselves a killer tonight."

"How could I argue with that?" Nate brushed her blond hair back and stared into eyes so blue he would write a freakin' poem about them if he could string two words together. Which he couldn't. But if he could, he would. "You're an amazing woman."

"And you're not so bad yourself."

Not the best or most effusive compliment he'd ever received, but since her hand was stroking his cock, he'd take it.

Then she yanked her hand away suddenly. "Oh! I just had a thought."

Somehow he didn't think it was of an intriguing sexual position they could try. He tried not to sigh. "Yeah? What's that, beautiful?"

"Does Sasha know Chechikov is dead?"

"Not that I'm aware of. That was supposed to be my job to go over and inform her of her husband's unfortunate demise. But I got a little sidetracked." By the realization that he was a vampire. He saw exactly where Gwenna's thoughts were going.

"Let's go tell the little missus now."

He liked where she had been going with her hand better, but she was right. Sasha needed to be told and they needed to witness Sasha's reaction to the news.

"Sounds like a good plan."

The smile she gave him was smug, no doubt about it.

"How convenient that Slash wanted to meet at the Bellagio tonight, which is where Chechikov lived with Sasha." Gwenna thought it was all just a little too convenient as they cut through a patch of spring grass, dewy from the night moisture.

"You sound downright sarcastic, Gwenna." Nate smiled at her.

He seemed to be taking to the change better now. He was having a strength issue—he'd ripped the car door off its hinges—but otherwise that earlier sickness he'd experienced seemed to have gone away. That alone made her feel a huge sense of relief, despite the fact that they were walking into a potentially dangerous situation. Going up against a killer of mortal vampire slayers seemed less intimidating after watching Nate bleed out in his Ford Explorer.

They had skirted the front of the Bellagio and the fountain, not wanting a chance encounter with Slash, whoever he might be. Gwenna wasn't scheduled to meet him for another hour, but who knew if he was lurking about already, so they'd gone in the side door to the hotel from the parking lot.

As they headed for the elevator, Gwenna shrugged. "I admit I have a bias against Sasha. Brittany told me that when Gregor kidnapped her—and keep in mind Brittany was five months pregnant at the time—Sasha just sat in the room and read a book while Gregor slapped Brittany around. That makes me sick."

Nate hit the elevator button. "Maybe she was scared of her husband. The dude didn't sound like a nice guy."

She made a face. "That's true. I guess Sasha could be a victim here, too, though my gut says she isn't."

"Well, let me do the talking, alright? I'm the detective with the badge. And we're going to approach this initially in an official capacity."

"Then why am I with you?"

"You're not. You're going to wait down the hall."

Gwenna glanced over at him as the elevator opened and they got on. "Oh, really? I'm glad we discussed it and came to that conclusion together."

She sounded snappish and knew it, but Nate needed to understand she was not going to do the submissive girlfriend routine with him. She was done with that dreary scene and they needed to start as they intended to go on.

Not that he looked the least bit offended or put off. He was grinning down at her and his fingers had started to make inroads into her inner thighs, just brushing along the zipper of her jeans. "Let's discuss it."

"Great. Since you're here in an official capacity, I probably shouldn't be seen. I'll wait down the hall." It wasn't the idea she had objected to, just the delivery.

"Excellent."

He hauled her over to him by yanking on her waistband with his large man hands. It was easy to see where the expression *manhandled* came from, and now that he was a vampire, too, she couldn't even resist his force. Not that she wanted to. There was something about the way Nate touched her that was sexy, not controlling. He wanted her, but he wanted her to want him. He had no interest in domination. His woman would benefit from his loyalty, his sense of protection, and his instinctive urge to take care of her, but he would never control. Seduction was his style, not the quest for power.

Gwenna supposed she was Nate's woman—technically girlfriend. That seemed spot on, but strange to think of. She'd never been a girlfriend before. But whatever the hell she was, she was going to be the recipient of that protection, loyalty, caring. Seduction.

"I want you," he said, murmuring into her ear. "We should have finished what we started before we left."

"We're on a time crunch," she said piously, even as she pressed her breasts against his chest and wished the elevator would die and strand them for a good thirty minutes. "We can manage all that later."

"We have all the time in the world, don't we?" he asked, his expression suddenly darkening.

Gwenna would have responded—with what, she had no idea—but the door opened and Nate strode down the hall. "This way."

"I'll hang back here," she said, flicking her finger over the faux flower arrangement in front of the elevators.

Nate stopped and looked back at her. He made as if to say something, then clearly changed his mind. "Yeah, okay. I'll be back in five."

"Let me know if you need me."

Giving her a wave, he went down the hall.

Damn it. Why had that somehow sounded needy on her part? She had meant it as a reassurance, but it somehow sounded clingy. Frustrated, Gwenna leaned against the console under the mirror opposite the elevators. She was lousy at this relationship thing.

A glance down the hall showed Nate and his very fine butt had disappeared around the corner. She needed to relax or she was going to scare the wits out of the man and send him running for a vampire chick who actually had her act together. And bigger breasts.

Gwenna scowled at her thoughts. Since when had she worried about her lack of a sizable chest? She had utterly lost her mind.

The elevator door to the right opened. She stood up straight, prepared to start walking and look like she had a purpose and wasn't just lingering in the hall. Then she saw who it was.

"David?" It was David Foster, the guitar player from The Impalers, looking freshly showered, his hair still damp. He must be staying in the hotel. "How are you?"

The knife was at her throat before she even realized he wasn't smiling back at her.

"Just come quietly with me if you want to live."

Bloody hell.

Sasha Chechikov was attractive, Nate would give her that. She had smooth skin, long legs, and full plump lips. The outfit was a bit much, in his opinion, tight narrow jeans and high-heel boots that went to her knees. Lots of gold chains and rings and a shirt that looked like it had gone a round with a cat and lost. Designer, obviously, but all a little over the top for his taste. She was pretty, maybe even gorgeous by some standards, but her eyes ruined the effect of her features. The eyes stared at him, cold and calculating, sweeping down the length of him and back up again.

Gwenna was right. Sasha was a bitch.

She said something in Russian. Nate flashed his badge. "Detective Thomas with the Las Vegas Police. Are you Sasha Chechikov? I need to speak to you about your husband."

Though Nate suspected she understood every word he said, she shook her head and shot off another round of Russian.

"Would you like me to get a translator?" he asked, irritated to still be standing in the doorway, and not enjoying the feeling that she was playing him for a fool. "I'm sorry to be the one to inform you of this, but your husband, Gregor Chechikov, is dead."

Sasha went pale. "Dead? Gregor is dead?"

Yeah, he thought so. Her English was accented, but perfectly coherent. "Yes, he's dead. I'm sorry. He was found murdered poolside at the Ava hotel and casino."

Gripping the doorknob tightly, she frowned, shock on her face. "I do not understand . . . are you sure it is him?"

"We got verbal confirmation of his identity from Roberto Donatelli. When was the last time you saw your husband, ma'am?"

"I do not know." Sasha looked distracted, but not particularly grief-stricken. "Very early this morning I imagine."

Nate knew he wasn't going to be able to trust a damn thing she said. "Did he mention his plans for the day?"

"No."

And there it was. The shutdown he'd been waiting for. The moment her shock wore off and her sense of self-preservation kicked in. She had pursed lips and a frown line on her forehead, her eyes narrowed and intense. Nate could practically see her assessing her options, running through them one by one mentally, looking for an escape.

He stepped inside the room, forcing her backward by his bulk. "Who killed your husband, Mrs. Chechikov?"

She grabbed her throat and played with the delicate gold chain hanging there. "I do not know. But it was not me, if that is what you are asking."

"No, that's not what I was asking. You might have wanted to kill him, but you couldn't have. He was a big guy, and you're so skinny you'll disappear if you turn sideways." Nate pointed to her hands. "And small hands like that could never have choked the life out of a burly guy like your husband."

"You are not really the police, are you?" she asked, crossing her arms over her chest.

"Actually, I am. Newly switched to the night shift."

Nate saw she was going for a weapon, though he'd have been hard pressed to believe anything could fit in that skintight outfit. "I wouldn't do that if I were you," he said as a dagger emerged from her shirt. That would explain the weird shredded effect to the clingy top. It allowed her to look stylish and hide a weapon at the same time. He was almost impressed with her cunning. But he still yanked it out of her hand before she could so much as arch it.

"You're a vampire," she said, chest rising and falling rapidly, fear spreading across her exotic features.

"Precisely. And I want answers. Are you on the slayers' loop?"

She gave a slight nod.

"Do you know who killed those men from the loop?"

Looking away, her hands going into the back pockets of her jeans, she shrugged. "It was not me."

"No one said it was. You're just a mortal, and again, look like you could use a juicy burger or two to boost you past a size zero. You couldn't have done to those boys what I saw. But you know who did." That he was convinced of.

Tears flooded her eyes. "You have to protect me. He'll kill me." She even managed to pull off a lip tremble, her fingers plastered over her chest.

It was decent acting, but Nate wasn't buying it. "Tell me who did it, and sure, I'll protect you. I won't press charges against you for being an accessory to murder, either."

Nate expected her to prevaricate. To stall for time. But she just looked him straight in the eye and said, "It was David Foster who killed the boys on the loop. I do not know who killed Gregor, but perhaps it was David as well."

The name was the one Gwenna had mentioned earlier. Something about David Foster warning her not to meet Slash. "Really? And how do you know that?"

"Because he told me. He has been pursuing me, uh, romantically?" She looked like she needed confirmation on her English so Nate nodded.

"Okay, so why did he kill them? And why the hell would he tell you about that?" It didn't exactly sound like flirt material. Hey, I whacked these guys, let's go out for pizza and a movie. Nate wasn't buying it.

But she just shrugged. "How should I know? He is strange. And the more I consider it, the more I am convinced he killed Gregor. To free me, you understand, because he wishes me for himself."

"Sure, I understand." That it was all a load of bullshit. "So where can I find David Foster?"

She blinked, her head tilted down, eyes looking up at him from under those mink-colored eyelashes, her glossy red lips parting slightly. It might move another man, but Nate was way too far into feelings for Gwenna and too much of a jaded cop to be even the slightest bit impressed. He reached into his back pocket and pulled out his handcuffs. "Or we can talk about this at the police station."

The pout drooped. "He is at the club downstairs. The band is having a private party for a hundred vampire friends and fans and several hundred mortals. Five of which are slayers who are planning to use this party to kill as many vampires as they can."

Was she serious? Nate frowned. "How the hell could they manage that at a casino club? And what kind of party starts at one in the morning?"

"A vampire party. And it's all been planned. Each of the slayers is willing to die to purge the earth of the evil of the vampire."

"Like suicide bombers?"

"Exactly."

And she looked pleased at the thought. Nate could see that. She wanted death. Whether it was for all vampires or one in particular, he wasn't sure and didn't care. "So why would you reveal this little plot to me?" She wasn't stupid, so she had to have a reason.

"So you will go and try to stop the plan, and you will be killed, too."

Wow. She was one bitter little thing. Quick on her feet. And vicious. Too bad Nate had no intention of dying. Not when he'd just escaped that very fate earlier in the day. Not when Gwenna had risked herself and recrimination from her brother and Donatelli.

"Well, let's get to it then, shall we?" He gestured to the door.

She brushed past him. "And you might wish to know that the slayers are determined to see Gwenna Carrick die tonight. They know who she is, how important she is in vampire politics. They know how much her death will anger vampires."

That stopped Nate cold. "No one is going to touch Gwenna."

The smile she gave him was smug. "She is probably meeting Slash right now, yes?"

Damn it. That had never even occurred to Nate. But it was exactly something Gwenna would do, to prove her independence.

He went into the hall, dragging Sasha with him. She squawked in protest at the pressure on her arm, but he wasn't really hurting her and he wasn't in the mood to care about her sensibilities.

The elevators were closed. And there was no Gwenna in front of them.

Eighteen

Gwenna found it really irritating that David Foster, the quintessential nice guy, with a wide smile and chewing gum in his mouth, could be a cold-blooded murderer. It just boggled the mind.

It was wrong and she intended to get to the bottom of it. As David ushered her off the elevator on the second floor, she glanced at him. "Why did you do it?"

"Do what?" He looked around—nervously, she suspected.

"Infiltrate the loop and kill those boys. They were just playing around, it was a hobby to them. And you killed them." That distressed her beyond belief. It was never fair to involve some innocent bystander in vampire business and politics. And surely that's what this was.

She didn't really expect him to answer but he stopped walking, the knife hidden in his waistband. Gwenna thought she could probably break away from him and run, but he would catch her. They were in a quiet mirrored hallway with only one other couple twenty feet away, though God knew she didn't want to involve any more mortals in the mess. Besides, she was curious as to where he was taking her.

"I didn't enjoy doing that. But I had to."

"Why? Were they threatening you? They're just mortals, David. They can act out their slayer fantasies all they want, but it's very difficult for even the most skilled slayer to kill a vampire. You know that." None of this was making any sense to her. "How does Sasha play into all of this?" And what was Sasha currently saying to Nate upstairs?

Saying Sasha's name made David even more agitated. Sweat was on his forehead and he shifted anxiously. "Chechikov was going to kill her. But first, he was going to torture her, unless she took out the slayers. He's already been knocking her around . . . right since the first day they were married. So I was helping her, taking care of Chechikov's nasty requests so he would leave her alone. I followed Chechikov to the Ava out of curiosity, and watched him sneaking around the pool. And I realized he was mortal. It seemed like an amazing opportunity, you know? So I killed him, too. Problem solved. Sasha free, slayers left alone . . ." He leaned forward, so close to her she could see the shadow of his beard and smell the cinnamon of his gum. "I'm going to take you into this club and you're going to dance and drink and have a great time. Just like you did at The Impalers concert."

Gwenna ignored that. She was still floored from the obvious realization that David was Slash, and he was absolutely and utterly in love with Sasha. Poor sot. That would be a cold bed to lie in, she imagined. And he had killed for the witch. Maybe she wasn't being fair to Sasha, but somehow she doubted there was a hidden heart of gold.

"You're in love with Sasha, aren't you?"

David's eyes narrowed, then he just scoffed. "I'm not discussing anything else with you."

"Love makes you do insane things, doesn't it? But trust me, David, some people are not worth our devotion. They just drag us down to their level. I should know. I was married to Roberto Donatelli for three hundred years."

"I'm not interested in this conversation," he said and took her elbow, pulling her back down the hall.

"Why are you taking me into a club?" What the hell did any of this have to do with her? A thought occurred to her. "Is Kelsey here?"

But he looked genuinely confused by that. "No, why would she be?"

Gwenna dug her feet into the carpet. Her mind was racing, struggling to keep up. "The slayers are here, aren't they?"

He just wiped his free hand on the bottom of his black T-shirt and yanked her harder. "I wouldn't drink so much this time if I were you."

Since she couldn't decide if that was meant to protect her or send her up the proverbial river, she said nothing. But he had to have a decent reason for hauling her with him, and she wanted to know what it was.

There was a doorman scanning IDs through a computer and verifying they were on the guest list. "I'm on the list," Gwenna said stupidly when he scanned her license and her name popped up. Now why was that exactly? Who would gain from having her attend what obviously wasn't just open night at the club, but a private party. One she knew nothing about.

Then it occurred to her. The slayers knew that killing her would invoke a lot of anger from vampires. Ethan. Alexis. Roberto. All of them with enormous amounts of power and people at their disposal. They wouldn't take her murder lightly. They would retaliate. So in essence, killing her would start a war.

What a special feeling to know her stupidity might be responsible for exposing all of her species to mortal condemnation, ensuring the death of hundreds if not thousands of vampires and mortals alike.

The doorman handed her identification back. "Thank you, Ms. Carrick."

When he moved, Gwenna saw that he had a gun tucked under his button-up shirt, which was open to his T-shirt. And he was mortal. "Thank you," she told him with a polite smile, stripping him of his weapon before he was even aware she had moved. A quick thrust of her hand and she had him down on the ground in a glamour, breathing heavily, eyes closed.

She rounded on David, gun aimed at his chest. "Explain what the hell is going on here."

He cursed colorfully. "You can't kill me with that."

"And you can't kill me with that knife. But we can both cause each other some pain and slow each other down. Which puts us at a stalemate."

"I'm stronger than you."

"I'm smarter than you."

"Someone's coming down the hall," he said.

Gwenna could hear them, too. "Get behind the desk. And drag the doorman with you."

"No!"

"Yes, you idiot. If someone sees us, they'll call the cops and that will ruin whatever nefarious deeds you have planned for inside that club."

That spurred him into action. He grabbed the doorman by the feet and hauled him behind the desk, tugging on Gwenna's shirt as he went by. She went with him, just because she wanted to keep an eye on him. The whole situation was ridiculous. Squatting down behind the desk, the gun still loosely in her hand, she glanced at David next to her. He looked tired. Resigned. The doorman was drooling, crumpled up on the floor. And she felt the urge to giggle, but restrained herself.

Then she realized who was coming down the hall. It was Nate. She could hear his voice, low, angry. Smell him. It was instinctive to stand, but halfway up she dropped back down. If he was speaking to someone, odds were it was Sasha, so it would be wise to see what they were doing first. She shot David a stern look to ensure his silence, but he looked too miserable to say anything.

"If you're lying to me, I'll be very, very angry," Nate said, and Gwenna was glad she wasn't the one who had ticked him off. That was not a pleasant tone he was using.

"I am not lying," a woman replied, her voice almost as cold as Nate's, her accent Russian. Definitely Sasha.

David's eyes widened when he realized who it was.

"David will be here at the club and you can arrest him. He deserves to rot in jail for murdering my husband and for harassing me."

There was a sharp intake of air from David and he whispered, "That . . ."

Bitch. Exactly what Gwenna had thought. She was sorry to be right in this case. David looked like he was going to revisit his dinner, and he looked absolutely heartbroken. Utterly crushed.

"He killed the others to incite the slayers to violence, and he has been stalking me with his unwanted attentions."

They opened the door and went into the club. Gwenna heard laughter and music float out. She and David sat still for another second, until she reached out and patted his knee. He had killed three men, but he had thought he was doing so to protect the woman he loved from her monster of a husband. She actually felt a certain amount of pity for him.

"I'm sorry. She isn't worth it, you know."

"Yeah." David squared his shoulders. "Guess I should have known a woman like that wouldn't be into me."

"You don't want her into you. She has issues. Serious issues."

"Whatever. It's fine. My online name isn't Dumb Fuck for no reason." He turned to her. "Don't go in there. They're going to kill you."

So David was both Slash and Dumb Fuck. That was clever. "Who are the slayers?"

"There's five of them, all wearing T-shirts that say, 'Get Impaled, You Know You Want It.' "

Gwenna blinked, and again had the completely inappropriate urge to laugh. "That's creative."

He gave a brief smile. "I think they call that a double entendre."

She had to ask, had to confirm what she thought, because she was convinced David wasn't really a bad sort after all. "The boys on the loop . . . did they suffer?"

His eyes shifted away from her. "No. I put a glamour on them, killed them, then drained them. Worst thing I've ever done . . . it was a horrible feeling. But I thought I was protecting whatsername from her husband."

"You need to make restitution in some way to those families, because what you did was wrong, even if your reason was noble."

He didn't answer. He just stood up and was gone.

Gwenna wrinkled her nose. She really needed to work on the lack of badass-ness in her personality. Gigantic softie that she was, she'd just let a murderer zip away to God knows where.

What was she going to tell Nate? *He seemed like a nice guy, honest.*

Somehow she didn't think that was going to go over well.

She stood up and went into the club to find the man she loved and explain herself.

And take out five vampire slayers wearing ironic T-shirts.

Nate wondered why people weren't dropping from seizures nightly from the irritating strobe lights flashing in the dance club. It was one of those Vegas hot spots that he normally wouldn't get within ten feet of and wouldn't be allowed entrance to anyway. His shoes weren't cool enough. But there had been no one at the door tonight and it was a private party, though it was still filled with skinny half-dressed women and pretty men. The purple velvet sofas were all stuffed with people, tables in front of them littered with exotic drinks, the DJ pumping out loud music with words he couldn't understand.

Sasha kept trying to get away from him, so he was holding her hand like they were lovers, but with an iron grip on her.

"You will never figure out who the slayers are," she said, trying yet again to yank herself to freedom.

It was sheer stubbornness. He was amazingly strong now that he was immortal. "Which is why you're going to tell me who the slayers are, because if you don't, you're going to die right along with everyone else when they carry out whatever their plan is."

"I am not afraid to die."

Man, she was irritating. Nate glared at her. "Well, maybe I should just strangle you right now and get it over with."

She made a sniffling sound and stuck her chin in the air.

For ten long exasperating minutes he wandered around the room, wondering what exactly he was doing, and when a plan would miraculously occur to him, when Sasha suddenly made a sound. He turned to look at her, suspicious. "What?"

"Nothing." She shook her head, but couldn't quite prevent her eyes from darting to the left.

Nate turned in the direction she was looking and wondered if vampires could have a heart attack.

Gwenna was getting a piggyback ride from a guy with a shaved head and a goatee, her long hair flying behind her as he bounced her around.

Whatever possible explanation there could be for that, he was pretty damn sure he didn't want to hear it.

"I don't want to be here," Ringo complained to Kelsey as she led him through a throng of dancers at a lux nightclub in the Bellagio. There was some kind of vampire party going on and Kelsey was running on and on about how she knew the band and wanted to see them before they left Vegas.

Ringo had a headache and was already questioning his conviction to go clean, made a whole freaking five hours earlier. Everything was so much easier in the haze. The real world was loud and painful and demanding.

"Come on, silly, it's fun." Kelsey was wiggling to the music as they moved through the crowd.

"Yeah, well, I'm not having fun."

"Dancing is a better high than heroin."

Now who was the one on drugs? Was she serious? "I'm afraid I have to disagree with you, babe."

Which made her pout, her bottom lip jutting out. "Come on, sweetie, try to have a good time."

"Try to be normal, you mean." Well, he wasn't normal, whatever the hell that was.

"I didn't say that."

"You meant it." And that was the fucking pot calling the kettle black. Kelsey wasn't normal, either. She wouldn't know normal if it walked up and kissed her ass. That was why they were a good pair.

"Don't put words in my mouth," she said, snuggling up against him, her breath teasing across his lips.

"I could think of something better to put in your mouth."

She laughed. "You're naughty and rude."

"That's why you love me." She did love him. And he loved her, in whatever way he was capable. He went to kiss her, but she pulled away, giggling.

Her giggle was probably the best thing about her, it was so carefree and vibrant. He reached for her, intent on holding her, but she squirmed away and spun on her high-heel shoe.

And ran straight into Sasha Chechikov.

The guy who was holding her arm tightly shoved her at Kelsey and Ringo. "Watch her. Don't let her leave. I'll be right back."

He disappeared into the crowd and Ringo narrowed his eyes at Sasha. "Well, well, well. Look who stopped by to visit."

Sasha tried to mask the fear, but Ringo could smell it. She also tried to run, but he caught hold of her hand and pulled her in between himself and Kelsey. "Leaving so soon? I don't think so. I want to talk to you. Let's find a table."

It had seemed like a good idea to let Drake the guitar player hoist her on to his back so she could scan the room better, but she hadn't expected him to react so enthusiastically. They were doing a horse and rider interpretation as he ran across the club humming the theme song from *The Lone Ranger*. It was all she could do to keep from being flung off and sent sprawling. There was no way she could actually focus long enough on anyone's shirt to read it.

As it was, half the women in the room were probably suspecting Gwenna of hitting on them, since she was studying their chests so assiduously.

"I think we can slow down," she suggested.

Drake reacted with a battle cry of "To the bar!"

Or they could go to the bar. Sure, that was fine, too.

They skidded to a halt, and Gwenna took the opportunity to slide off Drake. She took a deep breath and shoved her hair out of her eyes. And saw Nate standing in front of her.

"Hi!" she said, feeling more than a little ridiculous.

She introduced Nate and Drake to each other, grateful when Drake handed her a martini glass and excused himself.

"So, how are things?" She set the martini down on the bar, knowing it for best for everyone if she didn't drink that.

Nate just looked at her in that unnerving way he had. She shifted uneasily, glancing around the room. "I found out what the slayers are wearing—"

"Gwenna," he interrupted her brusquely.

"Yes?" Here came the lecture, about improper behavior and the seriousness of what they were doing, etc., etc. She should probably deliver it first and spare him the breath.

"You know how I said I wasn't sure if I could trust my feelings? That I wasn't sure if I'm in love with you?"

Of course she remembered that. It had been a really lousy moment for her, so thanks for bringing it up again. "Oh, yes, I remember."

"Well, I was wrong. I *am* completely and totally in love with you." He moved closer to her and took hold of her waist. "When I saw you bouncing on some other guy's back, I suddenly realized that I love everything about you, and I don't want to lose you. Ever." He touched her cheek. "I want you to move in with me."

Honestly, she had not seen that one coming. Perhaps she should ride on men's backs more often if it brought about the very thing she wanted. She grinned at Nate, heart swelling. "Are you sure?"

"Absolutely."

Kissing him lightly on the lips, she said, "Then I would love to move in with you. And I love you, too."

More than she could believe possible. But then again, she was ready to love fully and forever, and this time she was absolutely certain she had chosen a man worthy of that kind of devotion.

"Aren't you going to lecture me for my inappropriate behavior?" she asked, pulling back slightly and smiling at him.

"Hell no. I have no intention of telling you how to act. You're a grown woman."

Good answer.

His eyebrows went up and down. "Besides, I think I needed a little jolt of jealousy to make things clear. You're an amazing woman and I want to be with you, live with you, love you. Now let's rope up these slayers and get the hell out of here so I can get you naked and do wicked things to your body."

Even better answer. "I like the way you think. So here's the deal. David Foster said the slayers are wearing T-shirts that say, 'Get Impaled, You Know You Want It.' "

Nate tilted his head a little. "Are you sure?"

"Yes, why?"

"Because I see four guys and a girl standing right in the freaking doorway wearing shirts with that catchy little phrasing on them."

Gwenna stopped herself from turning around by sheer willpower. "Are you serious?"

"Yep. So let's go take them out."

"How?"

"They're mortal, we're immortal. Shouldn't be too hard." Nate squeezed her hand. "This is your takedown, babe. You're first man in, and I'll take your back. Get them in the hall and the rest should be easy."

Easy. Sure. He was trained in combat and she was trained in embroidery. She looked up at him, about to protest.

But he gripped her shoulders and said, "You can do this. I know you can. You are badass, Gwenna. And you'll be saving hundreds of lives in the process."

Well, hell. If he could trust her abilities, then surely she could, too. She nodded. "Let's do it."

And she turned and moved toward the door, confident that Nate was right behind her.

"I have nothing to say." Sasha pushed away the drink Ringo had ordered for her.

"You're going to sit with me until you explain why you tried to kill me. I have all the time in the world." More than he really wanted to think about, given that every day—well, night actually—was a struggle for him.

Kelsey was sucking down a cosmopolitan to his right, looking ditzy and disinterested, gaze fluttering around the dance floor. But Ringo knew better. Kelsey was watching everything they did, and if he needed assistance, she would be there. She was good at convincing people to dismiss her as a dumb brunette and that always worked to their advantage. It caught people off guard when she made a move.

Sasha just stared at him.

And Kelsey, without even turning toward them, said, "It's because of Kyle."

Ringo started at the mention of his brother's name. He should be used to it. Kelsey dropped Kyle's name randomly, sometimes even calling him Kyle as a nickname, which he both despised and liked. But the stab of pain he always felt whenever his brother was mentioned was insignificant next to the realization that Sasha had reacted to Kyle's name.

Tears popped into her eyes and her lip trembled. "Do not bring Kyle up. Ever."

"You knew my brother?" he asked, horrified.

For a second he didn't think she would answer, but she smoothed her hair, which was pulled back tightly, and pressed at her temples. Then she lifted her eyes. "We were engaged. I met him online. We were in love. We were going to get married, and you killed him."

Ringo felt rancid bile rise into his mouth. "That's true," he said. "I did kill him. Accidentally."

It had happened so fast, it had been reactionary on his part. He was a trained killer, first in the Marines, then as an assassin, and he couldn't hesitate, never hesitate, or he would wind up dead. So when he'd been living in California and Kyle was visiting, he had never paused, defending himself with his semiautomatic when a competitor had opened fire on his house in a drive-by. The smart thing to do probably would have been to lie low and let it go, but

Ringo didn't want to give the impression that he could be intimidated. Threatened. So he had shot back, to make a point.

Kyle was just a nice kid, a college student, raised in a suburban neighborhood with none of the demons that his older half brother had been exposed to. He had panicked. Stood up.

And when the noise settled and Ringo picked up his brother's dead body, it was obvious that the fatal bullets had created entry wounds on Kyle's back, not front. Shot in the back by his own brother. Dead.

"I do not care what happened. All that matters is that Kyle is dead and you killed him. And he was a better man than you could ever be." Tears were streaming down her cheeks now. "I do not understand how a man with so much love and potential had to die, when you—despicable, lazy, a disgusting drug addict with no thought for anyone but yourself—you get to live forever."

Ringo's hands and feet felt cold and there was a buzzing in his ears. He did not need this bitch pointing out the truth to him. "Well, life ain't fair, is it?"

Rage coursed through him, alive, pulsing, determined and frantic and demanding. "Come with me."

He stood up and grabbed her by the arm.

Kelsey stopped watching the dancers. "What are you doing?"

His wife looked alarmed, and she should. He was a man—a vampire, a monster—on the edge. He couldn't stand to look into Sasha's face and see his shame. "Why did you marry Chechikov?"

"To get access to vampires. To kill them."

"That had nothing to do with me."

"No."

Ringo moved her across the club, jostling people out of their way. "So you hate vampires?"

"With every bone in my body."

He paused to look down at her beautiful face. There was nothing but hatred there. This woman had married a man she despised, had let Ringo himself touch her, put his hands all over her body. She was willing to use whatever she had to exact whatever revenge she had planned.

"That's such a shame. Because you're about to become a vampire."

If she could punish him, stab and scar and mutilate him with that look, with his guilt, with her hatred and profound disgust and disdain, then he was entitled to punish her in return. Let her be shoved into what she claimed to despise, let her be forced to drink blood and hate herself for enjoying it, let her stare ahead into an endless future with no hope, no love, no fight left.

Then she could look at him and see the mirror image of herself, and she would have no right to judge.

Nineteen

Love was an amazing thing. Gwenna should have been shaking in her shoes as she ran full vampire speed into the group of slayers, yet she was so pumped up on happy hormones from Nate's words that she charged with no hesitation, slamming into them like a bowling ball making contact with the pins.

Two hit the floor. Two went careening backward, tumbling into the hallway. And one unfortunate soul got knocked unconscious when his head made immediate and solid contact with the wall. Gwenna followed the two into the hall, sent them into a glamour, and trussed them together with her belt.

By the time she was finished, Nate was shoving the other two out in the hall, both looking dazed, confused, and altogether unhappy. He went back for the fifth while Gwenna tied the others up.

It was over in less time than it took Gwenna to floss her teeth. Five slayers up, five slayers down. For the first time in nine hundred years, she felt the true power of her immortality, and it was a heady shot of adrenaline.

She did have a sudden thought. "Now what the hell do we do with them?"

Nate was patting them all down. Under their various denim jackets and zip-up sweatshirts, they were all carrying explosives, which he was careful not to touch.

Bloody hell. They really had been serious about their task. Good thing she hadn't known that when she'd run pell-mell into the lot of them.

"Now I call for backup and we haul them to prison, where all mortal criminals get to rot."

"Oh. Right." She hadn't thought that one all the way through to its logical conclusion. It had a fabulous circular sense of justice. Vampires couldn't punish mortals unless they killed them, and she could never advocate that. It was the softie thing again. But this way justice was served and the Vampire Nation got to stay entirely out of it.

"What happened to David Foster, by the way?" Nate asked conversationally as he pulled his phone out of his pocket. "I thought you had been kidnapped but I found you in here playing cowgirl with the guitar player instead."

He made it sound so thoroughly undignified. "I was scanning the room from the height advantage of Drake's back," she said in her haughtiest voice.

"Of course," he said, with a smirk, before he got serious and waved her away. "Now step away from these guys. We need a bomb team to remove these explosives so the whole building doesn't go up with a bang. And you didn't answer my question."

"David Foster got away," she said as she backed up. That was the truth. He *had* got away. "And the poor sap did it for Sasha. He thought she was being tortured and abused by Chechikov, so he did the killing she told him she was supposed to do. But then he figured it was a better idea to just kill Gregor than to keep killing innocent victims. He thought that's what she would want, but she wasn't being abused by Gregor, was she?"

"She might have been. But she walked into her marriage with a motive. She wants to kill vampires, though I'm not exactly sure why. I left her with Kelsey, by the way. I hope she hasn't disappeared, though I doubt we're going to get any more information out of her. And she hasn't committed any crime that we can prove."

"Kelsey doesn't like her, so she might still have her. Though I find the whole thing rather odd." Gwenna wasn't sure why Sasha would want to kill vampires, either. Maybe they would never know. She listened to Nate make the call to the police station and appreciated the picture he presented, the strength of his stance and his convictions, the way he spoke with confidence and professionalism, the fact that he seemed to have accepted his change to vampirism with aplomb. He had the attitude that it was what it was, and sometimes you just had to deal with it.

She was grateful to him for that attitude. She was in love with him. And she was very much looking forward to whatever the future held in store. Living together, him working the night shift, her launching her Internet people-search business. It was a pleasing, pretty picture, and when he hung up the phone, she approached him from behind and slid her hands around his waist, leaning her head on his back.

"You're a good man, Nate Thomas," she told him. But there was something she had to offer, and even though it frightened her, she had to.

Turning around, he gathered her into his arms and kissed her forehead. "Hey, have I mentioned that I love you?"

"Yes, but I expect you to keep mentioning it on a nightly basis." Playing with his T-shirt, smoothing it out over his chest, she took a deep breath. "You know how I told you that Corbin had a vaccine that changed Gregor to mortal? Well . . . he gave me one dose. I can return you to your mortal life if you want. The choice is yours."

She needed the choice to be his. The thought of going through eternity with the guilt that she had altered his life, made him immortal without his permission, was daunting.

Nate didn't say anything for a second. Then he tipped her chin up so she would be forced to look at him. Her heart was beating wildly and she was scared as hell that this would be it. That they would have this week, and that would be all.

Knowing why Gwenna had made him the offer, Nate searched for the right words to explain to her how he felt, how he wouldn't trade the opportunity to be with her just for the known life that had been taken away. He had never expected, really, to find this kind of love with a woman. Certainly not now, when he was grieving for his sister, and his life had felt so empty, so lonely.

It wasn't an accident that they had met each other, and they needed each other in a way that wasn't sad or pathetic or clinging, but enriching, fulfilling, wonderful.

"Gwenna. I want eternity with you. Do you understand that?" He touched her soft lip with his thumb as her eyes filled with tears. "I look at you and I just know it's right. I had doubts before, but that's because I'm a guy and I'm an idiot. There's no doubt now. What I want is you and me, forever."

"Forever is a long time," she said, though she smiled, a blood tear trailing down each cheek.

"I'm counting on it."

And he kissed her.